"I have to say, Mr. Turner, you were quite impressive back there.

"I don't believe I've ever seen you quite so...tough. Warrior-like," Emma said.

Jake snorted. "Oh, yeah. So tough...against a woman and teenage boy."

"They had a shotgun. And you took command of the situation without anyone getting hurt. It was...kinda sexy."

Jake blinked and shot her a grin. "Really?"

She moved her hand to his leg and squeezed his thigh. "Really."

He inhaled deeply and cleared his throat. "You were pretty badass yourself, Mrs. Turner."

"For a housewife slash design consultant, you mean?"

"For anyone. You were impressive. I have to say... You surprised me, babe." He lifted her hand from his leg and kissed her palm. "We make a good team," he said.

"We used to," she said under her breath...but clearly loud enough that he heard.

Jake shot her a dark look. "What does that mean?"

Emma leaned her head back on the seat and sighed. "Forget it. Now's not the time."

Dear Reader,

Marriage, raising kids, balancing work and home life—this stuff isn't for the faint of heart! It is hard. It requires commitment and patience and a whole lot of love. Is it any wonder sometimes even the most loving and earnest couple find themselves facing hard times? But what if, at your marriage's most vulnerable moment, a crisis threw your life into chaos? Jake and Emma Turner find themselves at just such a touch point in *Kidnapping in Cameron Glen*. Their eldest daughter has been kidnapped by human traffickers, and Jake and Emma will stop at nothing to rescue their firstborn.

As difficult as the subject of marital discord is to tackle, this book was one I felt I had to write. Happily-ever-after is a commitment to every day, especially when life gets hard. Even harder to address is the ugly truth of sexual predators. But through public awareness and the terrific work of organizations like A21, www.a21.org, we can end human trafficking. We must.

As always, wishing you the best and happy reading,

Beth

KIDNAPPING IN CAMERON GLEN

Beth Cornelison

HARLEQUIN

ROMANTIC
SUSPENSE

HARLEQUIN®
ROMANTIC SUSPENSE™

Recycling programs
for this product may
not exist in your area.

ISBN-13: 978-1-335-75979-5

Kidnapping in Cameron Glen

Copyright © 2022 by Beth Cornelison

For questions and comments about the quality of this book, please contact us at CustomerService@Harlequin.com.

Harlequin Enterprises ULC
22 Adelaide St. West, 41st Floor
Toronto, Ontario M5H 4E3, Canada
www.Harlequin.com

Printed in U.S.A.

Beth Cornelison began working in public relations before pursuing her love of writing romance. She has won numerous honors for her work, including a nomination for the RWA RITA® Award for *The Christmas Stranger*. She enjoys featuring her cats (or friends' pets) in her stories and always has another book in the pipeline! She currently lives in Louisiana with her husband, one son and three spoiled cats. Contact her via her website, bethcornelison.com.

Books by Beth Cornelison

Harlequin Romantic Suspense

Cameron Glen

Mountain Retreat Murder
Kidnapping in Cameron Glen

Colton 911: Chicago

Colton 911: Secret Alibi

The McCall Adventure Ranch

Rancher's Deadly Reunion
Rancher's High-Stakes Rescue
Rancher's Covert Christmas
Rancher's Hostage Rescue
In the Rancher's Protection

Visit the Author Profile page at Harlequin.com for more titles.

For Paul, who has been sharing the ups and downs of marriage with me for *mumble mumble* years and counting. Thanks for being my happily-ever-after, Pup!

Chapter 1

Jake didn't get home until 11:00 p.m. that night. He'd missed dinner entirely. Both of the girls were in bed, which was good. They didn't need to hear their parents arguing. Again.

Four-year-old Lexi had drifted off at around 8:00 p.m. while waiting for her daddy to come read her a book, and fifteen-year-old Fenn had retired sometime around ten after Emma had turned off the Wi-Fi.

As much as she hated to get into it with Jake for the zillionth time, Emma was fed up. More and more often he was absent from family time. He'd come home late three of seven nights at first, then four, five. Weekends. This was the fourth straight night this week that he'd missed dinner and Lexi's bedtime. The girls deserved better. She deserved better.

But beyond being absent from their home, Jake had been absent from their marriage for months, had turned off communication with her, shut her out, walled himself off. No matter how many times Emma tried to reach him, exhort him, break through, he moved farther away emotionally, physically. She was tired of the limbo. If she was going to be alone in the marriage, she might as well make it official. She needed closure.

Emma sat at the kitchen table, her heart aching, her jaw clenched and her gut in knots when he came through the back door. He paused at the threshold when he spotted her. Sighed. After dropping his keys on the counter, he closed the back door and raked fingers through his thick black hair. He needed a haircut, but he had neglected that in recent weeks as well.

"You're still up," he said, stating the obvious in a dark, defeated tone.

"Yep." Emma fought to tamp down the emotion strangling her. "We need to talk."

Concern swept over his face. "Why? Did something happen to one of the girls?"

Emma gave him credit for being worried about his daughters' welfare. But then, he'd always been a caring father. Which made his missing the girls' bedtime all the more disheartening. She shook her head. "We need to talk about *us*."

He rolled his eyes. "No. We don't. I'm tired, and I just want to go to bed."

When he turned to head down the hall, to walk away from her, she gritted her teeth. God, she hated when he did that!

"Not here you won't," she said loud enough to stop him.

He hesitated at the kitchen threshold. Flexed and balled his hands. Turned with a glare. "What's that mean?"

She shushed him. "Keep your voice down. The girls are asleep." With a directional nod, she indicated the duffel bag she'd packed for him. "I want you out. I can't do this anymore."

Jake scowled. "Seriously? You're kicking me out? For… what? Breaking my back all day to put a roof over our heads? Food on the table?"

"Don't give me that! You're not *breaking your back* until eleven o'clock at night. You're avoiding us. You're killing time until you think we're in bed. Brody said he saw you picking up food at the diner for supper, even though I texted to tell you we were having tacos at Lexi's request." Jake loved tacos as much as their four-year-old did, and she'd hoped the dish would be enough to entice him home for a meal with his children. But no.

He drew a slow, deep breath, his nose flaring, his jaw stony. Finally, he shook his head and muttered, "The key words there are 'picking up food.' I took it back to the office to eat. If you remember, I'm doing the job of two people, since I haven't found a satisfactory replacement for Peter yet."

"So hire someone!"

"Don't you think I'm trying to? I've worked my butt off repairing the damage to our reputation that the scandal with Peter caused, and, thanks to the slowdown in the economy, no one is building retail space right now. I'm sending out dozens of bids all over the state hoping to land anything I can. But along with that come long hours. I've worked too hard to build my company to let it slip away now. So yeah, I'm working late a lot, Em. Deal with it!"

"What I'm *dealing with* is my own job, plus raising our girls without you *and* running the house—"

"Geez, Em! Stop! You've done nothing but gripe at me for months. No one wants to be around that kind of negativity."

His comment stung—because she knew she'd been grumpy and complaining more recently. But after suppressing as much of her frustration and unhappiness as she could all day, she tended to blow up at Jake, taking out her fatigue and anger on him. He'd always been her safe place to vent and find comfort before. When had her venting *to* him become venting *at* him, *about* him?

She drew a deep breath, mustering her composure. "You're right. No one likes to live in a negative environment." Emma paused, flattening her hands on the tabletop and giving him a level look. "That's why I've filed for divorce."

His face slammed into a deeper frown. "You what?"

"All we do is fight, Jake. I'm tired of it. I've talked to a lawyer and started the paperwork."

He stared, clearly stunned. Good. She'd taken the drastic legal step as a last-ditch effort to grab his attention, to make him see she was serious—things had to change or she was gone.

She wished she could know what was going through his mind, but his face was frozen in a mask of shock and anger.

"So that's it?" he rasped. "You're quitting on us?"

She balled both hands, moving them to her lap, and swallowed hard. This was *not* her fault. "Didn't you quit on us months ago?"

His eyes widened. His back stiffened. Spinning on his boot heel, he stalked down the hall.

"Jake, stop! Don't walk away like that! We have to—" But he was gone. Down the hall. He slammed the bedroom door, and she cringed. Damn it, if he woke Lexi or Fenn...

Emma shoved her chair back and pursued him. This was why they needed time apart. They couldn't even have one conversation without blowing up at each other. Why couldn't he just accept the inevitable and do this peacefully? They'd both seen it coming for weeks, maybe months. Why did he have to make a scene, risk the kids hearing them? Lexi already came to her crying from nightmares at least once a week due to the tension in the house.

She opened the closed bedroom door and shut it again behind her. Quietly. "Jake, I hate it when you leave in the middle of a discussion like that."

He was stripping off his work clothes and paused to cock his head as if puzzling over something. "And yet, you just told me you want me to leave the house. That you're divorcing me. Which is it, Emma? I get so many mixed messages from you. How the hell am I supposed to know what you want?"

She gritted her teeth and crossed her arms over her chest. "Maybe you'd know what I want if you ever listened to me! Or, I don't know, spent more than five minutes here per day."

He barked a dark laugh. "See, there you go again." Jake jabbed a finger in her direction. "Spend more than five minutes? How am I supposed to do that if you *kick me out of my own damn house*!"

She shushed him again when his voice rose.

"Do *not* tell me to shush!" He whipped his shirt off over his head and threw it aside as if pitching a fastball. "It's my house, too, and *I'll shout if I want to*!"

Emma hurried across the room and aimed a finger in his face, whispering harshly, "Stop it! You'll scare Lexi and Fenn. Or don't you care about your children's feelings?"

"Of course I do. Do you?" Heat poured off him, his bare chest laboring with deep breaths of fury and frustration. "Is that why you've banished their father from their home?"

Emma lowered her gaze, unable to meet the burning accusation in her husband's dark brown eyes. But encountering his naked torso and the small tattoo on his left pectoral—a heart with her name in the center—only deepened the ache and guilt in her own chest. Her hand trembled at her side, and a powerful yearning to touch that decorated spot on his skin swelled inside her.

Damn her traitorous self for still feeling the potent allure of Jake's muscled chest and flat abs. But sexual attraction had never been their problem. They could fall in their bed now and have sex that was as passionate and fulfilling as the first months of their relationship, when discovering each other's bodies and personal pleasures had been new. But hot sex didn't fix the growing distance and dissonance between them.

Emma drew a careful breath, took a step back from Jake and raised a pleading gaze. "I am doing this *because* of Fenn and Lexi. You said it yourself. The atmosphere around here has become toxic. They need to be protected from the—"

"Doing this because of Fenn an—?" he roared, and she clapped a hand over his mouth. He pulled her hand away, and in a strained whisper, he said, "I'm working my butt off, trying to save my company and provide for my family. Yes, it's more hours than I'd like! I'm exhausted when I get home, but it is worth it to me, because I'm doing it for my family. For you. For the girls. I'm trying to give them—" he pointed toward the bedroom door, beyond which their daughters slept "—the financial security I never had. My family lived paycheck to paycheck. You know that, Em!" He drew a slow breath, his nose flaring, and she saw moisture glint in his eyes. "I will not let my company fail and let my family down!"

Emma swallowed past the knot in her own throat, and in a small voice asked, "And what if by putting your company first, you are failing your family?"

Jake growled and raked fingers through his hair. "This is stupid. We're going in circles."

"Jake, Fenn and Lexi don't need to hear us fighting

anymore. It's hurting them! We just need a little time apart to—"

"The girls are fine."

"No. They're not. And you'd see that yourself if you were ever here to—"

He cursed under his breath, snatched his shirt back off the floor and shoved past her, striding toward the bedroom door with long, stiff steps. "Fine. You want me gone? You want a divorce?" He jerked open the door and headed down the hall, once again leaving her to follow. "I'm sick of this crap. Sick of coming home to the same harping every night. Well, no more."

"I'm sick of fighting with you, too! Sick of you not hearing me! The girls are the only reason I—"

He grabbed the handle of the bag she'd packed him and marched through the kitchen to retrieve his keys. "Save it, Em. I. Am. Out!"

And then with a slam of the back door, the only man she'd ever loved was gone.

Fenn roused from a shallow sleep when she heard the loud voices down the hall. Her parents. Fighting again.

Nausea sawed in her gut, and she clenched her teeth. She was so, *so* sick of them shouting and blowing every little thing out of proportion. She wanted to shout at both of them to grow up. She was tired of hearing them grumble about each other, then lie and say everything was fine. But worse was seeing the tears in Lexi's eyes when Dad missed story time. Or the worried look Mom wore every evening as she watched the driveway, waiting for Dad's truck to pull up—a look that shifted to anger and disappointment as the minutes passed. And she'd had enough of the tension in the house when there was no yelling. It was like waiting for a bomb to go off. She'd spent most of the last few months pretending, adding her own lies to her little sister that everything was fine, when the acid in her stomach said otherwise.

She rolled over to grab an extra pillow to hold over her ears to muffle the shouting when she heard Mom say her name.

Then Dad shouting, "Doing this because of Fenn!"

She froze. They were yelling about her? What was Dad doing because of her? Had she made him angry? Was she why Dad was so late tonight?

She crawled out of bed and tiptoed to the door of her bedroom, pressing her ear against the cool wood to listen. Her heart was pounding so hard, she could barely hear anything over the panicked thumps. The floor shook as her dad stomped down the hall.

Sick of coming home. No more.

Girls are the only reason...

I am out.

Out? The door slammed, and then the house was filled by a chilling silence. A moment later she heard her dad's truck engine. She hurried to her window and peeked through the blinds in time to see the F-150's taillights departing. Her dad left in a hurry, the gravel in the driveway spraying as he raced away. Angry. He'd sounded so angry.

Because of her?

She'd clearly heard "the girls are the reason," and "because of Fenn." Her dad had left, and it was her fault?

She thought about Lexi. Normally when their parents fought, Lexi would get scared and cry in her bed or come climb in bed with Fenn. Creeping to the door and cracking it open, Fenn listened for Lexi. Should she go check on her?

She heard a sob, stepped into the hall to go to Lexi. And froze. The sobs were coming from the kitchen. Her mom.

Heart in her throat, Fenn eased to the door of the kitchen and peeked in. Her mom was sitting on the floor, back to the cabinets, her face buried in her hands as her shoulders heaved.

Fenn's heart rose to her throat. This was serious. Mom was usually so strong. She'd seen Mom cry at Great-grandpa Cameron's funeral a few years ago, but that was the only time. Well, except for certain TV shows. And when Lexi was born.

She swallowed hard and rasped, "Mom?"

Her mom stiffened, jerked her head up and swiped her face with her hands to dry her tears and runny nose. "Fenn. Honey, I—"

Fenn moved closer to her mom and sat beside her quietly.

"I thought you were asleep," Mom said, adding the worst attempt at a smile ever, as she wrapped an arm around Fenn.

"I was. Kinda. I heard you and Dad yelling."

Her mom huffed a humorless laugh. "Of course you did." Another pitiful smile as she stroked Fenn's hair. "I'm sorry. I—" Her voice cracked, and she glanced away, dabbing her eyes again with her sleeve.

"Are you...okay?"

"Yeah." Mom nodded. Not real convincingly, but... "I'm fine. Oh, Button, everything is fine. We're going to be...fine." She nodded again as if to reassure herself.

Fine? Fenn seethed inside. Did her mom think she was stupid?

"But Dad left," Fenn said flatly. A statement. Stunned disbelief and confusion.

Her mom glanced at her with wet eyes. Hesitated. And nodded. Again. God, she wished her mom would stop that ridiculous nodding like a broken bobble head.

"For the night or...for good?"

Her mother's shoulders lifted and fell as she took a deep breath. Shook her head. "I... I don't know, Button. But... you don't need to worry about...anything." She paused.

Sniffled. "Your dad and I just…need some time apart to—"

"No!" *Need some time apart* was adult code for divorce. For giving up. Pain slashing her chest, Fenn shoved out of her mother's arms and jumped to her feet. "How do you expect to fix this if you split up?" Emotion clogged her throat, but she battled it down to squeak. "Lexi needs both of you here. She's so little! She doesn't understand! How can you do this to her?"

To me! was what she wanted to yell, but she already felt guilty about what she'd overheard. If her parents separating was in any way her fault, she had no right to ask them for anything.

…doing this because of Fenn!

"Fenn, I know you don't understand, but…there are things your dad and I have to work out before he can move back in."

Her stomach rolled. "So he's really gone? He moved out? For good?"

Mom's face crumpled, and she shifted to her knees to get off the floor. "Honey, I'm sorry. I know this is hard for—"

Fenn shouted a curse at her mother that would normally get her at least a week of restriction. Mom's face went white. Hurt and shock seemed to physically knock her back.

"Fenn!"

Tears blurred Fenn's view as she raced back to her room and closed the door behind her. She almost slammed it, but at the last second, she pulled up, remembering Lexi was asleep. Instead, she lashed out at her pillow, beating it so hard and so long she was surprised not to see stuffing fly out. Then when her arm got tired of thrashing the pillow, she hugged it close and cried silent tears into it.

Her fault. *The girls are the reason. Because of Fenn.*

But why? What had she done? Sure, she talked back to her mom and dad sometimes, sassing them when she got frustrated with their nagging. She had friends who talked way more smack than she did, and their parents didn't split up over it.

Although…there was that time last summer she'd snuck out and drunk beer with Eric. And kept a big secret about witnessing a break-in at one of the family cabins. Of course, her parents had argued heatedly over how to punish her for that. And she'd cut class once right before Christmas with her friends to go see a movie in Asheville. Mom and Dad had yelled at each other about that, too, blaming each other for her "acting out."

Her heart was a rock. Hard and heavy and dragging her down in a pool of guilt. Okay. She'd given them several reasons in the last year to be mad. Maybe she *was* the spark that set her parents' marriage on fire. Maybe it *was* her fault. She knew they'd gotten married to begin with because her mom had gotten pregnant with her during Mom's senior year of high school. They'd skipped college to start a family. Did they resent her for that? Maybe all of her parents' troubles dated back to her birth, how she ruined their plans and forced them to marry too young.

Maybe the family would be better off without her.

Nausea swam in her gut, and she thought her heart might crack. If her parents were fighting, breaking up the family because of her, she had no choice but to find a way to make things right. But how?

The light on Brody's front porch flicked on in response to Jake's late-night knock. When his brother-in-law opened the door, blinking at him sleepily, Jake grimaced. Brody went to bed crazy early because he got up crazy early to start his landscaping work before the hottest part of the day.

"Jake? What's wrong?" Brody croaked, rubbing his tousled hair.

"Sorry to wake you, man." Jake shoved his hands in his back pockets and sighed. "Can I crash here tonight?"

"Here? Why?" Brody shook his head as if realizing the question sounded inhospitable and quickly amended, "I mean, yeah." He pushed open his screened door, inviting Jake in. "But also, why?"

"Em kicked me out." Jake heard the despondency and defeat in his tone, and pinched the bridge of his nose. He didn't want to dump his troubles on Brody, putting his brother-in-law in the middle of his marriage issues with Emma. He and Brody might be as close as blood brothers, but he knew Cameron blood was thicker than any in-law bond. Brody's first loyalty would be to his sister.

As he edged past his brother-in-law and moved into Brody's den, he choked down the bitterness that rose in his throat. How had his marriage come to this? Where had he gone wrong? How did he course correct?

Did he even want to? Maybe he and Emma were better off divorcing. That notion sent a chill through him, shook him to his core.

"So…wanna tell me what's going on?" Brody asked from behind him.

"Not really. Just…an argument. We both needed time to cool off." He waved a hand to the sofa. "I'll just sleep out here. I don't need anything fancy."

"Good. 'Cause I don't do fancy. I can get you a blanket, though." Brody disappeared down the hall and returned a moment later with a thin quilt. After handing the quilt to Jake, Brody frowned. "You two have been going at it a lot lately. The family has noticed, and we're worried."

Jake blew out a long breath that made his lips buzz. "Yeah. I'm worried, too."

Brody stared at him silently for a long time, his hands on his hips, his brow furrowed.

Jake knew Brody was waiting for some explanation, but Jake was too tired, too distraught, too confused by the turn his life had taken to try to unpack it all. How could he when he understood so little of what was happening himself?

"Have y'all talked to a counselor?" Brody finally asked.

Jake snorted. "Seriously?"

Brody's expression hardened. "Yeah, seriously. I'd say it's time. Past time if you're showing up here in the middle of the night to sleep on my couch."

A counselor? Jake winced internally. Seeing a shrink was tantamount to admitting he and Emma had real problems that they couldn't solve by themselves. That he'd failed. That he had lost control of his life. He hated the idea of airing their dirty laundry to a stranger. Or worse, someone they knew. Which was pretty much everyone in their small hometown of Valley Haven, North Carolina. "Em suggested it a few weeks ago, but I don't know. I can't see it."

Brody sighed. "Don't be a stubborn blockhead about this, Jake. Isn't your marriage worth it? Isn't Emma worth it? Do it for her. For your kids!"

Jake toed off his shoes and sank down on the couch.

Emma. Fenn. Lexi. His girls. He'd walk through fire for his family. Face a firing squad.

So go see a counselor, nimrod.

His lungs seized so hard he couldn't breathe. He squeezed the quilt in his fists and struggled to draw oxygen. Why did getting help feel like defeat? Like failure?

"Well, think about it." Brody exhaled a frustrated sounding huff before he strolled out of the den and turned off the overhead light. "I'll be up at four, but I'll try to be quiet. Night."

Think about it.

He did. All night.

When his brother-in-law stumbled down the hall to the kitchen at 4:00 a.m., Jake was still awake. And still had no answers.

Four o'clock arrived, and Fenn still hadn't slept. All night, one thought had repeated in her brain again and again. She just wanted it all to be over. She wanted to get away from the yelling. She wanted an end to the anger and fighting. For her parents' sake, for Lexi's sake. For herself.

If not for her, maybe her parents would have a chance. *Because of Fenn.*

Dread and sadness dragged at her as she rolled out of bed and did what she knew she had to. For her family's sake. Because she couldn't stand another night of listening to her parents battle and her sister cry and doors slam. She stuffed a few clothes in her backpack, added her purse and all the money from her secret stash. Fifty-two dollars wouldn't go very far, but she'd figure something out. She put her phone and charging cords in an outer pocket then stopped. Sarah Beth said her folks had tracked her location using her phone even without the spy app. She hated to be without it, but she didn't want to be found either. Taking it back out, she dug in a drawer for her mom's old iPod and jammed it down a front pocket of the backpack. At least, she could still have tunes.

In case Mom peeked in her room when she got up, Fenn dumped a pile of her dirty clothes on her bed, like they did in the movies, and pulled the cover up to make a lump that looked like she was in bed. Finally, she took a picture from her bulletin board of the whole Cameron-Turner-Harkney family at Aunt Cait's wedding last month. A pang twisted in her chest looking at the smiles of her aunts and uncles and grandparents and great-grandma

Nanna. And her mom and dad. For one day, her parents had at least acted happy, even if the smiles were fake. She loved her big, loud, crazy family. She'd miss them. She'd come back and visit once things had settled down for her parents. But until then…

She sniffled and wiped her eyes. If she was going to do this, she had to get going. Before Mom heard her, stopped her.

She zipped up the backpack, slung it over one shoulder, jammed her feet in her sneakers and tiptoed out of her room. She stepped over the squeaky board in the hall, squeezed through the partially closed kitchen partition so it didn't screech on its runners. As she made her way to the back door, she spotted her mom's purse on the counter and hesitated. Debated. Mom would want her to have enough money to eat, to survive. Right?

Quelling the kick of ill ease, Fenn opened her mom's purse, found the wallet and removed the debit card. Replacing everything the way she found it, Fenn pocketed the debit card and hurried to the back door.

The spring morning was cool, and she thought for a moment about going back in for a jacket. But the sun would be out soon enough and riding her bike would warm her up. Their feral cat, Magic, roused from her sleep and appeared out of the bushes with a stretch and a yawn.

"Sorry, Magic. Not breakfast time yet," she whispered.

The black cat sat down, her tail curling around her feet, then lifted a paw that she licked.

After securing the backpack on her shoulders, Fenn pushed her bicycle down the gravel driveway. Her chin trembling as she remembered Dad speeding down the same path last night, and she had to blink to clear the moisture from her eyes. At the end of the drive, she glanced back at the house, still and quiet in the predawn darkness, and whispered, "Goodbye."

Climbing on her bike, she set out. She could be all the way into Valley Haven before anyone knew she was gone. And she knew buses left the Valley Haven bus depot for Asheville and Charlotte early in the morning, for business commuters. She planned to be on one of them.

Chapter 2

Jake was fumbling with the filters at the coffee pot in the Turner Construction break room when his administrative assistant arrived. Darla, a fifty-something widow with dyed black hair and rimless glasses, hesitated in the door with a startled gasp.

"Land sakes!" She pressed a hand to her bosom and chuckled. "You scared me silly, Jake. I'm used to being the first one here, having the run of the place for a half hour or so before folks arrive."

"Sorry. Left my cowbell at home." *Along with everything else that means anything to me.* He grew frustrated with his attempt to separate the thin layers of paper and waved the filters at Darla. "Will you do this?"

He threw the stack on the counter with a peevish huff.

"Certainly." Darla gently nudged him aside with her hip and went to work with the speed and agility of rote.

Jake pinched the bridge of his nose where a headache was building. "I couldn't sleep, like...*at all*, so I figured

I'd come in, get something done." He leaned against the counter, his shoulders sagging. "But without any coffee…" He let his sentence trail. He wasn't even sure what he'd meant to say. His thoughts, no matter where they started, always circled around to Emma. To finding her at the kitchen table last night.

We need to talk. Were more terrifying words ever spoken in a relationship? He sure as hell hadn't wanted to go down that treacherous path. But Em couldn't leave it alone. She'd pushed him when he was already stressed and tired, and he'd exploded.

Regret washed through him as he squeezed his eyes tighter shut, replaying the argument in his head, the sour tones exchanged. Not his finest moment. A groan rumbled in his chest as he acknowledged he had a lot of "not his finest" moments lately.

A hand touched his shoulder, and he jolted.

"Are you all right?" Darla asked.

He scrubbed a hand over his face. "Yeah. No. Hell, I don't know."

She angled her head and gave him a look of motherly concern. "Why don't you go on in your office, and I'll bring you a cup of this when it's ready." She waved the coffee carafe before sticking it on the burner and flipping the power switch to On.

Jake gave her a grateful nod and retreated to his office, closing the door behind him. He propped his arms on the desk and buried his face in his hands. *What do I do? How did my life end up here?*

Memories of a boy watching his father grow prematurely old, burdened by too many bills and too little pay, haunted him. He remembered nights his siblings cried because they had no supper. He remembered the embarrassment of wearing clothes to school that were too small, the pinch of shoes that were too tight because they couldn't

afford new. He thought back to the tears his mother had
shed on Thanksgiving when a charity had delivered hot
plates of food. Tears of gratitude for her, while his father
had shed tears of shame.

Promise me, Jake, Dad had said. *Study hard, go to college. I want more for you, for your kids than this life.* Jake
had tried to reassure his father that he had nothing to be
ashamed of. His work ethic, his love for his family, his
sacrifice were things to be proud of. But his father could
only see want. Need. Lack.

The stress of trying to provide for his family drove
his father to drink, to despair and eventually to his grave
when a heart attack stole him too soon. Jake had sworn
to himself, to his father, that he would be the success,
the provider that his father had dreamed of for him. He'd
learned how to work hard, give his all and set high goals
from his father. And then…

Emma had gotten pregnant when they were eighteen.
He'd had to skip college, jump straight into work-a-day
life to take care of his new wife and child. And somehow,
through sweat and sacrifice, he'd built a thriving construction company.

Every day, when he entered his office, he paused to
touch his father's hard hat, which sat on a shelf in a place
of honor in Jake's office. A reminder of all his father had
sacrificed for his family.

Now Jake stared across the room at the battered old
hard hat and sighed. He wished his dad was still around
to ask for advice. Jake had done the hard work of making Turner Construction a thriving operation like his
father would have wanted. But how did he save his family?

He knew he needed to make a plan. You didn't build
a house without blueprints, and he hadn't built the best
construction company in the county without planning and
management skills. Emma liked to call him bossy and a

control freak, always grinning and adding, *In a good way*. But at the moment, one of the most critical crossroads of his life, he had no idea which way to go, what the next steps were.

Did he get an apartment? Meet with Emma and try to talk sense into her?

Emma said she'd already filed for divorce.

A cold chill raced through him that such an idea had even crossed her mind. Did that mean she'd lost faith in him? Quit loving him?

How did he live without Emma and the girls? Sure, things had been sour with Emma for a long time, but he'd never been a bad husband. He worked hard to provide for them, never cheated on her and would defend them with his own life. And Emma thanked him by kicking him out of his own home?

A fresh wave of anger and hurt swept through him, and the acid in his gut roiled. His fists balled tighter, and his jaw clenched.

The light rap on his door jerked him from his gloomy musing, and Darla sauntered in without waiting for his response.

Relaxing his tensed muscles took conscious effort as he sat back in his office chair.

"Here you go, hon." She set the steaming mug of coffee on his blotter and studied him with a tipped head again. "Anything else I can do? Have you had any breakfast?"

He shook his head, answering both questions. "Thanks, though."

She heaved the kind of sigh he'd heard his mother sigh throughout his teen years when she was concerned and disappointed. Darla often treated him more like a son than her boss. Not that it bothered him. He kinda liked the warmth and kindness she offered, especially since his own mother had passed away a few years back. Damn cancer. He could use some maternal advice about now, but was wary of crossing a line with Darla and dumping his personal problems on her. That would just be…awkward and *wrong*.

"Well, all right." She walked to the door where she stopped and cast a sad glance back at him. "Don't forget you have a meeting at nine with Mr. Shapiro about the Wildwood contract."

Jake groaned and dug the heels of his palms into his eyes. "No. Not today. Cancel it."

"Uh…are you sure?"

Jake dropped his hands to the desk and nodded. "Yeah, cancel it. And…hold my calls today. I've got other stuff to deal with."

With a reluctant frown, she bobbed her chin once and closed the door behind her as she left.

He didn't feel good about canceling the meeting, but his head was too messed up, his thoughts too splintered to be on point in any business meeting. *Thanks for the unwanted distraction, Emma*, he thought grouchily.

He wished he knew why Emma had become so harsh, so full of complaints and demands lately. Didn't she see how hard he was working to keep his business afloat? Of course he spent more time at the office lately. Who wanted to be around her negativity and judgmental attitude?

He thought about Brody's suggestion they get counseling. Did he want to sit in a falsely cheery office listening to Emma list all his shortcomings and her gripes to a stranger? Hell no. Would he for his daughters' sake? For his marriage's sake?

He heaved a deep sigh. What choice did he have? He had to do something before it was too late.

It was getting late. Well past normal breakfast time. Emma passed Fenn's closed door for the umpteenth time and hesitated, wanting to knock, wanting to check on her…

then stopping herself. If Fenn was sleeping, she needed to let her daughter sleep. Being Saturday, Fenn didn't have to rush to catch the school bus. She knew Fenn had likely been awake much of the night, as she had. Besides, she wasn't looking forward to the conversation they'd have to have when Fenn did wake up.

Maybe just a peek? Biting her bottom lip, Emma turned the knob of Fenn's door as quietly as she could and opened the door a crack. She spied the still lump of her daughter's form in a tumble of sheets and the quilt Nanna had made. Fenn had clearly had a rough night, judging by the twisted knot of bedclothes. With a sad sigh, Emma closed the door.

How did she explain to Fenn why her dad had left the house last night? How much had Fenn overheard?

Her daughter had found her crying. She hated that. Emma wanted so much to be strong in front of her girls. To protect them. Seeing their mother in the deepest throes of heartbreak and frustration would surely frighten them and undermine their sense of security. She didn't want them wondering, "If Mom is cracking and Dad is gone, where does that leave us?"

Where, indeed?

After peeking in Lexi's room to assure herself her youngest was playing quietly, she wandered back into her own bedroom and sat on the bed, replaying the shouting match that had unfolded here last night. Where had Jake gone when he left? Where was his head this morning? Had her stand shaken him enough to wake up to what was happening between them?

She reached for her mobile phone on the bedside stand and pressed the speed dial for his cell. He answered with a gruff, "What?"

"I thought we could talk."

He scoffed. "Well, we can't. I'm busy." And he hung up.

She sucked in a deep breath, bunched the bedspread in

her hand and counted to ten. To twenty. To fifty. When she thought she had her temper under control, she hit Redial.

"I'm not doing this now, Emma," he grated when he answered. "I have work to do."

"Fine. Then when?"

"I don't know." And he hung up.

A tremble raced through her. She'd asked for this when she kicked him out. She'd known he'd be hurt, angry, bitter. None of that made his curtness any less painful.

The ache in her chest swelled until she couldn't catch her breath. Nausea swamped her, and she darted to the bathroom where she lost what little breakfast she'd managed to choke down.

Rising on shaky legs, she rinsed her mouth at the sink and met her haggard reflection in the mirror—and winced. When had thirty-four started looking so…old? Her shoulder-length brown hair was beyond rumpled, and her cheeks were wan. Leaning closer, she noticed her Cameron-blue eyes—Saltire blue, Nanna called it, referencing the flag of her homeland, Scotland—were bloodshot and had bags as big as suitcases underneath. Her gaze was steeped in regret. Maybe she'd made a terrible mistake filing for divorce, telling Jake to move out. Maybe…

She shook her head and pinched the bridge of her nose. No. He'd forced her hand. She'd done what was best for the girls. She couldn't—

"Mommy?" Lexi's voice roused Emma, and she turned to find her youngest tangled in her shirt. "I'm stuck."

Emma forced a wobbly grin and crouched to help her. "That you are, silly goose. You have your head in an armhole." She tugged the skewed T-shirt off, straightened it and guided it back over Lexi's head correctly.

"There you go." She kissed Lexi's nose and finger-combed her daughter's silky, caramel hair. "There's my pretty princess."

"Why are your eyes all funny?" Lexi asked, wrinkling her nose.

"They're all funny?"

Bobbing her head, Lexi squinted at her. "All red and stuff."

Emma swallowed hard, determined not to start crying again. She said the first thing that came to her. "Well, because... I haven't had enough Lexi and Fenn hugs this morning, I guess."

She opened her arms, inviting Lexi in, and when her daughter fell trustingly against her, Emma's heart swelled and her throat clogged with emotion. She squeezed Lexi tightly, clung for as long as the four-year-old would allow. When Lexi pulled away, Emma rearranged her face with a smile. "There. Much better."

"Now Fenn's turn!" Lexi wiggled past her and ran toward Fenn's bedroom.

Emma chased her and caught Lexi's wrist before she could knock. "Whoa! Sissy's still asleep. Let's leave her alone for a while. She's really tired. Okay?"

"But you need a Fenn hug to fix your eyes."

Emma chuckled despite her mood. Lexi's innocence and four-year-old logic was refreshing. And poignant.

"And I will get a Fenn hug as soon as she wakes up. But right now, I need to feed my princess. What do you want for breakfast?" She stood and offered her hand to Lexi, leading her down the hall toward the kitchen. She set her phone on the counter and opened the refrigerator to survey the contents. "French toast and bacon?"

French toast and bacon was Fenn's favorite breakfast, and Emma hoped the scents of cinnamon and smoked meat would cheer Fenn a bit when she woke. But an hour later, when she'd still not heard a peep from her teenager's room, Emma put away the leftover French toast and bacon. Three hours later, with still nothing from Fenn's room, Emma felt the first stirs of concern. Though it was not uncommon for her fifteen-year-old to sleep late on a Saturday, knowing Fenn had heard the argument with Jake, had seen her breakdown, put a different light on the situation.

If Fenn was hurting, confused, angry, Emma wanted to be there for her daughter. Maybe Fenn was awake and just hiding from confrontation. Maybe Fenn didn't know how to face her mother after witnessing Emma's meltdown last night. Maybe…

Shoving aside her nagging thoughts, Emma walked to Fenn's door and tapped quietly. "Fenn, honey? Are you up?"

No answer.

"Fenn?"

Still nothing.

"Mommy, I can't get Elsa. I wanna watch Elsa." Lexi handed her an electronic tablet with the parental block page glowing, waiting for the password to allow Lexi to view her favorite movie again.

Emma took the tablet but hesitated. "Kitten, why don't you go play outside? It's a pretty day."

"Nooo," Lexi whined. "I wanna watch Elsa!"

"Maybe Grandpa will take you fishing or to play on the tire swing?" Emma cringed internally, knowing too often she depended on her parents, whose yard adjoined hers on the family's one-hundred-and-fifty-acre retreat property, Cameron Glen.

Lexi shook her head and pointed to the tablet again. "Elsa! Pleeease!"

The whiny plea grated on Emma's raw nerves. Usually she could juggle working from home and her youngest daughter's needs for attention. She had never wanted to use electronics as a babysitter and had developed a litany of creative outlets for Lexi's energy and curiosity. Emma made the most of that uninterrupted time for video consultation with her clients or online research regarding the latest remodeling materials, color trends and product designs.

When puzzles, dress-up, coloring and books failed to distract her little girl, Emma also had most of her family living a short walk away on the grounds of Cameron Glen. Lexi's doting grandparents, who loved to show Lexi how to bake and fish and knit and throw a baseball, were next door. Emma's sisters, who showed Lexi how to make clover chains and played hide-and-seek among the Fraser firs of the Cameron Christmas tree farm, lived in cabins on the family's retreat property. Brody, who gave Lexi the best excuse to get muddy, helping plant and weed and water the plethora of landscaping around Cameron Glen, could be found somewhere on the property daily tending the Christmas trees and flower beds.

And Fenn was usually willing to help entertain and look after her sister on weekends and school nights in return for a weekly allowance. Emma glanced at Fenn's closed door and dismissed the idea of waking her teenager to babysit while Emma helped Caroline Penshaw choose cabinets, back splash tile and countertop marble for her kitchen remodel.

"Okay. Elsa it is," she said with a relenting sigh. She tapped in the password to unlock the tablet and start the Disney movie playing. After getting a few cheese crackers and grapes in a bowl for Lexi to snack on, Emma headed to her office and closed the door to work.

Ninety minutes, dozens of stain colors and tile designs later, Emma emerged from her work cave in time to hear the refrain of the end credit's music from the living room. Fenn's door was still shut. Emma rolled her eyes. It was after 1:00 p.m. Even if Fenn had been up most of the night, sleeping all day didn't bode well for getting rest tonight.

"Fenn?" Emma knocked on her daughter's door before

cracking it open and glancing around the dim space. "Time to get up, darling. It's better not to sleep all day if—"

Emma paused, squinting at the bed. The rumpled sheets she'd thought were Fenn looked different in the brighter light of the afternoon sun. She marched to the bedside, flipping back the covers to be sure. No Fenn.

"Fenn?" She turned to see if she'd missed her daughter lurking at her closet or huddled over her desk or… But no. No Fenn. *Huh.*

She headed to the girls' bathroom, but the light was off, the door open. No Fenn.

"Fenn!" she called, all the more confused as she checked the other bedrooms, the laundry room and kitchen without finding her oldest daughter. She moved to the living room where Lexi was starting the movie over. "Once is enough, Lex. Go play in your room or go outside for a while."

Emma took the electronic tablet from her youngest, who flopped backward on the sofa with a dramatic sigh. "Uh, Mommy! Please?"

"Have you seen Fenn today?" Emma placed the tablet on a high shelf and faced Lexi again.

"She's still asleep."

"She's not. I checked her room, and she's not in there. You haven't seen her, then?"

Lexi shrugged and pulled the plush lap blanket off the back of the couch. "Mommy, watch this." She wrapped herself in the blanket, mummy-fashion and lay stiff on the sofa cushions. "It's my cocoon." She threw the blanket off and sprang up. "Now I'm a butterfwy!"

Emma gave her daughter a smile of approval. "Good job, honey."

Something moved outside the window in her peripheral vision. She moved closer and pushed the curtain aside for a better look. Magic, their black feral cat had chased

a squirrel up a tree and sat on the lower limb of the dog-
wood, her tail thrashing.

So…not Fenn. But…

Emma headed outside to check the yard, the tree house,
the tire swing. She circled the house. "Fenn? Fenn!"

No answer. Frustrated, Emma marched toward the back
door. She opened the screened door and reached for the
doorknob…then paused as a strange prickle nipped her
neck. She glanced back at the yard, the tool shed, the car-
port, wondering what had seemed off. Her gaze settled
on the empty spot next to Lexi's tricycle, and her pulse
jumped.

Fenn's bike was gone.

Using one hand to shield the keypad like she'd seen her
mother do, Fenn typed in the PIN number to her parents'
bank account, then glanced around warily while the ATM
clicked and whirred, processing her withdrawal.

A shifty-looking guy in sagging khakis and a ratty gray
T-shirt leaned against the outside wall of the convenience
store, a cigarette pinched between his lips. But it wasn't
anything about his clothes or smoking habit that made him
shifty in Fenn's book. It was the less-than-subtle way he
watched her. He made her neck itch and her pulse scam-
per. He didn't approach her, but when she looked his way,
making sure he was keeping his distance, he winked at
her and flashed a leering smile.

When the machine spit out her cash, she snatched the
bills and receipt, jammed them in her tiny change purse,
then stowed the change purse in the main pocket of her
backpack. She hadn't intended to get cash quite so soon,
but her bus ticket had cost more than she'd anticipated.

The earliest bus she could get on left in another hour
for Knoxville, so she was killing time, trying to plan and
prepare for her trip, her future. She'd left the house with-

out eating, and her stomach had started growling a couple hours ago.

Avoiding eye contact with Shifty, she hustled inside the convenience store to buy lunch. Nothing much in the store looked very good—overcooked hot dogs, dried-out chicken- and egg-salad sandwiches that would almost certainly give her food poisoning—but she didn't have a lot of choices in this part of town. Maybe she could ride her bike over to the Bi-Lo on Rutherford Road, but that was down a really busy street and close to two miles out of her way. So a prepackaged turkey and Swiss on white bread and a nearly expired bag of chips it was. She selected her items and headed to the register to pay. While she waited for another customer to pay for their lottery tickets and beer, she studied the candy display. Butterfingers were her favorite—

"Hey! Hold up, you!" a woman shouted, startling Fenn from her perusal of the chocolate offerings and drawing her attention to the front door. A middle-aged woman in a store apron grabbed the arm of a girl a little older than Fenn with hair dyed bright magenta and a nose ring in her left nostril.

"Get off me!" the girl snarled back, trying to shake off the woman's hold.

"Empty your pockets. I saw you put something in your jacket." The aproned woman waved a finger toward the bright-haired girl's pockets.

The girl replied with an anatomically impossible suggestion for the woman.

"Fine. Gerald, call the police!" Ms. Apron grabbed the girl's frail wrist and clung tight. "You can wait for them in my office."

Magenta's dark eyes widened, and her expression was nothing short of panic. "No! No, cops!" She dug in her pockets and pulled out a small bottle of Tylenol, some beef jerky and a box of condoms. "Here. I was gonna pay. I just—" She broke free of Apron's grip and stormed over to the register, elbowing Fenn out of the way. "Just be cool." She fumbled in the pocket of her jeans and pulled out a few dollars. "That's all I got."

"Three bucks?" the cashier, presumably the Gerald Apron had asked to call the cops, spread the bills the girl offered in his fingers with a sneer.

"Call the cops," Apron repeated.

"No!"

Fenn could feel the fear rolling off Magenta Hair, and her own heart beat faster. She didn't like the idea of the police showing up either. What if they recognized her as a runaway and called her parents?

"Wait!" she blurted. "She's with me. I'm paying for both of our stuff."

All eyes shifted to Fenn, and she held her breath. Well, she'd dived in. Nothing to do but follow through now. She pushed past Magenta and dropped her purchases on the counter.

"You're with her?" Apron sounded dubious.

Fenn squared her shoulders and tried to sound sincere. "Yeah. So everything's good, right? It was just a misunderstanding."

Her eyes met Magenta's as she slid her backpack from her shoulder, dug out her change purse and extracted one of the twenties the ATM had just fed her. The corner of Magenta's mouth twitched in appreciation.

Once she'd paid for the items, Fenn walked out of the store with Magenta, under the twin skeptical glares of the cashier and the aproned woman. On the sidewalk in front of the store, she opened the bag and handed Magenta the Tylenol, jerky and condoms. A funny tickle wiggled in her belly. She'd just purchased condoms. Condoms! Even if they weren't hers, it gave her a feeling of being mature and sophisticated.

Magenta took the items with a sheepish grin. "Thanks."

"Sure. Happy to—" But before she could finish, Magenta spun away and stalked off to the older model sedan idling at the far end of the parking lot. Smoke curled out from the front passenger's window, and Fenn squinted to make out the smoker's face. Shifty. Staring at her still. Another guy sat in the driver's seat and a girl about Magenta's age was in the back seat.

Curious, she watched Magenta approach the sedan and talk to Shifty. Was Shifty her boyfriend? Then Magenta glanced back at Fenn. An uneasy feeling stirred in her gut. She stuck the sandwich and chips in her backpack and headed for her bike, which was propped against the concrete block side of the convenience store.

"Hey," Magenta called to her.

Fenn slowed and faced Magenta. "What?"

Magenta stopped halfway across the parking lot and held out some cash. "Here's your money back."

Fenn hesitated, a weird prickle on her neck. She knew pretty soon she'd need that twelve bucks she'd spent on Magenta, but why wasn't the girl bringing it to her? Narrowing a suspicious glare on the other girl, Fenn crossed the pavement and reached for the money.

At the same time her hand closed around the bills, Magenta's other hand closed around Fenn's wrist.

"Hey!" Fenn tried to jerk her hand back, but the other girl clung tight.

"C'mere a minute. I want you to meet my friends."

"No. I—" Fenn braced her legs as panic swelled in her chest. "I don't want to! Let go!"

In an instant, Shifty was there. He moved behind Fenn and wrapped his arms around her in a way that penned her arms to her sides. He lifted her as the sedan darted forward.

"No!" Fenn shouted, thrashing her legs, kicking at Shifty as best she could.

But Shifty and Magenta combined their efforts and pushed Fenn in the back seat, even as she loosed a scream. Someone struck her jaw, and shock silenced her as her ears rung from the blow.

Shifty shoved in beside her, closed the door. And the sedan sped away.

Chapter 3

Emma's jaw tightened with frustration. Fenn knew better than to leave the house without permission, without at least telling someone where she was going.

With a grunt, Emma shouldered the back door open and found her phone on the kitchen counter. She called Fenn's cell phone, ready to read her daughter the riot act. She heard one ring through her phone and, almost immediately, the pop tune that was Fenn's ringtone sounded down the hall. Emma followed the music to Fenn's room. Her daughter's cell phone was on her dresser.

Disconnecting the call, she dropped on the rumpled bed, confused. Fenn never went anywhere without her cell phone. It didn't make sense. Fenn's bike was gone, but her phone was here. What was going on?

Her panic rising, Emma retreated to her bedroom behind a closed door and called her parents. They hadn't seen Fenn this morning, didn't know where she was.

"Have you called the police?" her mother asked.

"It's too soon for that. I haven't tried her friends or any other family yet. Maybe she's just walking around the lake or…something."

Next she called her sister Cait in the Cameron Glen office. Fenn often hung out down there when she wanted distance from Lexi's pestering. But Cait hadn't seen Fenn either.

She called her sister Isla, then her brother, Brody. Neither of them knew anything about Fenn's whereabouts.

"Your husband spent the night on my couch, though. You wanna talk about that?" Brody asked.

"No. I don't," Emma said, her tone clipped.

"You know, my letting him crash here doesn't mean I'm taking sides, Em."

"I know. I'm…I'm sorry if I sound brusque. I'm worried about Fenn."

"I get that. But shouldn't you be a little worried about Jake, too? He was pretty torn up about—"

"Brody, stop. I—" Emma's throat constricted, and she shoved her fingers through her messy hair as she struggled for a calming breath.

"I'm just saying—"

"I can't do this right now. Yes, I'm worried about my marriage, about Jake. About *a lot* of things. But right at this very moment, I have to find Fenn. I can't do…can't think about anything else right now or…I'll lose it."

Her voice cracked, and on the other end of the line, she heard her little brother's gentle, "Aw, Em."

She sniffed. Wiped her eyes. Checked the door to make sure Lexi hadn't come in to overhear. "Keep an eye out for Fenn, okay? Send her home if you see her."

"Of course. And, Emma?"

"Hmm?" She was already deciding which of Fenn's friends to call first.

"I'm here, if you need…anything."

Emma squeezed her eyes shut, overcome with emotion, a tear dripping from her lashes. "Thanks," she squeaked as she disconnected. She jammed her fist against her mouth to muffle the sobs that rose inside her. Once she'd battled down the wave of self-pity and fear, she called every friend saved in Fenn's phone contacts. Nothing.

She knew Jake was the obvious, logical next call. Her gut knotted, remembering the bitterness in his tone when she'd called him earlier. But no matter. Finding Fenn was paramount. She tried reaching him on his cell, and the call went straight to voice mail. After leaving a message for him to call her back, she phoned his office landline.

"Turner Construction," the office administrator's voice chirped brightly. Turner Construction was open six days a week, during the busiest building months, and Jake's administrative assistant was paid time and a half on Saturdays and had Monday afternoons off.

"Hi, Darla. It's Emma. I need to speak to Jake."

"Well...he asked me to hold his calls."

"Please, Darla. It's an emergency."

"Oh. Goodness. I— Let me try his line."

Emma waited on hold until Darla returned with a gloomy tone, "He says he's busy, and, quote, for you to leave him alone. I'm sorry, hon."

Emma's face warmed. Her marital problems with Jake were no secret at the construction office thanks to a recent argument in his office and the hours Jake kept, but Darla's witness to Jake's flagrant dismissal was humiliating. Irritation spiked in Emma. His refusal to talk to her was so typical of the distance and disinterest in the family he'd shown lately. Once again, she was left to deal with everything related to the house and the kids, on her own. No input or assistance from her husband. She swallowed the curse word that sat on her tongue. "Right. Well, thanks for trying."

"Any message for him?"

Emma shoved aside any number of scornful comments she wanted to fire at Jake. "No. I guess not. But, Darla? You haven't seen or heard from Fenn today, have you? Did she maybe come by the office or anything?"

"Fenn? No. Why?"

Emma's shoulders drooped. She was running out of ideas and options. "She went out this morning and forgot her phone. I haven't been able to reach her. So…have her call me if she comes by there? Please?"

"Of course."

Emma groaned as she disconnected. "Blast it all, Fenn! Where are you? This is the last thing I need today."

She tossed her cell phone aside and flopped back on the pillows, draping an arm over her eyes. She would *not* cry again. She'd already worried Lexi with her red, puffy eyes, and tears were a waste of time when her daughter was missing.

Missing. The word sent a chill to her core. She glanced at the bedside clock. The screen read 2:37 p.m. She'd spent the last ninety minutes calling everyone she could think of, scouring the yard and house.

Was it time to call the police? Had she missed something, someone, some place obvious?

Jake would have known exactly what to do. He'd always been the anchor, the calm in storms of the past. Emma realized that she missed him in that moment. Missed his steadying presence. Missed his arms around her and his whispered reassurances. A sharp pang stung her chest when she thought about facing the future without him. But *that* Jake had been gone for some time, had been missing in action for the marriage in recent months. And right now, she needed *that* Jake more than ever.

Rolling off the bed, her limbs feeling leaden, Emma

found Lexi in the living room watching *Frozen* again. "Come on, baby. Let's go see Grandma and Grandpa."

Despite her four-year-old's protest, she trundled Lexi across the two grassy lawns to her parents' house. Once her mother had guided Lexi into the kitchen to help make cookies, Emma told her father, "I'm going to drive into town to look for Fenn. She couldn't have gone far on her bike."

He jammed his feet in his shoes with a nod. "I'm coming with you."

"No."

He raised a startled frown.

"I mean...take your own car. Cover the south end, and I'll go up toward the bowling alley."

Her father nodded. "All right. But, Emma...just for an hour or so. Then we really need to call the police."

Emma's heart twisted, and a shudder swept through her. Calling the police was acknowledging that Fenn was truly gone. Missing. In danger. It was a scary last resort. But she swallowed the bile that rose in her throat and bobbed her head in agreement. "An hour."

Sixty-five minutes later, when their search of town streets and businesses yielded nothing, Emma sat on her parents' couch, flanked by her mother and father. Her hand trembled as she tapped her screen to make the call she dreaded. "Yes, I—I need to report a missing minor."

When a car out his window backfired, shaking Jake out of his stupor, he realized he'd been staring at a blinking cursor on his computer screen for—he glanced at his cell phone to check the time—more than an hour. Geez. He needed more coffee, more sleep, more *something* if he was going to accomplish anything today.

Heaving a sigh, he rolled his chair back and carried

his empty coffee cup out of his office. He paused and met Darla's worried look. "Is there any coffee left?"

"It's old and gross. But I can make a fresh pot."

"Would you? Please?"

She stood and took his cup from him. "Jake, you haven't heard from Fenn today, have you?"

"Fenn? No. Why?"

"When Emma called earlier, she said she couldn't locate Fenn and that Fenn had left her phone behind."

Jake frowned, processing this news. They teased Fenn about her phone being a barnacle that was growing on her hand. She always had it with her. Then the rest of what Darla had said registered. "Wait…she can't find Fenn?"

"Last I heard. But that was a couple of hours ago."

Jake pulled his phone out of his pocket and scrolled through his notifications. He'd silenced the phone, not wanting the distraction of Emma constantly calling or the trivial updates about his social media, incoming texts or commercial push notifications bothering him.

He had a number of new texts, most from business associates, one from his mother-in-law, and a couple from Emma that simply read, CALL ME!

He opened the one from Grace Cameron, Emma's mother, and read.

Please come home. Fenn is missing, and we've called the police. We need all hands on deck.

Jake's heart dropped to his toes. They'd called the police? As in Fenn was officially *missing* missing?

He thought about Emma hushing him time and again last night, warning him not to be so loud that the girls heard him. He'd been so irate, so dumbstruck by Emma's eviction demand and divorce bombshell that he'd ignored Em's warnings. He'd flouted them. Fenn had almost certainly heard them arguing. And now his daughter, his precious firstborn, was gone.

He swallowed hard as bile and self-reproach rose in his throat. He muttered a scathing word and stalked toward the door. With his head preoccupied with worry, he drove on automatic, muscle memory, habit as he made his way to Cameron Glen, the private acreage outside of town where his in-laws' family had built a vacation retreat. As newlyweds, he and Emma had built their house atop a picturesque hillside on the property, just down the one-lane road from her parents' one-hundred-year-old home. Emma's sister Isla lived in another small house near the property entrance. Her sister Cait and Cait's new husband Matt lived in a guest cabin while Turner Construction built the newlyweds a home on the family property. The other ten cabins on the Cameron Glen property were rented year-round to travelers looking for the quiet and beauty of the small Smoky Mountain retreat.

When he saw a police cruiser parked in his driveway, his gut swooped. He parked behind the cruiser and raced inside. "What's going on? Where's Fenn?"

All eyes in the living room shifted to him. In addition to two uniformed police officers, the majority of his wife's large family was clustered in his den.

Emma stood and approached him, her eyes red-rimmed and her mouth pressed in a thin line of fury. "Well, look who finally deigned to show up."

He didn't want a shouting match in front of her family and the cops. He wanted answers. He wanted a status report on Fenn and something concrete to do to bring his baby home. He drew a slow breath, shoving down his jangling anxiety. "I came as soon as I heard."

Emma scoffed. "And you'd have heard hours ago if you'd bothered to take my calls or answer my texts. But in typical Jake fashion, you shut me out, and we've lost precious time finding our daughter."

Placing a hand on each of her shoulders, he pitched his tone low and leaned close. "I don't want to fight with you now. Can we please focus on Fenn? Tell me what happened. How long has she been gone?"

Emma's frown deepened, and tears flooded her eyes as she wrenched her shoulders free of his grip with a sharp twist. "This is your fault, you know."

Jake stumbled back a step, her words poleaxing him, stealing his breath.

"Emma!" Her mother appeared at her side, shaking her head. "Don't say things like that in anger. Casting blame is cruel and completely unproductive. We need to come together, work together to find Fenn."

Her brow furrowed and her breathing harsh, Emma turned her face away and fell silent.

"Jake, come in and talk to the officer, please. He wants to hear from everyone about when they last saw Fenn and so forth." His mother-in-law, Grace, waved a hand toward the living room then returned to her seat.

When he last saw Fenn. Jake stared at the floor, trying to remember when he'd last seen his older daughter. What had he said to her? Would the last time he'd seen Fenn be the last time he saw her?

The thought sucker punched him, slammed him with a horror and grief that made his knees buckle. "Oh God," he rasped, his voice choked with the onslaught of emotion.

Emma turned back toward him, and he met her eyes with his. He couldn't be sure what his expression revealed, but Emma had always had a knack for reading him. In a heartbeat, her own expression melted from cold disdain and resentment to compassion. And in the next second, her face crumpled with the same sort of grief and terror that raged inside him.

The shoulders she'd snatched away moments ago now shook as sobs racked her body.

"Jake," she whispered as her entire countenance crumbled. "Where could she be?"

He stepped forward, wrapping her in an embrace, and Emma curled into him. He held her, clung to her really. He needed her at that moment as much as she needed him. He buried his face in her silky hair, and inhaled her familiar apricot-scented shampoo.

"We'll find her, Em. We will." They had to. He couldn't accept that anything bad might have happened to his precious Fenn.

Emma sniffed heavily and, backing out of his arms, she wiped her nose with her arm. "You don't know that. What if—"

He tightened his hold on her shoulders. "We will. We have to believe that."

Some of the starch returned to her spine, and heat filled her glare. "We'd better find her, or I will never forgive you."

"The best thing you can do now is get the word out to as many people as possible," Officer Smith said.

Emma nodded. "I called all of Fenn's friends in her contacts this morning, and I asked them to have Fenn get in touch with me if they saw or heard from her."

The policeman ducked his head once in a polite affirmation. "That's a good start. I recommend you call them again, impress the urgency of the situation on them. Friends will often lie and cover for other teens. They have more loyalty to their friend than to the parents."

"I understand." When she'd been a teenager, Emma had relied on friends to keep secrets, help her sneak out and see Jake after hours or help her get beer. She knew the strength of teenage girlfriend bonds. But mothers could be tough, determined and relentless, too. She gritted her teeth, resolved to impress upon Fenn's friends the stakes involved. "Whatever it takes."

"Not just her friends," Officer Smith added. "Call neighbors, call her friends' parents, call church acquaintances and teachers. You never know who she might turn to, who might cross paths with her. The more people you call the better."

Emma drew a breath for strength. "I will. I'll call them all."

"*We'll* call them all," her mother said, emphasizing the plural pronoun. "You're not in this alone, dear. We'll all do our part."

Her heart gave a thump of love and appreciation for her mother's voiced support. She'd always been able to count on her mom, even in the most trying times. Times like coming home from the doctor at age eighteen to tell her she was pregnant, skipping college and marrying her unemployed, teenage boyfriend. Her parents' disappointment and frustration with her had been tempered with unbounded love and support and encouragement. At eighteen and many times before and since.

Had she not been that sort of mother for Fenn? Why had her daughter felt it better to run away than talk to her? Why didn't Fenn trust her to help with whatever was bothering her?

A sick feeling balled in the pit of her stomach. *Because you are what is wrong. You and your inability to work out the differences with your husband without shouting, anger and late-night evictions.* No wonder Fenn didn't trust her.

She glanced at Jake, and he met her gaze with a strange cocktail of grief, guilt, resentment.

"But calls aren't enough." Officer Smith continued, "We need to blanket the community, far and fast."

Jake's mouth tightened, and he faced the officer again, asking, "How so? What do you mean? Posters?"

"Posters and flyers are a good start. But you'll want to use social media. Phone chains. Search parties."

"Dogs?" Jake asked, his facial color growing paler, as if he were beginning to understand all the implications. What a search entailed. How searches for missing children sometimes ended with…a body bag.

Emma drew a sharp breath as she quickly squelched the image that came to mind. No. Not Fenn. Not her baby. Fenn was out there. Safe. Alive. Needing her mother. She shoved to her feet, unable to sit still any longer. She needed to be *doing* something. Anything.

"I'll need a couple of recent pictures of Fenn, if you could gather them. Different hairstyles if she wears it different ways. Different moods, different clothes."

Energized by a productive task, Emma headed toward the kitchen for her purse.

"I have a recent picture of her, her school picture, in my wallet. And more on my phone I can text to you."

"I'm going to start making a file we can send out on social media and print up as flyers," Brody said, clearly glad to have a task as well.

"I'll start calling the church folks and her friends' parents," Emma's mother said.

Emma heard more voices divvying up tasks, asking questions of the policemen, discussing plans, as she made her way into the kitchen to retrieve her purse. She pulled out her wallet, her phone and a tissue to dab her damn leaky eyes and nose.

Pull yourself together!

Fenn needed her mother to be strong and set aside the emotional displays until her girl was found. Back home and safe. *Dear God, please keep my baby safe! Please bring her back to me!*

She took a few moments to breathe deeply, compose herself as she scrolled through her phone, creating a text message for Officer Smith and attaching the selected pictures of Fenn.

A posed picture with Lexi from Easter. A candid shot by the family's fishing pond when they'd been feeding the ducks. Another image from Matt and her sister Cait's wedding a few months back. Fenn had been laughing about something with Matt's son, Eric, and the pure unbridled joy and mirth radiating from Fenn caused a bittersweet stab in Emma's heart. She touched the image on the screen whispering, "Oh, baby girl, where are you?"

"I thought she asked you to stop calling her baby girl. She's not a baby anymore."

Jake's soft admonition was followed by a warm, wide hand on her shoulder. A firm but gentle squeeze.

Emma hated to admit how good the hand, the deep rub of her knotted muscles felt. She gathered her anger around her like a shield. "Well, she's not here to hear me, now is she?" She faced him, lifting her chin. "And you know she will always be my baby. You've said as much yourself."

His face grew sad. "I have. She is. She'll always be that sweet pink face that peeked out when the nurse handed her to me, wrapped like a burrito. I was nothing but a dumb teenager, too stupid to know anything about being a father, but I knew immediately that I would kill to protect her."

Emma huffed her frustration. "And yet...we're the ones who hurt her. Drove her away."

"We?" Jake said, lifting an eyebrow. "So you don't blame me alone, then?"

She pulled away from his touch and put her phone back in her purse. "I don't have the desire or energy to argue semantics or...anything with you right now, Jake." She dug out her wallet and unsnapped it. "So don't. Just...don't—" She paused, sensing immediately that something was off, but so distracted by Jake, by the situation, that she couldn't put her finger on what didn't feel right at first.

"Fine," Jake said with a huff. "Finding Fenn comes first. I know that. But give me a chance to—"

She raised a hand to shush him, and her brow dented as she studied her purse, her wallet, her phone…

"Jake, please, stop. Give me a second to think. Something's…not right."

"A lot's not right," he mumbled, and she shot him a glare. Then it hit her, and she jerked her gaze back to her purse, the wallet in her hand. She flipped through the divided sections of her wallet, twice. Caught her breath. "It's not here. I always put it back right here." She pointed to an empty card slot. Lifting a stunned look to Jake, she said, "I bet Fenn took it."

He canted closer, lifting an eyebrow as he focused on what she was saying. "What did Fenn take?"

"My debit card. I don't *know* that she took it, but…it's gone and so is she."

"Does she know your PIN number?"

The reply that leaped to her tongue was along the lines of, *Of course, she does. She runs errands for me all the time. You'd know that if you were ever around long enough to—*

At which point she shut the thought down. She'd meant it when she said she didn't want to fight with Jake now, and acrimony in her retort would only raise his hackles. She schooled her expression, relaxed her mouth and exhaled. Nodded once.

Jake's face brightened. "Well, good. Then we have a starting place."

Emma bit her bottom lip, and her stomach ached with a sinking weight, knowing that with the pilfered debit card, Fenn had access to the money she needed to pay a taxi driver, or get a bus ticket, or otherwise fund her escape plans indefinitely, so long as she had access to one of the bank's ATM mach—

She gasped as she got it. Emma turned to Jake with a renewed sense of hope thrashing in her chest. "Oh my God! Yes! A starting place…if she used the card to get cash…"

"The bank could tell us which ATM she used!" Jake finished, his eyes bright with calculation and strategy. "I'll let Officer Smith know this piece of information. You call the bank."

Emma already had her phone out checking their bank account for recent withdrawals.

Jake had only made it as far as the kitchen door before she spotted the entry on their account summary that made her heart skip. "Jake! The Stop N Shop on Highway 6. Two hundred and fifty dollars was withdrawn this morning at 10:14 a.m.!"

Jake angled his gaze to the clock on their microwave. "That was almost six hours ago," he muttered as if holding his breath, his dark eyes widening. "But maybe…"

They sprang into motion at the same instant.

Chapter 4

Fenn's jaw hurt. She came to slowly, the images around her confusing and blurry. The sour smell of unwashed bodies and stale cigarette smoke filled her nose. She gagged and found a cloth of some sort stuffed in her mouth. Her hands were bound behind her. A strange room...

Panic washed through her like a tidal wave. Acid flooded her stomach, and bile surged up her throat. She gasped, sucking the cloth farther down her throat, and started choking. She sat up, fighting for air, eyes wide, heart thrashing. Something came out her nose, making her sinuses burn.

"Hey, easy!" The girl with magenta hair appeared at her side and snatched the ball of fabric from her mouth.

Fenn vomited, coughed, wheezed air through her paralyzed throat.

Magenta jumped out of the way as Fenn got sick, then with a look of disgust, disappeared into another room for a minute before returning with dingy white towels. She tossed them at Fenn. "You can clean that up for yourself. I ain't doing it." Then as if remembering Fenn's hands were bound, she added, "If I undo your wrists, you gotta promise not to run, not to fight me, not to scream or try nothing that will get both you and me in trouble. 'Kay?"

"Don't trust her," a voice behind Fenn said in a flat tone.

Fenn, still struggling for a full breath, still battling to keep from throwing up again, twisted to see who'd spoken. The second girl Fenn had seen in the old sedan was lounging on the second of two messy beds.

A cheap motel room.

"DJ said not to let her loose until he got back," warned the second girl, whose hair was streaked with bottle-blond stripes and her eyes lined with more mascara and eye shadow than Fenn would wear in a month.

"Shut up, Kristy," Magenta said. "She was choking. You wanted me to let her die? You think DJ would like that?"

Fenn felt a tug on her arm, and then Magenta was snipping the zip ties that held Fenn's wrists. Her numb hands started tingling, then aching, as blood flowed back into them. Fenn rubbed her wrists, dividing a wary gaze between the two girls.

"Who are you?" she rasped, then coughed as her throat burned from the bile rising from her stomach. Fenn swallowed hard, determined not to throw up again. "Where are we? Why did you take me?"

"So many questions." Magenta pointed at the mess Fenn had made and wrinkled her nose. "Clean that up. It reeks."

"This whole room reeks," Fenn grumbled but started cleaning up. "Who is DJ? Why would you help him kidnap me?"

"Shut up, kid. You're getting on my nerves." Kristy sneered at her and got up from the other bed to find the remote for the television. The tight miniskirt she wore rode up and revealed that she wasn't wearing underpants.

Fenn looked away quickly, shuddering. After wiping up the vomit and pulling the dirty sheet off the bed, Fenn carried the soiled linens into the bathroom to dump them in the corner. As she dropped the pile of sheets, a roach skittered out from behind the toilet. Fenn shrieked.

Magenta appeared at the bathroom door as Fenn tried to charge out, and they collided.

"What the hell?" Magenta asked gruffly. "Can you keep it down? We don't need anybody calling the cops!"

"Sorry… I— There was a roach." Fenn saw the condescending look that crossed Magenta's face and added, "It…startled me."

"Well, get used to roaches, princess. We don't got the funds to stay at fancy places, so you'll see lots of crawly things from now on."

From now on…

The clear implication being Magenta thought Fenn would be with her and DJ and Kristy for a long time. Another swell of panic brought up the rest of the contents of Fenn's stomach, and she whirled to upchuck in the toilet.

"Geez, girl. Get that outta your system quick. DJ will be back with your first customer any minute."

Fenn shot a wide-eyed look at Magenta as she wiped her mouth on a wad of bathroom tissue. "Customer? What do you mean?"

Magenta scoffed and looked at Fenn as if she were the stupidest of little girls. "A john. A trick."

If Fenn had had anything left in her gut, she'd have lost it then. Her lungs seemed to freeze, and she struggled for a breath. "B-but…"

Magenta jerked her head toward the sink. "Get cleaned up. Hurry."

Fenn shook her head, her thoughts skittering a thousand directions at once. "N-no. No, no, no!"

Magenta grabbed her wrist, hard. "Don't fight me. I swear, you don't want to mess with me."

"You're...hookers?" Fenn asked, distraught.

"That's one term for what we do. You, too, now." Magenta gave a sardonic smile. "Welcome to the family."

Tears rushed to Fenn's eyes. "No! Please! I can't. I..."

"You can, and you will when DJ gets back. Don't cross him neither. You do not want to piss DJ off. Trust me."

"But... I don't... I've never..." Fenn started hyperventilating. Shaking from head to toe. *Oh God, no! Please, please, please, no!*

"You never what?"

Fenn didn't get the chance to explain. The motel room door banged open, and a voice shouted, "What the—? Where's the new girl?"

Panic sent blood pounding in Fenn's ears, drowning out Kristy's response. Fenn imagined she could feel the floor shaking as Shifty stomped to the bathroom and appeared like a bad dream to hover over her. "Ruby? What's going on back here? Why are her hands free?"

Magenta faced Shifty/DJ, waving a shaking hand as she started, "She woke up and started—"

DJ lashed out, backhanding Magenta—Ruby, he'd called her—and sending her stumbling backward. "I told you not to let her loose!"

"I w-was choking," Fenn muttered softly in Ruby's defense, finding the courage to defend her from God knows where.

DJ turned a glare on Fenn. "What?"

Fenn quaked and backed as far away from DJ as she could. "I... I threw up. I c-couldn't breathe."

"I freed her hands, so she could clean up," Ruby added, touching fingers to her bleeding lip. "She'd—"

DJ cut her off with a grumbled curse. "Whatever." He made a slashing motion with his hand calling an end to the topic. "She's got her first job on his way. Get her in clean clothes and take her to room five. Fast."

DJ turned and stormed away, and Ruby moved to follow her orders.

"No!" Fenn's plea was little more than a squeak from her constricted throat. Terror raged through her, and she knew she had to calm herself in order to think clearly. Her current chaotic thoughts and shallow breathing only made it harder to process the rapidly changing situation.

Run! one voice in her head shouted.

Fight back! another voice said.

Don't fight! Stay alive! a third countered in rapid succession.

Ruby grabbed Fenn's arm and dragged her from the bathroom. "Strip. Everything. Shoes, too."

Fenn glanced down at her jeans, T-shirt and high-top sneakers. She'd soiled her shirt, but didn't even care. Those were her clothes, and she was not about to give them up. Shoes…shoes! They wanted her shoes. Her best chance to run was now, while she had—

Without completing the thought, Fenn bolted.

"Hey!" Ruby's shout rang out behind her.

Fenn made it to the door, had a hand on the knob—

And DJ hooked an arm around her waist from behind and threw her onto the nearest bed. Disappointment crushed Fenn, even as DJ stepped to the edge of the mattress to loom over her, his eyes hot and his mouth twisted. "You little bitch!"

A stinging slap found her cheek. He leaned close to snarl in her face, and his fetid cigarette breath fanned her face. "If you ever try that again, I'll break every bone in your legs."

Fenn found her breath and launched a second attempt, slashing at his face with her fingernails. She left a gash on his cheek, and when he jerked back, clapping a hand to his wounded face, she rolled away from him and darted for the door again.

Kristy stepped from the shadows and blocked her path, allowing DJ to grab her again. He hauled her back to the mattress.

His expression twisted with rage, and he balled a fist, reared back.

Fenn gasped, cringed. Braced for the blow.

Ruby leaped forward, shouting, "Wait! You said she's got a job. Someone's coming? If you mess up her face now, he might not want—"

"Then one of you two will take him!" DJ growled. "She's gotta learn her place."

He raised his fist again, but a knock sounded on the door. DJ glanced over his shoulder, huffed his frustration. Stepping back from Fenn, he snarled, "You'll do what you're told, or you'll regret it. We know where your family lives, and we can take out your mama and anyone else if you don't cooperate. Completely."

An icy cold filled Fenn's core. Would he really kill Mom? If he'd gone through her backpack, found her address...of course, he could hurt Mom or Dad. Or steal Lexi, the way he'd stolen her. The thought of little Lexi in these monsters' grip sent chills through her. Revived the nausea that had never totally gone away. She swallowed hard to keep from barfing again. *Ohgeezohgeezohgeez!* What did she do?

The knock came again, and DJ put a finger near her nose. "Understood?"

"DJ?" Kristy said, motioning to the door with a question in her eyes.

He jerked a nod. "Let him in."

Kristy answered the knock and pasted on a simpering smile. "Howdy, handsome. C'mon in."

The man on the threshold hustled in, looking irritated.

His balding head was beaded with sweat, and his rail-thin arms and legs reminded Fenn of a scarecrow. His eyes were pale behind his glasses, in keeping with his sallow complexion. "What the hell took so long?" He blinked as his attention shifted from Kristy to Ruby, to Fenn, then to DJ. "What's going on? Do I get three for the price of one?" His leering grin was like oil in Fenn's already queasy gut.

DJ gave a stiff laugh. "You wish. Naw… You get to test-drive this one." He hitched his thumb toward Fenn. "Layla. It's Layla's first time out."

Fenn furrowed her brow. Layla? What the—?

Duh. Of course, DJ wouldn't use her real name. If he even knew it.

"First timer, huh? Unspoiled goods. I like that!" The man poked his scrawny chest out and rubbed his hands on his stomach like he'd just eaten his favorite meal.

The room spun around her, and she squeezed the sheets in her fists. She opened her mouth to tell the man she'd been kidnapped, that her name was really Fenn and please, oh please, call the police. Help her get back home! But the words stuck in her dry throat, still burning from the bile of her vomit. If she said anything, if she gave DJ trouble, she had no doubt he'd beat her…and that he might, in fact, hurt her family. She couldn't risk her family. So she swallowed the words. Swallowed the rising acid. She had to find another way to save herself…

"DJ? Can I talk to you?" Ruby said quietly.

DJ frowned at Ruby and snapped, "In a minute. Can't you see I'm busy?" He shot a stern look to Kristy, who quickly grabbed her shoes and headed out to the sidewalk. "You, too, Ruby."

Fenn met Ruby's gaze, pleading silently for help. Ruby's brow dented, and her shoulders hunched as she chewed her lip. She started out of the room but hesitated at the door. "DJ, I just—"

"Shut up and get outta here!" DJ cut her off, growling through his clenched teeth.

Still Ruby hesitated, shuddered. Fenn held her breath, praying silently Ruby was doing something to help her.

"Well, Mr. Jones…" DJ flashed a knowing grin at the man as if acknowledging his name wasn't really Jones. "I'll leave you to get acquainted with—"

"If she's a virgin," Ruby blurted, talking over DJ, "she's worth a whole lot more than whatever this guy's paying for her. You could auction her."

Fenn gasped. Auction her? Like a farm animal or piece of property? She gaped at Ruby. What was she thinking?

Beside her, DJ stiffened, his mouth thinning. He narrowed his eyes on Ruby as if deciding how to punish her.

"But if this guy spoils her…" Ruby let her words trail with a wave of her hand toward Mr. Jones.

Fenn held her breath, realizing what Ruby was trying to do for her.

DJ's expression changed, cooled, as he, too, seemed to consider all the angles of what Ruby was saying.

Mr. Jones squared his shoulders and waggled a finger. "Hey! Now we had a deal. I already paid for an hour with—"

"With one of my girls," DJ finished for the john. "I didn't promise you which one. And I just decided you get Ruby."

He grabbed Ruby's arm and tugged her toward the bed so hard she stumbled and fell onto the sagging mattress.

Fenn blinked. She was fighting to keep up with the changing situation while a thousand bees buzzed in her ears and stung her gut. Adrenaline had her heart pounding nearly out of her chest, and her body shook from tip to toes, as Nanna put it. Her chin trembled when she thought of her Scottish great-grandmother, who always had smiles and hugs and peppermints for her. Tears stung her eyes. Please, God, she just wanted to go *home*!

A hard grip closed around her upper arm, and she was yanked to her feet. "Come on, Lana, you and I are going to have a little chat."

Lana? Fenn didn't miss the fact that DJ couldn't even keep straight what fake name he'd used five seconds earlier. But even with the gruff bully's hand clamped on her arm like a python, Fenn released her breath. She'd been spared. For the moment.

As DJ dragged her out the motel room door, she sent Ruby a sad look and mouthed, *Thanks.*

Emma stumbled out of Jake's truck in a rush, even before it stopped moving. They'd been so eager to follow the lead, they'd rushed out of the house without telling anyone where they were going. Not even the policemen. Emma remedied that as they drove across town.

Armed with pictures of Fenn pulled up on her phone, she sprinted inside the convenience store where her bank record showed the withdrawal had been made.

Jake followed on her heels, his long legs covering the ground at a clip that allowed him to pass her as they reached the vacant checkout counter. He slapped the back of the register with the flat of his hand, craning his head to search for the employee that should be monitoring the front end. "Hey! Anyone there?"

Emma pivoted on her toes, scanning the store for anyone who seemed to work there. "Hello?"

A woman near the refrigerator section poked her head up to gaze over the bags of chips and popcorn like a gopher peeking out of its hole. "Can I help you?"

Emma rushed to her. "We're looking for our daughter. We think she was here this morning." She shoved the phone toward the woman wearing an apron with the store logo.

The woman wrinkled her nose as she took the phone. She shoved her glasses to the top of her head then studied Fenn's image.

"We think she's the one who used my card in the ATM machine outside," Emma blurted, unable to bottle up her restless energy and anxiety. "She's only fifteen, but she left on her bike sometime overnight. We're worried sick."

Emma kept her eyes trained on the woman staring at her phone and sensed more than saw Jake move up behind her.

Finally the store clerk offered the phone back to her with a jerk of her chin and a scowl. "Yeah, she was here. Her and her no-good thievin' partner in crime."

Jake stepped forward, his eyes narrowed. "What partner in crime?"

The clerk straightened, pressing a hand at the small of her back as she stretched slightly and grunted at the effort. "The girl with purple hair. She was shoplifting stuff, and that girl—" she wiggled a finger toward the phone screen "—said they were together and paid for the shoplifter's things."

Jake cut a confused look toward Emma. "Does Fenn have any friends with purple hair?"

The urge to snap *You'd know the answer to that if you were ever around to talk to your children and meet their friends!* welled in her throat. But Emma knew a sharp rebuke, starting another argument, was not what the situation called for. Instead, she shook her head.

Until Fenn was found, she had to set aside all her hurt and anger and focus on the only thing that mattered until Fenn was safe—finding Fenn. She needed Jake to help get their daughter home. She needed his intelligence and strategic thinking. She needed his calm rationality and long-view approach to matters. She needed the balance that his critical, logical thinking gave her creative and impassioned view of things. And hell…she needed his broad shoulder to cry on, his arms to hold her and promise her things would be okay, and his strength to get her through this disaster. And honestly, she even needed his take-charge attitude, because right now she was holding herself together with spit and a prayer. Her shaking hands, trembling heart and wobbly knees gave evidence to how close to shattering she was.

As if reading her thoughts, Jake edged closer to her, wrapping his arm around her shoulders as he faced the store clerk again. "Do you have a picture of this other girl? The one with purple hair? It's important that we find her."

"It was more kinda bright red than purple, like the color for South Carolina."

They all shifted their attention to the middle-aged man who strolled up, his white dress shirt wrinkled and a loosely tied necktie that had definitely seen better days, and perhaps a run-in with the soft drink dispenser.

"In fact, I figured she was a Gamecock fan. You see people with their hair dyed like that in the stands at football and basketball games. You know, the wacky stuff college kids do to show team spirit. When I went to Appalachian State, I shaved all my hair off except for an *A* and *C* on the top of my head. Wore it home like that for Thanksgiving, and my mom 'bout laid an egg, she was so appalled."

Jake took a breath, but the flexing muscle in his jaw told Emma he was struggling for patience. "Do you know who this girl with red hair was? Had you seen her before? Have a picture of her?"

Messy Tie Guy twisted his mouth. "Don't know her name, but I've seen her hang out 'round here before."

The other store employee cut in. "She's probably on the

cameras, at least one of 'em. We got one that watches the
front door, others outside, more for the back of the store."

"Cameras?" Emma repeated, hope swelling.

The woman with the apron pointed to the corner of
the ceiling where a security camera was plainly visible.
"Security."

Jake stiffened. "We need to see the video, confirm it
was our daughter who used the ATM, get a picture of the
girl she was with."

Messy Tie squared his shoulders. "You a cop? Got a
warrant?"

Jake gritted his teeth, and Emma could feel the quiver
of anger that pulsed through him. She placed a hand on
his chest as he surged toward the other man as if spoiling to pick a fight.

"Please!" Emma said, dividing a look between the two
men—a plea for calm to her husband and an appeal for
help to Messy Tie. "Our daughter is just fifteen. She could
be in danger. Please help us get her back. The police are
on their way. We just got a…head start." She shared a
sheepish look with Jake. "But if we could just look at the
video recording—"

The woman was shaking her head. "It's against store
policy. We could be fired."

Emma faced the woman, hoping she could appeal to any
maternal instincts she might have had. "But my daughter is—"

The woman's hand shot up to cut her off. "Now if you
can get the cops to bring a warrant, that's a different matter."

Jake huffed, his hand fisting before he snatched his
phone from his back pocket. "Fine," he snarled, then
glanced at Emma. "I'll call Officer Smith. You go next
door to the McDonald's and see if anyone in there saw

Fenn or the girl with red-purple hair and which way they went when they left here."

Emma jerked a nod and took two steps toward the door before the woman in the apron called. "I can tell you which way they went. I was watchin' from the window up front to make sure the girl with the dyed hair and her friends left after she tried to steal from us. Didn't want any more trouble out of 'em."

"Them? She was with someone else?" Emma asked. She stepped back over to the woman, her heart racing, and struggled not to scream in the woman's face, *Why didn't you say so to start with?* "Who? Where did they go?"

Apron Woman rolled her shoulders and folded her arms across her bosom as if she didn't like Emma's tone. "There was three or four of 'em in the car. The driver was a skinny guy, short brown hair. Smoking. Once they were all in the car—all of 'em, including that girl—" she pointed to the picture of Fenn that Emma held "—they drove outta here fast. Turned left at the light and headed up toward the interstate."

Ice sluiced through Emma's veins, and, horrified, she cast a wide-eyed glance to Jake. Her husband looked equally gobsmacked and frightened for Fenn.

Jake regained his voice first. "Our daughter got in a car with the other girl and some man?"

The woman shrugged. "Yeah."

Jake stepped closer and leaned toward the woman, his expression stunned. "And you didn't call the police?"

With a scowl, the woman shot back. "She'd just told me she was with the purple-haired kid. Paid for her stuff. Why would I call the cops? I was glad to see 'em go!"

"Why—?" Jake sputtered, clearly aghast and his anxiety and frustration mounting.

Emma grabbed Jake by both arms. "She didn't know Fenn wasn't really with them. The important thing now is to get that warrant for the security cameras. We have to identify that girl, the man driving the car—" Emma spun back to the store employees, her whole body trembling. "Does one of the cameras cover the parking lot? Would it have captured the car? The license plate?"

Messy Tie and Apron Woman exchanged a glance.

"Yeah. Camera three does," Messy Tie said.

Jake aimed a finger at him, and in a tone that brooked no resistance he said, "We'll be back with the police and that warrant ASAP. Do us a solid and have the video cued up to the images of the red-haired girl and the car. Time is critical, and we can't waste a minute finding our daughter."

Chapter 5

"This is bad," Emma said the moment they were back in Jake's truck. "Our daughters both know better than to get into a car with a stranger. I have been hypervigilant about drilling that rule into their heads. So if she got in that car like they said, then—"

"Then maybe she knew the girl with the purple-red hair after all." Jake could see the panic brewing in her eyes, and he reached for her. Cupping her jaw in his hand, he brushed his thumb along her high cheekbone. "Can you say for sure that none of her friends, not even some of her more casual friends at school have never dyed their hair? A lot of kids are doing it these days."

Emma closed her eyes and released a stuttering breath. "No. I guess not, but… I just…have a gut feeling about this…" She shook her head and used the pad of her finger to wipe the moisture at the corner of her eye.

Jake drew his hand back and started the engine. When they'd called Officer Smith's number it had gone to voice mail. Rather than wait an undetermined amount of time for a call back, Jake had decided they'd go to the police station in person. It was only a few blocks away. If they couldn't talk to Officer Smith, they'd plead their case to anyone who'd listen. "Let's not jump to conclusions. Maybe—"

"Jake, she heard us."

He put the truck in gear and shot her a side-glance as he backed out of the parking space. "What?"

Staring at her lap, Emma twisted her earring, a nervous habit of hers when she was worried or irritated. "Last night. When we fought." She sighed. "I told you to keep your voice down, and—"

He huffed loudly and jerked the steering wheel as he punched the accelerator. "So we're back to this all being my fault. Is that what you're saying?"

She hesitated a beat, then said softly, "No." Bending her head, she pinched the bridge of her nose. "No."

He stopped at a red traffic light and bumped the side of his fist on the steering wheel. "I mean… I know I lost my temper last night and acted badly."

She angled a sad look at him. "We both did."

He pressed his mouth in a grim line, his back teeth clenching. "And I'm sorry for that."

She swallowed. Nodded. "Me, too."

When the light changed, he gunned the engine, feeling the pressure of a ticking clock sitting on him. Didn't they say the first twenty-four hours are the most critical for recovering a missing child? That the odds of recovering the child safely go down dramatically in the hours after that, and that if—

"She found me, too."

Jake blinked and frowned at his wife, her comment seeming like a non sequitur. "Say what?"

"After you left last night, Fenn came into the kitchen." The fatigue and grief in Emma's voice broke his heart.

If he could rewind his actions and his quick-trigger temper from last night, he'd give anything to do so. "And?"

"And I was on the floor by the back door."

"Wh—"

"Crying."

Another gut punch. Jake squeezed the steering wheel and gritted his back teeth harder, fighting back his own emotions. "Aw, Em."

"I tried to reassure her. But I was still reeling myself, and I don't think I handled it well."

Jake divided his attention between Emma and the road. "What happened? What did you say?"

"I tried to reassure her that things would be okay, but it was hard to sound convincing, when I wasn't so sure of that myself. But a good parent would have set aside her own worries and problems and made certain Fenn knew she was safe and that we both loved her and that nothing would ever change that."

"You didn't say any of that?"

"She yelled at me, stormed out. I thought giving her space, letting her calm down and having our heart-to-heart in the morning, when I had my own stuff together, was a better plan."

"Hey."

"Clearly, I was wrong. I screwed up and—"

"Hey," he said louder. When she finally looked up at him, he said firmly, "You're a good mother. A great mother."

Emma twisted her mouth as if debating how to deny it. But then her gaze shot to the road, and she pointed. "This is your turn."

As if he hadn't also lived in Valley Haven his whole life and didn't know the streets and shortcuts like the back of his hand. He swallowed the sarcastic retort he might have said in other circumstances and swung the truck up the side road that led to the main street where the police station was located.

When they reached the police station, Emma didn't rush out and charge into the building the way she had at the convenience mart.

"C'mon," he said to light a fire under her as he climbed out from the driver's side. When he glanced at her, she buried her face in her hands, and her shoulders shook. "Emma?"

She peeked at him before covering her face again. "Go on in. I j-just need a minute."

He sighed. "Em." Jake fished around for what he was supposed to say. He wanted to rush her. *We're in a hurry here!* Wanted to gripe at her. *Can you save the breakdown until after our daughter is found?* Wanted to crumple to the pavement and bawl with her. Dear God, his baby girl, his precious Fenn was missing!

But he had to hold it together for the both of them, for the family, and especially for Fenn, who needed his focus and energy honed on getting her home safely.

But then Emma squeaked through her tears, "I'm just s-so scared!"

Like getting kicked to the ribs, Jake fell back a step, his breath leaving him in a whoosh. Slamming his truck door, he raced around to the passenger side and yanked open her door. He pulled Emma into his arms and held her, whispering, "Shh. I've got you. I know. I know."

She curled her fingers into his shirt and leaned into him, letting him support her. For the first time in months, maybe more than a year, he felt…needed. Like he mattered. Like she wanted anything he had to offer. That idea alone nearly brought on the waterworks he was fighting to shove down. The apricot scent of her shampoo filled him with a sense of familiarity that anchored him. This was where he belonged.

Except she didn't want that. She'd kicked him out of the house he'd worked his butt off to maintain. Filed for divorce, breaking the promise of them together until death do they part. A pain like a red wasp stung his heart, and he clamped his back teeth all the tighter, fighting to push the pain away. He had to ignore the hurt, the nagging doubts, the uncertain future. He had a job to do. He couldn't think of anything else until Fenn was found.

As if reading his thoughts, Emma pushed away from him, wiping her eyes and gulping deep breaths. "I'm sorry. We don't have time for this. I'm okay."

Jake knew the look that crossed her face well. She was in soldier mode. This Emma was the one who'd balanced earning a degree in interior design with a part-time retail job, raising a toddler and being a wife. The woman of practicality and strength, who'd rallied her steel core to muscle them, as if by sheer will, through the toughest times in their marriage. His mother's cancer. Lost income. Tornado damage to their first home.

Grabbing her purse, she sidled past him and jogged toward the door of the police station.

Exhaling his frustration, Jake set aside the nostalgia to follow Em inside. Whether their marriage was crumbling or not, he had to find a way to work amicably with Emma until they found Fenn.

Obtaining the warrant that allowed the police, Jake and her to view the security footage at the convenience store took excruciatingly long. It may have only been a couple hours, but every minute that passed tore at Emma with sharp claws of impatience. But when they finally, *finally*, were huddled around the desktop monitor in the stuffy office at the convenience store, Emma almost wished she could go back in time to the moment before she saw her daughter on the small screen.

Messy Tie, who turned out to be the store manager, Gerald Howard, had the security feed ready for viewing then stood off to the side as Officer Smith began reviewing the video. The fug of old grease, stale cigarette smoke and mildew hung redolent in the air.

Emma held her breath until she spotted her daughter on the monitor. Fenn arrived at the convenience store on her bicycle, got cash from the ATM, shooting nervous glances at something off camera. Viewing the other camera feeds and time stamps indicated she might have been noticing—there she was—the teenage girl with dyed hair who milled about in the store aisles. Even before Helen, the woman in the store apron from earlier, pointed her out on the black-and-white images, Emma could tell she was the girl with the dye job in question. Fenn hadn't approached the other teen, hadn't spoken to her until Helen had confronted Dyed Hair.

Emma glanced at Officer Smith, who sat in the desk chair with the best angle to view the security feed. His face was largely impassive, intently studying the images on-screen. She shot a look to Jake who seemed to feel her gaze and met hers with eyes full of worry and confusion. Clearly he didn't recognize Dyed Hair either.

Officer Smith hit Pause on the video playback, freezing the frame when the shot had a good view of Dyed Hair's face. "Save this screenshot as a separate file," he told Mr. Howard and the man hit a few buttons on the laptop in front of him. Then to Jake, Officer Smith said, "We'll circulate it with the pictures of Fenn. Are you sure you don't know who she is?"

"No. Never seen her before," Emma said, and Jake echoed the sentiment.

Officer Smith continued his review of the video feed rewatching the part where Fenn took money from the ATM and entered the store. This time, however, the policeman paused the video feed as Fenn opened the door. He stiffened and grunted. He cut a sharp look at Gerald Howard. "Are there other angles of the front door? The front walkway?"

A tingle raced down Emma's back, hearing the harsher timbre of the officer's voice.

"What do you see?"

Jake put a hand on her shoulder and squeezed, as if he wanted the connection to her as much as she needed that physical link to him at that moment. She eased closer to him, covering his hand with hers.

Officer Smith didn't answer. He raised a finger signaling, *Hang on a minute.* Then ducked his head for a closer look as Mr. Howard switched views to a different camera.

The image on-screen was of a thin, youngish-looking guy who loitered by the front of the store smoking. He kept staring at something off to the side of the front door.

The ATM, Emma realized. And Fenn. Was the guy planning to mug Fenn? Steal the cash? Or—Emma shivered knowing there were any number of horrible things a man could do to a defenseless young girl. She squeezed Jake's fingers harder.

When Officer Smith groaned, Emma's stomach plummeted. "Officer, you're scaring me. What do you see? Do you know that man?"

Officer Smith paused the screen again and shot a look to Mr. Howard. "I need a screenshot of this guy, too." Then turning the swiveling desk chair to face Emma and Jake, the policeman rubbed a hand over his face before he spoke. "I can't be positive, but this guy—" he aimed his thumb over his shoulder to the frozen screen "—looks a lot like a guy our department has been monitoring in recent months. His name is Daniel Monroe. Goes by DJ. He's…not a nice guy."

Jake mumbled a curse word under his breath.

Officer Smith looked at Howard. "Would you ask your assistant manager to come back here? The one who said she saw the Turners' daughter leave the premises."

"Why have you been monitoring this guy?" Jake asked in a tone that demanded an answer and also spoke of the same fear coursing through Emma.

Officer Smith pulled a reluctant face. "We suspect him of recruiting runaway teens, both girls and boys, for an interstate prostitution ring."

"Recruiting?" Emma said, her voice a rasp. "You mean kidnapping." A statement. Horror. A sinking revelation. "You're talking about sex trafficking!"

Officer Smith opened his mouth and raised his hand as if to refute her, but the expression in his eyes told her she was right.

Chapter 6

Emma's knees buckled, and if not for Jake catching her under her elbows, she'd have crumpled to the floor.

Officer Smith shot out of the desk chair to help guide her to Mr. Howard's vacated seat as she wobbled. When waves of nausea washed through her, she put her head between her legs moaning, "OhGodohGodohGod!"

"I'm not positive this is him. And even if it is Monroe, we don't know that he took Fenn," Officer Smith said in a rush.

Emma glanced up at the officer. "But it could be him. You think he has Fenn, that he grabbed her, don't you?"

Helen appeared at the door to the office and, clearly sensing the darker mood in the room, hesitated. "Mr. Howard said you wanted to see me?"

With a nod, Officer Smith waved Helen forward and pointed to the computer screen. "Is this the man you saw driving the car that the Turners' daughter got into with the second girl, the one with dyed hair?"

Helen studied the image. Frowned as she twisted her hands together in distress. Then jerked a nod. "That's him. They grabbed at her and pushed her into the car."

"Pushed her in?" Jake said sharply. "You didn't tell us she was forced into the car!"

"I... I didn't want to alarm you. I thought she knew them, and—" Helen swallowed hard. "I'm sorry. I..."

Emma's stomach rebelled, and she grabbed the trash can just in time. She emptied her stomach in the waste-basket, chills of terror rippling through her.

"Jake..." she whispered, and he knelt beside her. He was as whey-faced as she felt, and seeing her husband, the man who'd been a pillar of strength through previous family crises, looking so shaken sent another blow to her core. "Our baby... Our Button..."

"I know." Then his jaw firmed, his eyes grew flinty, and his mouth flattened into a line of resolve.

Mr. Howard had pulled video footage of the parking lot up for Officer Smith and the scenario Helen had described played out in black and white.

Emma moaned and Jake drew her into a tight hug. "We're going to find her, babe. I don't care what it takes or how much it costs. We will find her and bring her back home. I promise you."

"But sex traffickers, Jake! Our Fenn—" Her voice caught on a sob, and Jake's grip tightened.

"I know, Em. I know." He levered back to meet her gaze with one of steely determination. His gaze glinted with ferocity, and his nose flared. "But if they hurt her, if they lay a finger on her, I swear I'll see that they pay."

"Folks," Officer Smith said quietly, "I know your instinct is to rush out and look for your daughter, look to avenge her..." He divided a look between them. "But don't be rash. Let law enforcement do its job. We'll add these new players as persons of interest and issue an APB for them statewide." Turning to Mr. Howard, he said, "This video is evidence in a felony kidnapping. I'll need copies of everything recorded this morning. If you see any of these people return to the store, do not confront them. Call the police immediately. Understood?"

The store manager jerked a nod.

"What can we do?" Jake asked, squaring his shoulders as he faced the officer.

"Go home. Stay by the phone."

"What?" Jake shook his head. "You can't expect us to sit back and do nothing!"

Emma was following the conversation as if through a fog. Or from the bottom of a pool. Or some weird movie where she was there…but not there. Her head was muzzy, her gut roiling, her heart a rock that still managed to thud with dread.

"Not nothing. You can continue to make and distribute the missing flyers—"

Jake snorted derisively. "Flyers? If Fenn was kidnapped by sex predators, what good will flyers do?"

Officer Smith twisted his mouth. "I don't know. Maybe no good. But maybe she'll escape or they'll stop at a truck stop in Tennessee or a motel maid will see her through a window. You never know. And it will give you something to do besides sit around and wait and worry."

A wrenching need to be at home, to wrap protective arms around Lexi and surround herself with Fenn's things, the traces of her daughter that lingered within the walls of their home, swamped Emma. She raised a shaking hand to grab Jake's wrist.

He glanced down at her, his eyes darkening when they met her gaze. "Em?"

Fenn. Her little Button.

"Take me home. I need… I need—"

She tried to stand, and her knees didn't cooperate. She

wobbled, and Jake caught her. She clutched at him, his solid shoulders. When she sucked in a breath, searching for the composure to stand, her husband's familiar woodsy scent filled her nose. Sanded the rough edges off her frayed nerves. Gulping oxygen, she tried again to rise, but Jake bent to scoop her in his arms. She should have protested his coddling. Having kicked him out of the house and filed for divorce, she needed to learn to stand on her own two feet, both figuratively and literally. But at that moment, even if she'd gotten her feet under her, she wasn't sure how she'd find the strength to walk all the way back out to Jake's truck. So once more, like she had many times in the past, she trusted herself to Jake's capable care.

The overhead light in the dark bathroom flicked on, and Fenn squinted against the sudden glare. Sitting up in the bathtub where she'd huddled for hours with her legs drawn up to her chest, she cast a wary glare to the door where DJ stood.

"Get up. Time to go." His tone brooked no resistance, and the hostility in the set of his jaw and his narrowed eyes sent a shiver through her.

"Go where?"

"None of your business," he said, stepping closer to hover over the mildew-stained bathtub. "You work for me now, and you will go wherever I tell you. Now move it!" He hitched his head toward the door behind him.

Instead of getting up, Fenn scuttled to the other end of the tub and raised her chin. "No! I don't have to do anything you say. And I sure as hell don't work for you!"

"Don't you back-talk me, little girl. Show me some respect. Ya hear?" He aimed a menacing finger at her.

"My dad says respect has to be earned. I have no reason to respect you."

He grabbed the front of her shirt so quickly, she had no time to react.

"You will do what I say or you will pay for it!" he snarled. He released her suddenly and her head hit the wall as she fell back in the tub.

Fenn's eyes watered, and the back of her skull throbbed. She narrowed a look that shot daggers, hatred for her captor roiling dangerously inside her.

DJ crouched to get more on eye level. He cocked his head to one side and chuckled. "Sassy little thing, aren't you? Good. A lot of my customers like their girls a bit salty." His eyes drilled into her with a heat that made her skin crawl. "But you listen to me, princess. You will do what I say, or you'll get more of this." He held up his hand and wiggled his fingers.

Despite the fear that twisted inside her, Fenn glared at him, drawing strength from sheer mulishness and fury that he'd threaten to hit her. Her mother often said Fenn was so stubborn she'd argue with a mountain and tell it to get out of her way. She hated the thought of cowering to this bully, even though another voice inside her said fighting him was futile, risky.

Anywhere he moved her could easily be worse for her than this dirty motel bathroom. Farther from home. Farther from rescue. And closer to whatever evil DJ had in mind for her.

While she'd waited alone in the dark bathroom, she'd tried not to think about what was happening at home. That only made her sad and scared, and she needed to be brave. Instead, she'd replayed scenes from her favorite books in her head, trying to remember how the characters she admired had dealt with danger. Sure, they were fictional, but weren't there lessons she could take from them? Strength. Wisdom. Courage. If now wasn't the time to be heroic, what was? But try as she might to channel

Katniss Everdeen, each new sound beyond the bathroom door shot spikes of terror through her. She wanted to go home. Wanted her mom and dad.

She'd heard snippets of conversation—DJ talking to another man on the other side of the bathroom door. One-sided conversations—phone calls presumably—where she only heard DJ. Then various female voices and DJ. Most of what she heard made little sense to her or seemed random or unimportant. He'd ordered a pizza. Shouted at someone to shut up. To change the channel. Asked a girl why she was back so soon.

But she'd also caught "make us more money," "virgin fetish," "get her out of town."

Virgin fetish. The words shot ice to her core.

Ruby had earned her a temporary reprieve from whatever horrible stuff they were expected to do, but her time was running out.

After glaring at her for a long moment, waiting for her to follow his order, DJ seized her arm and hauled her up. Her muscles were numb after sitting so long, and with a fresh injection of terror coursing through her, she stumbled, bumping her knees on the edge of the bathtub. Her legs were like the floppy appendages of the rag dolls Nanna had made her and Lexi.

"Come on! Move it." DJ tugged harder, his fingers biting deeper into her biceps.

Struggling to keep up with his brisk strides, Fenn winced as tingling pain ran up and down her arm from his grip. When she spotted the man standing by the motel bed, a whole new sort of fear washed through her. He was tall and muscled, his arms as big as her legs and his chest thick and wide. He had no hair on his scalp, but his beard was thick and dark brown. His throat had tattoos all the way from his chin to the neck opening of his T-shirt and on his arms. The guy eyed her like a starving man might eye a steak, and judging from the gut hanging over his leather belt, he'd had more than his share of steaks in the past.

Fenn shuddered. Was this the man DJ had sold her virginity to?

"She gonna give me trouble?" the giant asked DJ. "I heard her bitchin' at you back there."

"Naw, man." DJ gave Fenn a hard shake. "You're not gonna give Tommy any trouble, are you, Layla?"

"Layla?" Tommy said and snorted a laugh. "You come up with that?"

DJ shrugged. "What of it?"

"Clapton fan are ya?" Tommy asked with a crooked grin.

"Bite me." DJ dragged Fenn forward. "Go on and get on the road. Kurt is expecting you before sunup."

Fenn glanced to the window where no sign of sunlight peeked at the edges of the dingy blackout curtains. How long had she been in the bathroom? The wait had seemed like forever, but if it was dark outside, it had likely only been a few hours. No more than twelve. Past dinnertime, though.

A pang reverberated deep inside her. Oh God, what she'd give to be helping Mom with the dishes right now. To be in her own room with her bed that smelled like laundry sheets instead of stale cigarettes. Was Lexi having her books read to her? What were they doing to find her? *Were* they trying to find her?

Doing this because of Fenn!

Her stomach cramped—and not just because she hadn't eaten anything in a long time. What had she done that had made Dad so mad, that had torn her parents' marriage apart?

The big guy moved closer to them and flashed a little bottle like the ones that held her grandmother's insulin. "…better if she slept the whole way," Tommy was saying.

"Sleep?" Wait…what were they saying? She should have been paying closer attention instead of worrying about home. She was on her own and had to stay sharp, keep her head, fight back with everything she had if she was going to get away from these creeps.

"Not too much. Kurt wants her awake and not stoned looking for her pictures," DJ said.

"Yeah, yeah." Tommy brushed past them to the counter where the sink was and rattled a paper bag as he took out a syringe sealed in plastic. He ripped into the overwrap with his teeth and stuck the needle in the small vial. "Hold her still."

Fenn gasped and tried to backpedal. "No! Stop! What is that?"

"Just a little somethin' to keep you quiet and out of trouble till we get you to your next stop," Tommy said in a dull tone.

"No! Get away from me! Stop!" She twisted and yanked against DJ's hold on her. With her free hand, she slapped and clawed and pushed at her captor.

In response, DJ snaked an arm around her waist and pinned her free arm. "Cut it out!"

Tommy closed in, and she kicked at him. "Get away!"

"Shut up!" DJ warned, clamping his hand over her mouth, then to Tommy, "Hurry up, man. Before someone hears her."

Someone might hear her…

Fenn took the cue, and despite the hand over her mouth, screamed as loud as she could. She screamed through the prick on her arm as Tommy shot her full of some tranquilizer. She screamed until her head spun, and her vision blurred. Until her knees buckled and the floor rushed up to meet her…

Chapter 7

Jake paced the living room. He had to *do* something.

After getting Emma back to their house, he'd asked her parents to watch Lexi just a little while longer. He and Emma needed time to process what they'd learned at the convenience store.

Darkness had fallen outside, a reflection of his soul, his dim hope. His daughter—their little Button—in the hands of sex traffickers! His gut roiled. He wanted to rage, to punch something, to howl like a wolf in agony and frustration. But none of that would be productive. None of that would solve anything.

Emma had disappeared into the master bedroom and closed the door, clearly signaling he was not welcome. So after wearing a path on the living room throw rug for several minutes, he retreated to Fenn's bedroom and sank down on the edge of her unmade bed. The familiar, yet empty, room shouted accusations, echoed with heartbreaking silence.

Anguish washed through him.

As Fenn's father, he had to do something to fix this situation. She was his responsibility.

Casting his gaze around the strange collection of things his daughter kept in her room—concert posters from music groups he knew nothing about, books on preparing for college entrance exams and bumper stickers pinned to her wall with slogans from current hot-button issues. Dirty T-shirts featuring product logos, movie references and cultural icons, lay strewn over her floor, witness to her sloppiness, but also signs his little girl was growing up, forming opinions, learning empathy, choosing a path.

And then there were the beloved reminders of her childhood. A dusty stack of Baby-sitters Club and Junie B. Jones paperbacks on the bottom shelf of her bookcase, newer favorites like The Hunger Games series, *Divergent*, and *Lord of the Rings* were prominent on higher shelves. A sad smile tugged his cheek remembering Brody teasing Fenn about being a book geek, and her retort, *And proud of it!*

In a tiny chair in the corner sat a retired, but not yet packed away and forgotten, American Girl doll. Jake had driven all the way to Asheville to get the exact doll on Fenn's Christmas list some eight years ago. On her wall over her bed, the hand-carved cradle cross her grandmother had gifted her on her baptism. Her tattered Corduroy Bear, whom she'd called "Dowo" for years, the closest two-year-old Fenn could come to Corduroy. The name had stuck.

When he shifted on the bed to blink at the well-loved bear, his hand found something soft and frayed poking out from under her pillow. The last threadbare scraps of her baby blanket. She'd carried it with her until she was four and had been coaxed to leave it behind when she went to preschool. He'd known that as late as age eight, during es-

pecially scary thunderstorms, Fenn had snuck the blankie
out of hiding for comfort. He'd found her hugging it one
evening when he'd checked on her during severe weather.
Had Fenn felt her life so stormy in recent days that she'd
needed her childhood source of comfort to help her sleep?

Keep your voice down! You'll wake the girls!

He winced, wondering if his daughter had heard his
yelling.

Bowing his head, he groaned. Of course, Fenn had
heard him shouting and spewing his anger and frustration! He muttered an earthy, curt word under his breath.
As he curled his fingers tightly around the scrap of soft
pink fabric, fresh guilt and grief slammed down on him.

On the day she was born, he'd promised his baby girl
to always love her, to always take care of her, to always
protect her. And he'd failed. Failed to keep her safe. Failed
to make her feel his love deeply enough, and she'd run
away from home. Anything, everything, that happened
to Fenn before they rescued her would be his fault. And
that knowledge tore at him like an industrial drill boring
his heart, his head, his soul.

Down the hall, he heard the bedroom door open, the
hall floorboards creak and rapid footsteps marching toward the front of the house. "Jake?"

He thumbed moisture from his eyes, tucked the scrap
of blanket in his pocket and took a fortifying breath as he
walked out of Fenn's room. "I'm here."

Emma looked past him toward Fenn's bedroom, then
seemed to need a moment before she could speak. After
squeezing her eyes closed and taking a deep breath, she
glanced at him and said, "I'm going to bring Lexi home
from my parents' house. I want her life, her routine to stay
as near normal as possible."

Jake scratched his cheek. "Are you sure you wouldn't
rather have—?"

"Yes! I'm sure." Emma drew her shoulders back. "I want at least one daughter here with me tonight, where she belongs…"

Rather than argue, he slid both hands in his back pockets and nodded. "Okay. Whatever you want. I'll go with you."

Emma held up a hand. "No. I want you to be gone when we get back. Go stay…wherever you were last night."

A fresh prickle of anger crawled through Jake. "Hell no."

Emma jerked her chin up. "What?"

"Have you considered that if you hadn't kicked me out last night, Fenn would still be here right now?" He jerked his thumb over his shoulder and narrowed his eyes as he added, "In there, in her room, listening to her weird EDM music and texting her friends?"

Emma's eyes widened in shock and fury. "You're blaming *me* for this?" Her tone was an octave higher than normal. "Are you freaking kidding me? It was your yelling that woke her up! If you hadn't stayed out until the middle of the night—"

"You'd ordered me to leave my own house! Told me you'd filed for divorce! You expect me to take that lying down? Not get mad and shout about it?" All of the day's tension and anxiety, last night's anger and hurt, the bleak unknowns hammered in his brain. He loosed a roar full of anguish and frustration. When he exhausted the air fueling his howl, Emma angled her head and glared her disapproval.

"If you're finished…" She huffed and spun away to march toward the kitchen.

Jake followed. "Damn it, Emma, come back here! I'm not going anywhere. Not tonight and not anytime soon. We have unfinished business—this divorce you're forcing on me deserves discussion, but more importantly, our missing daughter. Until we find Fenn—"

Emma whipped back around to face him. "Until we find Fenn, *she* is my number one priority. But that doesn't mean I will neglect Lexi. And I will not subject Lexi to the continued fighting and yelling between us. So go. Be gone from here before I get back. I need some semblance of peace and normalcy here tonight for Lexi."

So his absence equaled normalcy for Lexi? He opened his mouth to argue but realized with a dull gnawing in his chest that she was right. He'd missed far too many bedtimes and goodnight hugs in the last several months.

Emma started for the back door, and Jake took a few long strides to catch up to her. "Em, wait."

She stopped, her shoulders tensing, then before she faced him, he heard her draw a deep breath and shake the stiffness from her posture. To her credit, her venom was gone when she met his eyes and asked, "What?"

"I will go back to Brody's for the night—if he'll have me—but I want to be here to help put Lex to bed. She's bound to be scared. To have questions. She deserves to have both parents here tonight."

Emma lifted one sculpted eyebrow, and knowing what she was likely thinking, he added, "She deserves both parents every night. And, yes, I've been gone a lot lately. But don't punish her tonight because of my mistakes." He spread his hands in appeal. "Please, Em. I'll go after she's asleep."

He knew the moment she'd changed her mind, saw the softening in her gaze, the flicker of regret and sadness that passed over her face, before she whispered, "Fine. But no arguing. No accusations or raised voices. We have to present a united front and comfort to her. Understand?"

"Goes without saying."

She jerked a nod. "Let's go bring our daughter home."

Jake followed Emma out, wishing with every fiber of his being they were bringing *both* of their girls home.

Was Emma right? Was his fractured family his fault? Had he contributed to Fenn's running away? Damn it, yes. He had to shoulder a lion's share of blame.

But now was not the time for recriminations and guilt. He had to focus his energy and every resource toward finding Fenn. And then, Jake resolved, fisting his hands at his sides, he would win Emma back and restore his family. Nothing was more important.

"Where is Fenn?" Lexi asked after they'd trundled her into bed and led her in prayers.

Jake's gut swooped, and his mouth dried. He sent a cautious glance toward Emma as if to gain some clue about the best way to approach his answer. But his wife's eyes were wide and her brow furrowed, clearly as heartbroken by the question and as confused about how to answer as he. Although he knew Emma's parents would have been careful not to alarm Lexi with anything said in front of her or their general behavior while babysitting her, Lexi wasn't stupid. The four-year-old knew Fenn was gone and that her family was on edge.

"Uh…" Emma fumbled, taking extra time to tuck Lexi's stuffed cat, Tom, in beside her. Tom had been a stopgap the Christmas before last Christmas when Lexi had begged for a kitten. Lexi love Tom but had not stopped asking for a real cat.

"She went…away for a little while," Jake started, watching Lexi's face carefully for her reaction.

"Where?"

"She's…staying with some other people for a while," Jake said.

"Who?"

"Oh, well, you don't know them." Emma gave a weak, wobbly smile.

"Scoow friends?"

Jake hesitated a beat then bobbed a nod. "Yeah, school friends."

Emma's gaze shifted to him, burning with accusation for his white lie. Then turning to Lexi she said, "Fenn will be back in a few days."

Please, Lord, bring Fenn back, Jake thought as Emma added, "Meantime, you get to enjoy all of the attention from your grans and your aunts and uncles. Won't that be fun?"

"I guess."

"Now, no more stalling. Night night. Sweet sleep." Jake bent to kiss Lexi's forehead, and a wave of emotion blindsided him. A lump swelled in his throat when the scent of baby shampoo teased his nose and Lexi's soft hair tickled his cheek. He'd kissed both daughters' heads good-night a thousand times. Taken the sweet scent, the precious moment, the tender feelings for granted. Tonight, he couldn't wish Fenn a good sleep or tell her he loved her. His innocent child was in the hands of monsters who preyed on her vulnerability. He rose from the edge of Lexi's bed quickly, a fresh cocktail of grief, rage and disgust grabbing him by the neck. He rushed from the room before his daughter could see anything of his turbulence on his face.

He listened to Emma whisper love and comfort to Lexi before joining him in the hall and closing the bedroom door behind her.

"Open!" Lexi shouted, and with a sigh, Emma opened the door again, just a crack.

Emma took a few steps away from Lexi's door and buried her face in her hands.

Jake moved closer and put a consoling hand on her

shoulder…which she shrugged off. She stalked to the kitchen.

He followed. "What?"

Emma stood by the sink, her arms braced on the counter. "You lied to her."

With a snort, Jake folded his arms over his chest. "A white lie. Our four-year-old doesn't need to hear the truth."

"Not the full, terrifying truth, but she knows we're worried, that something's not right. Now she'll equate going to visit school friends with something bad, something worrisome."

"What about you? You promised her Fenn would be back in a few days. We don't know that!"

Emma straightened and whirled to face him, her eyes fierce. "Really? Just a couple hours ago you promised me we would get her back. That you'd bring her home, and she'd be safe again. Am I not supposed to believe that? Did you lie to me?"

Jake scrubbed a hand over his face, grumbling a curse word. "You know I am going to do everything I can to make that happen. But we have no guarantees."

Emma pinched the bridge of her nose, her shoulders shaking. The sight of his wife reduced to tears punched Jake in the gut.

"We have to believe we will get her back. We have to keep a positive, fighting attitude. If we don't tell ourselves she's coming home…" He didn't finish the thought. It was too wrenching to even consider.

Emma stepped away from the sink and reached in her purse. Car keys rattled in Emma's hand. "I'm going out."

He blinked, stunned. "Out? Out where? What about Lexi?"

"You're here. She's fine. But Fenn is…" She flailed a hand toward the front door. "Out there. Somewhere. I can't sit here while Fenn is—" Emma bit her bottom lip when it wobbled. "I have to look for her."

When she marched outside to her SUV, he followed. "Emma!"

"I have to go somewhere, do something, hand out flyers or…whatever. I'm going crazy here. I can't just…do nothing!"

"I get that. I'm stir-crazy, too, but it's late. And you're not in any condition to drive—"

"*Don't* tell me what condition I am in!" She aimed a finger at him, and her blue eyes blazed in the moonlight. "You don't get to tell me what I can or cannot do!"

He raised both hands, palms toward her. "I'm not telling you what you can't do." If he could do that, he'd tell her she couldn't divorce him. "But you're clearly upset, and you—"

"Upset?" She scoffed a brittle laugh. "You think? My daughter's been kidnapped and my marriage is over. Why wouldn't I be upset?"

Jake firmed his mouth and shook his head. "I can't talk to you when you get like this."

"No, you *don't* talk to me. Period. Not like you used to. I wouldn't be 'like this—'" she said the last in a gruff voice, mocking him "—if you *did* talk to me. All of this—" she waved her hands expansively "—comes back to you."

Her accusation both stung…and rang an alarm deep in his marrow. Because it echoed one of his deepest fears. Had he failed his family? Was the crumbling state of his marriage his fault?

But her taunt also lit a fuse, and sizzling with resentment, he shot back. "Fenn ran away on your watch, Emma!"

She tipped her head, her tone bitter. "And why do you think that is, *Jake*? Do you think she would have run

away if she were happy? If her homelife felt safe and loving and warm?"

Now it was his turn to scoff. "Exactly! You're the one
who's home with the kids all day! If they don't feel loved
and safe and happy, whose fault is it really?"

She gasped and lunged at him, jabbing him with her
finger. "Don't you dare throw this off on me! I do *everything* to care for the girls! I've bent over backward to make
excuses for you and gloss over your continual absence.
Between us, I'm the only comfort and stability they get!"

"Except for a roof over their heads. And food in their
stomachs. And clothes—"

She loosed a muffled scream. The sound, so full of
frustration and ire, cut him off and raised the hair on the
back of his neck. Her fingers curled in her hair, and she
began trembling from head to toe. Or had she ever stopped
shaking since they left the convenience store?

Despite the vitriol of their argument, the urge to pull
her close and absorb her shaking smacked into him broad-
side. His instinct was to calm her, reassure her. He could
take her anger, could give as good as he got in their spats,
but her fear and anguish tore him apart. Gravel crunched
under his work boots as he closed the distance between
them.

For several weighty seconds, he held her. She was
breathing shallowly, her jaw tight and hands fisted. Then
she raised her hands to his back and clung. For a few moments, with the nocturnal tree frogs serenading them, he
lost himself in the reassuring familiarity of her embrace,
the flicker of what was meant to be. But just when he
thought he might be breaking through her fury, she yanked
free, grumbling, "Stop. I can't—"

Frustration squeezed his chest, and in a low voice, he
said, "This is pointless. We need to focus on what matters most—"

"Our marriage matters," she interrupted in a quiet, surly tone.

Then why are you throwing it away? he wanted to snipe, but he swallowed the bitter words and began again, "Finding Fenn is what matters most right now."

She shuddered and stumbled back a step as if his reminder of the danger Fenn was in were a physical blow to her. Drawing a broken breath, she lifted her chin. "Which is why I'm *going out*. I have to look for her. I have to do something to bring her home!"

"Officer Smith said the best—"

"To hell with Officer Smith!" Emma's voice cracked, and he felt a fissure rending his own heart. "My family is making and putting out flyers, posting on social media, calling everyone in town. But I'm her mother!" She clapped a hand to her chest as tears poured down her face. "I have to do more than posting her picture around town!"

"I want to do more, too. But what?" He moved closer to her, putting a hand on each of her shoulders. "We can't fly off half-cocked. We need to think. Be logical. Make a plan. Come back inside, and let's make a logical plan. Driving aimlessly when you're upset is not a good strategy."

She blinked up at him, tears glistening on her eyelashes. She inhaled slowly. Let it out. "Fine." She sighed, adding under her breath, "Damn you and your analytical brain."

He twitched a half grin because the last had been said without malice. The line was an oft repeated refrain she'd teased him with throughout their years together. Her way of admitting when he was right.

Jake dropped his hands from her shoulders and led her back inside. In the living room, he moved Lexi's dolls out of his way and sank onto the couch. With his legs slightly splayed, he leaned forward to prop his forearms on his knees. Bridging his fingers, he focused on calming his thoughts, centering his mind on finding the answer they sought.

Emma took a seat beside him, wrapping her arms around herself as if cold. Again, he could understand why. He'd had a chill in his core from the moment he'd learned Fenn was missing. Refocusing his thoughts, he cracked opened the door on the vile ugliness he wanted to deny, could barely face without becoming physically ill. Enraged. Terrified.

Fenn was likely with traffickers who intended to prostitute her…

Swallowing a groan, he steeled himself. *Shut down the emotion. Lock it away. For Fenn. You have to be unflinching, logical and strong.*

But it was Emma who spoke first. "We have to look for her in the kind of place where they'd take her. Where do prostitutes find their johns?"

Chapter 8

The next day proved to be tedious with every second of no news stretching out like a rubber band pulled to its limits. Taut, stressed and ready to snap. Like Emma herself.

She spent the day surrounded by her family, who tried to buoy her hope that Fenn would soon be found safe and returned, but whose own worry was deeply etched in their faces. She found herself clinging to Lexi, as if afraid her younger daughter might disappear like Fenn had if she didn't hold her close at all times. But Lexi, who didn't fully appreciate what was happening—thank goodness—too often would wiggle away, whining, "Mommy, you're squeezing too much. I wanna go play."

Jake expressed his restlessness and frustration with the lack of progress by the police by alternately wearing a path in her parents' living room rug and staring out the front window with a desolate look on his face. After her suggestion of searching for Fenn in places where prostitutes were known to hang out, he'd left her to watch Lexi and headed out into the night. His leaving her behind, though necessary for Lexi's sake, felt like a slap to Emma. An abandonment or desertion. Shouldn't they be working *together* to find Fenn? Yet he'd taken off to some undisclosed location until the wee hours. He'd returned to the house exhausted, despondent and reeking of beer and cigarettes.

Emma hadn't slept a wink while he was gone. Waiting, worried, wondering what she would do if they didn't get Fenn back. When she'd met him at the back door sometime around 3:00 a.m., he'd only shaken his head as he brushed past her and collapsed on the den couch.

Emma had called Officer Smith as soon as she thought it reasonable that he'd be awake and begged for good news.

"Nothing new. I'm sorry. The best thing you can do now is continue to put out word to the community. We need eyes out there looking," he told her, repeating the advice he'd given her yesterday. "We're doing everything we can from our end. Please, just stay by the phone and keep spreading the word."

Growling her frustration when she got the same report that afternoon, she disconnected the call and threw the phone at a stuffed chair.

"Emma?" her father said, looking up from the flyers he was prepping to hang from doorknobs around town.

"He wants me to sit on my hands and wait for them to find something. His tone was like a condescending pat on the head." She exhaled a harsh breath through her teeth. "I'm her mother! I have to do something!"

Jake turned from staring out at the yard and met her gaze. She could see him changing with every passing hour. His mouth pressed thinner. His eyes shone more darkly. His hands fisted tighter. The waves of tension and frustration and grief rolled off him in ever more potent waves. She recognized the hum of turbulent emotion vibrating from him, because it matched her own.

Her husband didn't do *pause*. He hated *wait*. He needed control. Action. Progress. Being told to stay by the phone and fill the hours with mind-numbing busywork that anyone in the family, the community could do—and was doing—was to keep the lid on a boiler while stoking the fire. Jake was ready to explode. They both were at a melting point.

As if suiting her thoughts to action, Jake spun away at that moment and stormed out the front door of her parents' house. No one said anything when he left. Her parents, sisters and brothers looked from one to the other as if silently asking, *What do we do?*

Drawing every scrap of composure she had, Emma rasped, "Mom, I know I've asked you to watch Lexi a lot lately but could—"

"Go," her mother interrupted. Rising to pull Emma into a hug, she said, "Lexi has a big family surrounding her, looking after her for as long as you need us to keep her. You give your everything to Fenn right now. Lexi will be fine."

With a final squeeze for Lexi and her parents, Emma left for her own house. As she crossed the lawn between the two houses, she could hear a dull thudding from her backyard. Grunts. Shouts.

Jake had stripped off his shirt and was swinging a sledgehammer onto a steel wedge, splitting firewood. In April. They were well past needing firewood this season, but she understood his chopping was not about winter fuel. The task was about burning off restless energy. Releasing anger. Channeling his grief and unspent adrenaline. With each swing of the sledgehammer, he growled with exertion and frustration and sorrow. When she walked in a wide circle around him so that he'd know she was there, she saw that tears rolled down his face along with his sweat. And her heart cracked.

Without a word, she picked up the axe that lay in the grass near the pile of split wood and stepped over to an upended log.

And joined him in the task.

That night, Emma's muscles were as sore as her heart and her body was tired. But her mind wouldn't shut down. With Lexi at her parents', she tried to focus on practical steps, useful things she could do for Fenn. And her mind kept returning to the same idea.

She would never find Fenn by sitting here in her safe, warm house. She had to follow the danger that Fenn was in. Had to go to the places, talk to the people who were most likely to know, most likely to have seen her daughter. Or the girl with dyed hair. Or Daniel Monroe.

Dark was falling when she finally surged off Fenn's bed. She'd curled up in Fenn's rumpled covers after a shower, just to feel her daughter surrounding her, have Fenn's scent close to her.

Jake looked up from his post in a kitchen chair where a glass of ice tea sat forgotten on the table in front of him.

Emma grabbed her purse strap from the peg where it hung by the back door, and Jake shoved his chair back.

"Where are you going?"

Emma arched one eyebrow as if to say it should be obvious. "Out. To find Fenn. Or Daniel Monroe. Or the red-haired girl or—something!"

Jake moved quickly to block the door. "Alone? You expect me to let you go to the seediest part of town looking for some scumbags?" He matched her raised eyebrow. "I think not."

Emma chortled. "Think again, then. You went last night, and I *am* going now."

"It's not safe for you."

"I don't care. If it's not safe for me, then it's sure as hell not safe for Fenn! I'd walk through fire to save Fenn. You should know that!"

Jake's mouth firmed, and his shoulders leveled. She knew that expression. He could be annoyingly obstinate sometimes. "I will not let my wife put herself at risk in—"

"Let?" She stiffened, and an unamused laugh barked from her throat. "*Let?* You do not get to say what I can and cannot do!"

"Okay, but as my wife—"

"Not for much longer."

He visibly flinched, but rather than verbally acknowledge the reference to the divorce papers she'd filed, he added, "It is my job to protect you from unreasonable risk. You're not going."

Emma sighed and shoved past him. "Try to stop me."

"At least stay close to me, so I can keep the monsters at bay," Jake said, as he parked in front of a pool hall just outside of town. They'd already visited three other dives, asking questions and showing Daniel Monroe's and Fenn's pictures to the patrons with no results.

But the bartender at the last place they'd stopped had overheard the questions they were asking and flagged Jake over. "We don't allow that sort of business around here. We don't want trouble from the cops. Ya hear?"

When Jake had sworn he didn't want to cause problems, the older man behind the bar had leaned closer and whispered, "The Old Mule out on the state highway south of town. Word is they cater to that sort."

After thanking the older man for the tip, he and Emma had driven straight to the pool hall. The place looked more like a run-down garage than anything else. Probably had been a mechanic shop in its former days, Jake guessed as he shouldered open his truck's door. "Same plan as earlier."

Emma nodded. "Same plan."

The plan they'd employed at the previous stops had been to discreetly observe before choosing the most likely candidates to show Fenn's picture to and make inquiries. They didn't want trouble, so caution was paramount.

Cigarette smoke and stale beer were redolent in the air as they entered the concrete block building. Rock music blasted from speakers that hung on the walls at each corner of the pool hall. The clatter of pool balls and rumble of male laughter and curses rang over the whine of electric guitars. The percussive thump of bass and drums reverberated in Jake's chest, keeping time to his heart's anxious beat. *Please let this work*, he prayed silently as they wove through the grid of pool tables.

Heads turned as Emma crossed the floor, and Jake draped a possessive arm around her shoulders. He guided her to the bar at the back of the room and ordered her favorite beer without needing to ask what she wanted.

"Two. In bottles," he added, not trusting the cleanliness of the mugs in the place. Not that they were really drinking tonight, but not ordering something would only cause undue suspicion. Emma pulled out a stool at the bar, looked at it. With a frown for the crumbs and sticky-looking substance on the ripped vinyl, she pushed it back.

When the bartender, a thirtysomething guy with a shaved head, a sleeve of tattoos and ear gauges the size of nickels, returned with their drinks, Jake pulled out the picture of Daniel Monroe they'd printed out and slid it across the counter. "You ever see this guy around here?"

The bartender glanced at the printout but didn't look at it more than a split second. "You a cop?"

"No. I just…need to find him."

Emma angled her phone toward the barkeep. "And her. Mostly her. We have to find this girl. Have you seen her?"

The bald man's face hardened, and Jake saw him flick

the merest glance across the room. If he'd blinked, he'd have missed it. More a nervous tic than a look really. Then the man gave a small shrug as he turned to walk away.

"Wait!" Emma called, and Jake put a hand on her arm. "Em."

She frowned. "He barely looked at either picture."

"He's not going to help us."

"What? How do you know? Why—"

"Just…trust me." He leaned close to her ear to be heard as he pitched his voice low. "He doesn't want to be seen talking to us for some reason. Maybe just on principle, considering the clientele here. He doesn't want to be viewed as a narc, or maybe someone's here that is watching him. Or… I don't know." Jake picked up his beer and took a sip as he cast an eye to the men around the pool tables. More than a few of the pool players were watching him and Emma. Jake gave a subtle nod to one of the men whose stare was especially hard and dark. Distrustful.

"Maybe if we explained—" Emma started, but when he sent her a dubious side-glance, she sighed. Staring toward the end of the bar where the bald man had relocated, Emma frowned her disgust. "Jerk," she grumbled under her breath. Or at least that's what Jake thought she'd said. The noise level in the room made him unsure.

Jake clutched his cold bottle of beer, trying to keep his surveillance casual, wondering if any of the men shooting pool would be any more likely to talk to them than the reticent barkeep. After a few minutes, he sensed more than saw Emma stiffen. He turned to her just as she grabbed his wrist, her attention locked on something across the room.

"Oh my God! Jake, that girl. I think that's—"

Emma dropped his arm and started across the room, nearly running. His pulse spiked. Fenn? He darted after Em, scanning the dim pool hall for his daughter. But the focus of Emma's attention became clear when he spotted a portly man at a corner table. The man was in deep conversation with a young woman—who had hair dyed a bright magenta.

Chapter 9

Emma locked her eyes on the girl with brightly dyed hair, desperate not to lose sight of her in case the girl ran. Her heart thundered against her ribs, and she plowed past men and pool cues and sticky chairs, unmindful of who or what she bumped in her haste.

The girl looked up, her expression shifting from puzzled to alarmed as Emma homed in on her.

"You…" Emma fumbled out her cell phone and woke the screen to show the photo of Fenn. "You were at the convenience store on Highway 6 yesterday, weren't you?"

The girl's eyes rounded.

"Hey, do you mind?" the man with the girl growled.

Ignoring the man's protest, Emma shoved her phone toward the girl. "You talked to this girl. Where is she now?"

"Em." Jake arrived at her side and tugged at her arm. "Easy."

The girl's expression grew more panicked looking as

she divided her nervous look between them and shook her head.

"She's our daughter!" Emma added, hearing the emotion filling her voice.

"I don't— I can't—" Without warning, the girl jumped from her chair and bolted for the emergency exit at the back of the room.

Emma followed, scurrying to keep the girl in sight.

Jake knocked into Emma's arm as he darted past her and out the back entrance, three steps ahead of Emma. They paused in the back alley between the concrete block pool hall and another building with broken windows and cavernous open bay doors. Emma gasped her dismay, uncertain which direction the girl had gone.

"Split up," Jake called as he sprinted to the right.

Jamming her phone in her pocket, Emma raced to the left, her feet crunching over broken glass and splashing in shallow puddles that shimmered with oil. When she reached the corner of the pool hall, she spotted a flash of bright magenta hair just as the girl disappeared behind a line of large trucks parked in the next lot.

"Wait! Please! We just want to talk to you!" she called as she ran after the girl.

Rounding the trucks, Emma again scanned ahead of her, searching. There. Headed behind that motel.

Motel? Good God! Was that where they had Fenn?

She ignored the stitch in her side and charged toward the building where she'd seen the bright-haired girl dart. Jake appeared from her right, and she pointed to the corner of the motel. "Back there!"

Jake raced forward, beating her to the parking area behind the low-rent motel. When Emma caught up, he was engaged in a sort of cat-and-mouse chase with the young woman who was cornered due to a tall hurricane fence that ran along the property line of the motel on two sides.

The magenta-haired girl dashed behind a set of dumpsters, and Jake followed. When the girl darted back out, Jake circled the other way. Only when Emma finally reached the waste receptacles did they trap the panicked and wheezing girl between them.

Emma, too, sucked in air, winded from her sprint, and the rancid smell of rotting trash from the dumpsters filled her nose.

Jake caught the girl's arm and held it firmly. "Where is she? Tell me where my daughter is!"

"Let go of me!" The girl struggled, slapping and clawing at Jake, until Emma took the girl's other arm and gave her a small shake.

"Please!" Emma drew a ragged breath and gagged as the stench assailed her. Putting a hand to her face to block the stink, she hitched her head to Jake. "Can we move this upwind?"

With one of them on either side of the girl, they guided her toward the back fence across the parking lot from the motel.

"Get off me! Leave me alone!" Bright Hair fussed, bucking and struggling to wiggle free of their grasp.

"Why did you run? You know where Fenn is, don't you?" Jake put his nose close to the girl's, his tone commanding.

The girl spit in his face.

Emma gasped, and anger roiled in her veins. "Just tell us where Fenn is!"

Jake wiped his cheek with the sleeve of one arm without dropping his grip on their captive. "Maybe you want us to call the police? We could have them knock on every door in this rathole motel and see what we turn up?"

Bright Hair stiffened. "No!"

Emma tensed as well. "We *should* call the police, Jake. I—" She patted her pocket. "Crap. My phone's not here."

She glanced back at the parking lot they'd run across to get here. Her phone must have fallen out of her pocket during her sprint.

A door at the back of the motel opened, sending a screech of old hinges into the night. The girl shot a panicked look that direction before returning a glare to Jake. "Let go! I can't help you!"

"I don't believe you," Jake grated. "We saw the security camera feed at the convenience st—"

With a gasp and a lunge toward Jake, the girl cut him off by wrapping her arms—and one leg—around Jake and kissing him. Deeply. Seductively. Aggressively.

For a moment, Emma could only stare in shock and irritation as the girl made out with her husband. The womanchild's hands roamed from Jake's hair to his tush, grabbing at his crotch and squeezing his butt.

Jake put an end to it quickly, though. Wrenching away from the plundering kiss and untangling himself from her groping hands. "What the hell? I'm old enough to be your father, kid!"

She came at him again, trying to snuggle close and wind her arms around him. "Most men I know would love to have a young thing to play with."

"Play with?" Jake sputtered, wiping his mouth with his arm and grimacing as if the words were bitter on his tongue. "Good God! No decent man would—"

The girl snorted and curled her lip. "Who said anything about decent? Men are scum." She cut a nervous glance toward the motel. "Don't flatter yourself, thinking I want anything to do with you. I only thought I saw DJ—" She clamped her mouth closed and looked away.

"DJ? Is DJ your pimp? Daniel Monroe?"

The girl stiffened and took a large step back, her eyes wide with terror. "I didn't say nothin'!"

Emma snagged Bright Hair's arm again, her tone hopeful. "He's here?"

Jake flashed the printout with the picture of Daniel Monroe. "This guy. You were with him yesterday. Where is he now? Where is Fenn?"

"Look," the girl snarled through pinched lips and glanced back toward the motel. "He can't see me talking to you. He'll make me pay for it, make *your daughter* pay for it, even if I don't tell you anything!"

Just the intimation of Fenn being abused by the monster who held her captive brought a sob to Emma's throat.

"Tell us what we need to know, then, and we'll let you go, right now!" Jake said.

A visible shiver rolled through the girl that Emma was sure had more to do with fear than the girl's skimpy miniskirt and crop top. After a brief hesitation and a dark scowl, she blurted, "She's not here anymore. He sent her out of town. On hold."

"On hold?" Emma shook her head. "What does that mean?"

"He's selling her, her virginity, to the highest bidder. An auction. Online."

"Selling—" Emma's stomach rebelled, but she gulped oxygen and swallowed the bile in her throat. When her knees buckled, she sat on the cracked asphalt before she fell over.

Jake rushed to her. "Emma! Are you all r—"

The sound of feet slapping on the pavement brought Emma's head up in time to see the bright-haired girl sprinting away. "Jake, she's running!"

Jake jerked his gaze toward her, but sighed heavily. "Let her go."

"What! Jake—" She clutched at his sleeve, panic swelling as the magenta-haired girl disappeared around the building.

"Do you want her to get in trouble with her pimp?"

"Of course not! I don't want her with a pimp at all! We need to call the cops and—"

"And what? You heard her! Fenn's not here. And if word gets back to this DJ person that we called the cops, that we pumped that girl for information, think what he could do to her—or to Fenn!"

Her eyes filled with tears. She *was* thinking of what could happen to Fenn, and it was all she could do not to shatter in a million pieces. Her heart stung. Her nerves were raw. Her body shook so hard she couldn't even stand. "But she was our only lead, our best hope of finding our baby!"

"Not our only lead." Jake put a hand under Emma's elbow to help her to her feet. "Let's go."

Emma shook her head, baffled that Jake would so easily give up. "No. Daniel Monroe is here somewhere. I know he is. The girl was worried he'd see her which means—"

"Which means we have to protect her, just like we'd want someone else to protect Fenn."

"But…"

"We have another lead. We need to talk to Officer Smith."

"So you believe her? That Fenn's gone? Being sold for her virg—" With a hiccupped sob, she broke off.

"I do believe her. We need to pass that tip on to the police, and then we'll go online and search for the damn auction ourselves."

Emma leaned on Jake as he escorted her back across the parking lot toward the pool hall. Of course. "But this other girl… Don't we need to do something to help her?"

Jake's steps slowed. "I wish we could, but right now, our priority is finding Fenn. The best we can do now is make our report to the cops and let them sort this out." He jerked his head toward the motel. "They probably won't be here an hour from now, if DJ did see us hassling that girl."

Acid rose in Emma's throat. The mother in her couldn't let go of what she'd seen in the magenta-haired girl's eyes. "Then promise me that when Fenn is safe, we will see to it that what's happening out here—" she aimed a finger toward the decrepit motel "—right under our noses, in *our hometown*—" her voice rose with vehemence, passion and fury "—is stopped. Promise me we'll do everything we can to put these monsters out of business and behind bars!"

"That is a promise that is easy to make." Jake captured her face between his palms. "We will find Fenn and bring her home, and then we will stop Daniel Monroe and his cronies from hurting anyone ever again."

Emma nodded. She had filed divorce papers just days before because she'd given up on Jake's ability and willingness to keep the promises he'd made her. But now, for her daughter's sake, she hoped she could believe him in *this pledge* at least.

"And how did you come by this information?" Officer Smith asked, narrowing his eyes on Jake and Emma from behind his desk at the police station. The officer, who'd been off duty and relaxing at home when they arrived at the Valley Haven police station to make their report, had hurried back to the station to talk with them. He was out of uniform and had a mustard stain on the T-shirt he wore.

Emma glanced at Jake, then back at the officer. "We tracked down the girl with the dyed hair we saw Fenn talking to in the security footage."

"Tracked down...how?" The crease between the officer's eyes deepened. "What have you been up to?"

"Looking for our daughter," Jake said without hesitation. "Like you're supposed to be."

"Jake," Emma said in a warning tone under her breath.

To the officer, she said, "We couldn't just sit around doing nothing. We went to some bars around town and got a tip where we might find some...prostitution activity."

Smith sighed. "Vance's Grill? The Old Mule?"

Jake sat taller. "You know what's happening out there?"

"Give us a little credit for having our finger on the pulse of the community."

"Then why weren't there cops out there asking questions and looking for Fenn?" Emma asked.

Officer Smith leaned forward, propping his arms on the desk to glower at them. "Who says there weren't?" He sighed. "You two may have just set our efforts back, spooking our contacts, sending Monroe and his operation to ground. They'll move to another town, even another state maybe." Tapping one finger forcefully against his blotter, he said, "You two need to sit tight and let us do our job. Back off. You're not trained law enforcement. You have no legal authority. You can, in fact, do more harm than good if—"

"Did your people know Fenn was being auctioned for her virginity?" Jake interrupted. He would not be told what he, as Fenn's father, could or could not do to get her back.

Officer Smith met his eyes squarely. The man's jaw tightened. "No. But I will get with the state police and have their IT guys start looking for—"

"When?" Jake asked.

"What?"

"When will the state police start looking? If we know where Monroe was operating tonight, if we know what his plans are for Fenn, why are we still sitting here talking? You should have men mobilized *now*!"

Color rose in Officer Smith's face. "Are you going to tell me how to do my job?"

"Of course not," Emma said, scooting to the edge of her

chair and shooting another glare at Jake. "But we know time is critical. The longer we wait—"

"There are procedures we must follow. A chain of command. Jurisdictions..."

Jake shoved to his feet. "For God's sake! Even by telling you what we learned we could have put Fenn at risk! That girl we talked to warned us that—"

"Ruby Haynes."

"What?" Jake fisted his hands then flexed them. Fisted them. He bounced on his heels. Adrenaline and frustration had his entire body cracking with energy.

"The girl's name is Ruby Haynes. We *have* been working on the case. We identified the girl from past arrest reports." Smith rose from his chair and divided a stern look between Jake and Emma. "I know waiting for news is hard. I know you want to help. But the best thing you can do is give us the time and space to handle this investigation by the books. When we find your daughter, we want the charges against the people responsible to stick. We have to follow legal procedure. Go through proper channels."

Jake plowed his fingers through his hair and ground out a curse word. All he could hear the policeman saying was slow, slower and slowest. Time consuming. Delays. And he knew in his gut that Fenn didn't have time.

He'd go home, sure. But he'd be damned if he'd sit back and wait for his daughter to be sold to a pedophile or worse.

Later that night when they got back to the house, Jake draped his jacket over a kitchen chair and stretched his shoulders. He was exhausted, mentally and physically, not having slept more than a couple hours in the last two days. But he couldn't afford to rest, not when they finally had a solid lead.

They'd retrieved a sleeping Lexi from next door, and

Emma carried their baby girl to tuck her in bed. When she returned, her shoulders wilted as she faced the empty kitchen, where their family had gathered for so many meals, homework and game nights.

"I'm going to start searching online for that damn auction." He paused in the door to the hall and said over his shoulder, "You should try to get some sleep."

Her answer was a scoff. "Sleep? Really? You think I can sleep knowing what Fenn's facing? Knowing how terrified she must be?"

Too tired to argue—why did Emma have to make everything a fight?—he shrugged. "Fine. Do what you want."

As he headed to the spare bedroom where Emma had set up an office, he heard her muttering.

He pushed aside his irritation with her and rolled the mouse to wake the computer screen. The background image of the desktop was a photo from last summer of Fenn and Lexi grinning at the camera from the lake where they were swimming. Fenn held her sister on her hip and the two had their heads bent together, hamming for the photographer. Pain shot to his core, so swift and sharp it stole his breath. For several seconds, he could only stare at the picture and ache.

His girls looked so happy at the moment in time caught by the camera. He frowned, realizing he didn't know who'd taken the photo. Not him. He'd assumed it had been Emma, but in truth, it could just as easily have been any one of Emma's family members.

As he continued to stare at the image glowing on the screen, he realized another uncomfortable truth. He hadn't gone swimming with his daughters even once last summer. Summer was the busiest time of year in the construction game, and he'd had more on his plate than contracts and contractors to contend with last summer. He'd had that nasty business with an employee embezzling from the company. The matter of Jake, himself, being suspected of the theft by the police. And, of course, there'd been the cleaning woman's suspicious death at Cameron Glen to worry about.

Yeah, it had been a tumultuous few months. No time for swimming while trying to save Turner Construction and defend himself from criminal charges. Yet an entire summer had slipped away, a whole season of his girls' childhood had gone up in smoke while he fought fires elsewhere.

Compunction and regret kicked him in the gut. Hard. How did he balance work and home? How did he live up to the expectations he'd set for himself, the standard he had to meet in order to protect his family from…what his father had become?

Hearing a noise behind him he angled his head to find Emma watching him. "I…shouldn't have snapped at you like that. My only excuse is that I'm tired and worried sick and…" She raised both hands then let them drop loosely at her sides, her shoulders slack. "I will try harder to put aside my grievances with you until we find Fenn."

He nodded. "For Fenn's sake, we need to work together and not be at each other's throat."

A strange look crossed her face. She opened her mouth as if to say something but clamped it shut again. Her attention shifted to the computer screen. "Haven't gotten far, I see."

Her tone was lighter, more teasing now, and he curled up a corner of his mouth in a rueful grin. "No." He pointed at the screen. "This is a great picture. Can you send it to my phone?"

She lifted one eyebrow and moved a second chair closer to the computer desk. "I did. Last summer when it was taken."

"You did?"

"Pretty sure."

"Oh." He sighed. "'Kay."

"But I'll send it again."

He flashed a smile. "Thanks."

Emma rubbed both hands on the legs of her jeans and inhaled deeply. "Well, let's do this."

"Em, you don't have to help if—I mean, this could be pretty disturbing. I can do this alone."

Her eyes grew fierce, and firm resolve tightened her jaw. "Everything about this situation is disturbing. While I'm not looking forward to this—" she waved a hand toward the computer "—I can take it. I have to do this. I'm her mother." She met his gaze squarely. Stubbornly. "I won't be shut out."

He grunted. "All right, then." He faced the keyboard and poised his fingers over the keys. "Hell. What do I even use as search terms?"

She added a huff of disgust before suggesting, "No point being coy. Start with 'Virgins for sale.'"

He entered the despicable search and gave a shudder. "Even typing it makes me feel oily and nauseous."

She placed her hand on his wrist as he navigated through the list of search results, and the simple connection to her buoyed him for the heinous task. He both wanted to find Fenn on one of the sites and didn't.

No. He did. Of course, he did. Because finding a posting selling her innocence could bring them an important step closer to bringing her home. He swallowed hard and started following links. For the next two hours, they searched websites and bulletin boards and photo galleries that made his stomach sour and his chest hurt. Many were simply porn. Some required passwords they didn't have to enter. Most wanted credit card information, which, for the time being, Jake refused to enter.

Now and then, they'd happen upon sites that featured image after image of naked or seductively dressed girls—and boys—children!—with dead or frightened expressions. Together, he and Emma searched each pitiful, precious face for their daughter. Every race, size and age of child was available for purchase. It galled him. Infuriated him. Sickened him.

Beside him, Emma sighed, whimpered and gasped as the mind-numbing, nightmarish catalog of innocents continued. Many of the websites were in foreign languages, but far too many were clearly based in the United States. When his head began to throb, he realized he'd been clenching his jaw, grinding his teeth, harder and harder. He was surprised he hadn't broken a molar.

At one point, he slammed a fist on the desk and gritted out a curse. *"This horror show should not be happening in this country."*

"It shouldn't be happening anywhere," Emma countered, her voice barely a whisper and full of strain.

He glanced at her and found silent tears streaming down her cheeks. The bereft look on her face punched him in the gut. "Aw, honey…"

He raised a hand to dry the moisture from her face, and she groped for a tissue to wipe her nose.

Emma gestured vaguely toward the computer. "Every one of those children is someone's daughter. Someone's son. They're babies. They're… Oh, God!"

Heart sinking, Jake turned back to the computer and closed the browser.

"What are you doing?" Emma protested. "We haven't found her yet! We can't stop!"

"That's enough…for tonight. We don't know what we're doing, and we're only torturing ourselves."

Emma flopped back in her chair and closed her eyes. "Oh, Jake…"

As tired as he was, he didn't dare close his own eyes, afraid of the images that would haunt him. He might never sleep soundly again.

Jake rolled the desk chair back and tried to muster the energy, the will to get up. If he couldn't sleep, wasn't hungry, what was he to do at—he checked his watch—two in the morning?

"I'm going to check on Lex," Emma said, her voice cracking.

Even though they hadn't heard a peep from Lexi's room, he understood Emma's need to see their baby, touch her, reassure themselves she was safe, and happy, and...home.

Jake sent up a silent prayer for Fenn, for help finding her, for strength to get through this crisis. Then he sat staring at the floor as new memories filtered into his brain.

Over the years, as he'd traveled to builder conventions or to visit contractors, he'd seen billboards and posters in airports featuring women with bleak expressions. He noticed the signs asking people to keep an eye out for suspicious situations with fellow travelers. Human trafficking. Sex trade. Girls being smuggled in from other countries. He'd read the posters and given the vile subject only a cursory thought. A quick "how terrible" before carrying on with his search for a restroom, a cinnamon bun or a ten-dollar hamburger. The reality was too horrible to ponder long, and he'd had a connecting flight to catch.

But now it was his fight. His daughter. And he could never be so blithe about human trafficking again.

Chapter 10

Fenn sat up as the door rattled. She'd been locked up in the glorified broom closet since arriving at the old house, located, as best she could determine, in the middle of no-where.

Tommy entered the tight space and threw something pink and flimsy at her. "Put this on."

She plucked up the scrap of clothing and shuddered. A negligee. And a skimpy one at that. "Where's the rest of it?" she said, not bothering to hide her snark.

"Think you're a comedian, do ya?" Tommy crouched in front of her and flipped the nightie with his finger. "Wear this or nothing."

Fenn glared at him. "Why?"

"Because I said so," he snarled, using a phrase she'd heard her parents use more times than she could count. Just the thought of her parents made her chest ache—again—and she had to blink to fight back tears—again.

She was determined not to cry in front of Tommy or any of the jerks who held her.

They'd gotten to this new location the day before, while it was still dark outside. Whatever drug they'd given her had worn off before they reached this place, so she wasn't sure how long they'd been driving.

Her head hurt. Her stomach hurt. Her body hurt in any number of places after being knocked around by DJ, Tommy and another guy that had met them at this house, Kurt.

Scared and alone didn't begin to cover how she felt. They were specks in the rearview mirror of her emotions. Desperate and terrified to the point of illness were more like it. But she wanted, more than anything, to be smart, be brave. She thought of the heroines in all the books she'd read and movies she'd seen, from Katniss and Tris to the heroines in the spy thrillers her mom didn't know she read. Even in the worst circumstances, they never gave up. They were defiant and resourceful and mustered courage even when they didn't really feel it. She spent most of her time alone studying her surroundings, trying to devise ways she could use ordinary things as weapons, scheming ways she could outthink, outmaneuver Tommy and get free. Then where she'd go, how she'd get help…

Unfortunately, she hadn't come up with much that seemed realistic.

When she didn't move, didn't comply, for several long seconds, Tommy said, "Either you put it on, or I'll put it on you."

Swallowing hard, she turned her back to him and started taking off her own clothes and slipped the nothing nightie on. Clutching her clothes to her chest, she faced him again.

But Tommy snatched her shorts, bra and shirt from her and tossed them to the far side of the room behind him.

He tugged her out of the closet and toward a mattress on the floor. "Now lie back, arms at your sides. I gotta get a few shots of you."

"Shots?"

"Buyers want to see what they're bidding on."

She curled her lip at him. "Like I'm a piece of meat? That's…that's…"

Tommy moved toward her so fast, his expression so mad, she shrank back in fear.

"Shut your mouth, or I'll fix you so you can't talk at all." The menace in his tone sent a shiver through her. "Now give me a pose. Show me your assets."

Drawing a shaky breath, she sat down. As she curled into a tight ball, she set her mouth in a hard line. "No."

Tommy raised a hand as if to strike her then stopped. "Damn it. If DJ hadn't specifically said no bruises that show…you'd be a bloody heap right now, girl." He rubbed his bald head, his nose flaring as he glowered at her. Then, with a malevolent smile, he took the phone he'd been about to use for pictures of her, and swiped through some screens. A moment later, he squatted beside her, reeking of cigarettes and sweat, and showed her what he'd pulled up. "This look familiar to you?"

She glanced at the screen and froze. Her house.

"I…"

"Mmm-hmm. We found your address in that little backpack you were carrying. We know where your family lives." He swiped to another screen and pulled up a picture of her family she'd recently posted on Instagram. "Nice-looking folks." Tommy tapped his finger on the screen. "I especially like this little girl." He pointed to Lexi. "Maybe we could snatch her and put her to work for us, too. Some guys like 'em young. *Real* young." His tone was leering. Threatening. Sickening.

The ice that filled Fenn froze her lungs, her heart, while a rage fired in her gut.

Struggling for the breath to speak, she rasped, "Stay away from my sister."

"You want your sister to stay safe? Your parents? Then do what you're told. You fight me or give me lip again, I'll send DJ or one of our other guys to your house to kill your dad, rape your mom and take your sister for our operation." He showed her an unsent text that simply read, Go. "One tap of a finger, and this text goes to DJ. He knows what to do."

The tears she'd fought so hard to hide filled her eyes, spilled onto her cheeks. "No! Leave them alone. Please!"

"You gonna do what you're told?"

Fenn swallowed the bile in her throat and gave one small nod.

Someone knocked on Emma's front door early the next morning, when the sun was just peeking over the hills around Cameron Glen. Her brother stood on her porch with a box of apple fritters in his hands and a worried frown knitting his brow.

"Did I wake you?" Brody asked as he stopped in her foyer to study her with a keen look.

"Can't wake me if I haven't been to sleep," Emma said, shuffling toward the kitchen and dropping into a wooden chair.

Jake appeared from the hall, his expression hopeful. When he spotted Brody, his face fell and he groaned. "Oh. It's you."

Brody snorted. "Is that any way to greet someone who brought pastries?" He offered the white bakery box with a flourish, but his attempt at levity dropped like a lead balloon. Setting the food aside, Brody sat heavily in a chair across from Emma and scowled. "Oh, man. What have you heard? I can see by your faces you know something more, something bad."

By turns, she and Jake relayed the events of the past eighteen hours to Brody, who listened with a growing horror darkening his eyes.

"We tried to find the auction online last night and got swamped in the most unbelievable cesspool of indecency and exploitation—" Emma raised a hand to her mouth and shuddered. "Oh, Brody, it was horrible."

"I can imagine." He scrubbed a palm over his mouth. "Geez."

Jake shook his head. "I don't think you can imagine. I don't consider myself naive or prudish, but even I saw things that shocked me and made me sick."

"Damn." Brody swallowed hard. "Were y'all on the dark web?"

Jake raised his chin, straighten his back as if startled by what Brody had asked—and yet inspired. "Uh…no. I'm…not even sure how to do that."

"What are you talking about? What is the dark web?" Emma asked, narrowing a curious stare on her brother. But given the reluctant expression on Brody's face and the loathsome-sounding name, she wasn't sure she wanted to know. Dark web? How much darker and more vile could things be than what she and Jake and found last night?

"It's a whole other level of hidden and illegal activity on the web. Real subversive stuff. Not easy to access because of the nature of the activity that goes on there." Brody winced. "I feel sure there are sex trafficking sites and platforms on the dark web. But I have no idea how to get on there either."

A chill raced through Emma, and she rubbed the goose bumps that rose on her arms. "If…if Fenn is on there, we… we need to try."

Brody scrubbed a hand over his mouth and furrowed

his brow in thought. "I know a guy who might be able to help us. His specialty is computers. Ben's like the genius hacker type."

With swift movements, Jake stepped forward and pulled out a chair. He took a seat and leaned across the table toward Brody. "Call him."

Brody glanced at the clock. "It's still early."

"I don't care." Jake smacked his flattened hand on the tabletop. "Wake him up. This is an emergency!"

Her brother hesitated only a moment before agreeing with a nod and pulling out his phone.

Two hours later, after waking her sister Cait to come stay at the house with Lexi, they were on the front porch of a house across the county. Even without already knowing so, Emma could've guessed the home belonged to a bachelor. Though the yard was mowed and neat, the flowerbed was barren other than weeds.

Their knock was quickly answered by a man wearing stylish black-framed eyeglasses and who appeared close to Brody's age. Ben grinned at her brother, and the two younger men fist-bumped as they exchanged the expected greetings. Introductions were made, and Ben offered Emma and Jake an amiable smile.

"So y'all live in one of the cabins up at that family retreat—what's it? Cameron Cove?" Ben asked as he assumed a loose wide-legged, folded-arms stance, as if he planned to stand in his foyer and shoot the breeze for several minutes.

"Cameron Glen. Yes, we have a house on the property." She cast Jake an impatient look. Her husband wasn't smiling. His body was taut, and his fidgeting hands spoke for his nervous energy. Jake personified a live wire, cracking and snapping with the current surging in him, much as she was. The exception was that her nerves had always coalesced in her gut, pooling and churning acid, whereas Jake's made him jittery and grumpy.

"Cameron Glen!" Ben snapped his fingers and nodded. "That's right. My parents stayed there for a week a couple summers ago when they were in town to visit me. I told them they could take my bedroom and I'd sleep on the couch, but my lumpy mattress was no prize compared to the beautiful property and quiet cabins of Cameron Glen."

Brody chuckled stiffly. "As the primary groundskeeper and owner of the landscaping company that manages the property, I thank you."

Emma shifted her weight and glanced into the next room, hoping Ben would take the hint that they were anxious to get started. This was not a social call.

"Didn't I hear something about a woman being found dead in one of the cabins last summer?" Ben arched an eyebrow, the same sandy-brown color as his rumpled hair.

Brody started to answer, but Jake cleared his throat and said, "I'm sorry but…can we get started? I think finding our daughter is a little more important than—" he waved a hand vaguely "—these niceties."

Now both of Ben's eyebrows shot up, and he sent Brody a quizzical look. "Um…*find* your daughter?" To Brody he said, "When you said you needed help with the dark web for your niece's sake, I thought you meant she was doing some kind of bizarre report or project for school."

Brody shook his head, scowling. "No, man. I wish it were that simple. Fenn's been kidnapped. We think she's being sold by perverts on the dark web."

When Ben only gawked at the three of them with an expression of shock for several seconds, Emma added, "Auctioned to some creep with a virginity fetish. We're in a hurry. We don't know when the auction might be posted, how long it might run…if it's even on the dark web or if the buyer is being arranged some other way but—" She stopped short and caught her breath. "Please." She waved a hand toward the house beyond the foyer.

With a chastened frown and seemingly filled with their same sense of urgency now, Ben waved them toward the hall. "Right, right. Of course. Back here."

Brody's friend led the way to a back room in his house that was filled with every description of computer equipment. Some unplugged and gathering dust, other pieces set up in separate stations in opposite corners.

Their host took the high-back swivel chair in the middle of a C-shaped desk by the far wall and rolled a mouse to wake the three screens arranged around him. Before logging on, he plowed his fingers through his shaggy hair and blew through his pursed lips so that they buzzed. "Where to begin?" he muttered to himself.

Jake rolled a chair from the other computer station over for Emma and unfolded a metal chair that he set up beside Ben. Brody sat on the corner of the desk and tucked his hands under his armpits as he watched the computer screens over Ben's shoulder.

Ben went through several log-in pages, entering codes, passwords and encryption keys as he accessed the secret and nefarious pages of the dark web.

"So this isn't your first time on the dark web?" Jake asked, his tone held a dark edge. Emma poked her husband as if to say, *He's helping us. Be nice!*

Ben grunted as he typed in his first search terms. "No. Not my first time." He cast Jake a side-glance. "I help companies whose security has been breached. I've had to venture in here for clients in the past when their customers' personal data is stolen. Things like social security numbers and bank account information, passwords and email addresses are a hot commodity on the dark web."

"Oh." Jake sighed and scratched his chin. "Sorry, I just… The last couple days… You can't imagine how difficult it's been and… I still have images in my brain from last night."

"Images?" Ben asked while still typing, clicking and scrolling.

"We did our own online search of the regular web last night," Jake said, leaning closer to see the screen better as thumbnail images popped up on the screen.

"Mmm," Ben hummed distractedly, his attention focused on what had come up on the screen.

"There's horror and filth enough on the general internet. I hate to think what we're going to find today in this dark corner of the web," Jake said.

Emma couldn't look. She, too, had pictures burned in her brain that would give her nightmares for the rest of her life. She stared at her hands in her lap and picked at a hangnail while Ben, Brody and Jake grunted, huffed and mumbled suggestions to each other. "Try that one."

"What's that?"

"No, that's based in Bosnia."

"What about…?"

"Good God! That's sick!"

"Look at this…"

"Yeah, maybe."

Emma held her breath and peeked up at the screen, relieved to not find images, but instead what appeared to be a message board. She caught a few words as Ben scrolled through the entries and clapped a hand to her mouth as she wrinkled her nose in distaste. Fetishes of every description were being sought and offered. Vile language, demands for exorbitant payments, and blessedly small pictures of perverted sex acts rolled up the screen.

"Wait!" Brody reached past Ben to tap the screen. "There. Virgins."

Bracing herself, Emma angled her gaze to the screen.

Revulsion and heartache for the children being victimized swamped her anew.

Ben paged through several listings and sites. "Do you see her?"

Emma held her breath, her hand to her mouth as one bleak face after another appeared on the screen. Young girls in little or no clothes, the expression in their eyes dead, paraded before her, and it was all she could do not to scream.

Until, after thirty minutes, Fenn's picture came up. And Emma did scream. A choked, tragic cross between relief and horror. Brody, who was closest to her, drew her into his arms, while Jake dropped his head to his hands with a strangled sob. Then, lurching to his feet and radiating a palpable anger, he paced away from the computer, both hands fisted in his hair. He shouted an obscenity and slammed his hand against the doorframe. "I swear to God, when I get my hands on the bastards—!"

"Can you trace the source of this posting in any way?" Brody asked, his own voice full of tension. "Does it say anything about where she is or—?"

"Guys?" Ben said. The strange quality in his tone rang alarms in Emma's head.

She twisted in her brother's embrace to glance at Ben. "What?"

"Her auction..." He paused briefly as if knowing how vile the sound of those words would be to Fenn's family. "It's scheduled to end in three hours."

A tingle skipped down Emma's back. Her brain was so frozen with horror and grief, she didn't know what had Ben agitated, but she sensed he was several mental steps ahead of her, formulating a plan.

"And?" she prompted when he grew silent, his brow furrowed in thought.

Jake spun and rushed back to his chair. "What's the bid right now?"

Emma grunted her shock at Jake's question. "What!"

"Twenty thousand," Ben said. "How much can you stake? Payment is due immediately when the auction ends."

"I… I don't know." Jake met Emma's gaze. "What's our credit card limit? Our bank balance?"

"We're bidding on her?" Emma's voice rose an octave. "Jake, I—"

"If they don't know it's us bidding, they might give us information useful to recovering her." Jake scrubbed a hand over his mouth, his expression hopeful, calculating. "If we can conceal who we are until they deliver her to us…"

Her mind spinning, she turned to Ben. "Is that possible? Would that work?"

Ben shrugged. "I'm in new territory here, folks. I can try a few things, including reverse tracing the location of the computer that uploaded the auction, but it's likely they covered their tracks a number of ways."

"Why not take what we've learned to the state police?" Brody said. "The FBI? Whoever—"

Jake paced back to the door and returned. "We don't have time! You've seen how slow the cops are being. When we talked to Smith last time, he was all about red tape and procedures. There'll be questions about how we found her auction and…" He bent his head to his chest as he expelled a weighty sigh. "Maybe if we had more time, if the auction weren't ending in three hours…" Facing Emma, Jake said, "If we don't act now, we could lose our best chance at finding her, Em."

She was shaking from the inside out. "I don't remember what our credit card limits are. I don't know how much we have in savings, precisely, but… I know we can get the money, any amount needed, if it means bringing Fenn home. We'll sell the house, ask my parents, get a loan… I don't care. Just…" She turned to Ben. Swallowed hard. "Up the bid in increments of, I don't know…a thousand?"

Ben shot a consulting glance to Jake, who nodded his agreement.

Flexing his fingers, Ben got to work, setting up a user account, entering a guaranteed method of payment— Jake's online banking app—and waiting for account approval before he was allowed to bid.

Restless and heartsick, Emma stood and walked away from the computer. Silently she prayed that their efforts would yield the outcome they wanted, that they were doing the right thing. What if Jake was arrested for participating in the auction? What if Fenn's captors got wind that Jake was the bidder and hurt Fenn in retribution? What if they took the money and never released Fenn to them?

She mumbled an unladylike word, which, on the heels of her fervent prayers, rang discordantly in her conscience. But given the circumstances, she figured she could be forgiven the expression of her raw emotion.

"Okay," Ben said, "Done. Your bid is the high—"

He didn't even get the sentence out before Jake growled with frustration. "We've been outbid. Already!"

Emma moved up behind Ben to look over his shoulder. The user name hottamale556, who'd previously been the high bidder, once again held the high bid at twenty-four thousand dollars.

"Maybe it's set up with an autobid program based on this user's initial high bid." Ben stroked his cheek and glanced up at Jake. "I'll keep upping the bid until you tell me not to."

Jake nodded. "Do it."

Unable to watch any longer, Emma left the computer room and wandered back to the front of Ben's house. She

Treat Yourself with 2 Free Books!

Get ready to relax and indulge with your FREE BOOKS and more!

Claim up to FOUR NEW BOOKS & TWO MYSTERY GIFTS – absolutely FREE!

Dear Reader,

We both know life can be difficult at times. That's why it's important to treat yourself so you can relax and recharge once in a while.

And I'd like to help you do this by sending you this amazing offer of up to FOUR brand new full length FREE BOOKS that WE pay for.

This is everything I have ready to send to you right now:

Try **Harlequin® Romantic Suspense** books featuring heart-racing page-turners with unexpected plot twists and irresistible chemistry that will keep you guessing to the very end.

Try **Harlequin Intrigue® Larger-Print** books featuring action-packed stories that will keep you on the edge of your seat. Solve the crime and deliver justice at all costs.
Or **TRY BOTH!**

All we ask in return is that you answer 4 simple questions on the attached Treat Yourself survey. You'll get **Two Free Books** and **Two Mystery Gifts** from each series you try, *altogether worth over $20*! Who could pass up a deal like that?

Sincerely,

Pam Powers

Harlequin Reader Service

Treat Yourself to Free Books and Free Gifts.

Answer 4 fun questions and get rewarded.

We love to connect with our readers! Please tell us a little about you...

	YES	NO
1. I LOVE reading a good book.	◯	◯
2. I indulge and "treat" myself often.	◯	◯
3. I love getting FREE things.	◯	◯
4. Reading is one of my favorite activities.	◯	◯

TREAT YOURSELF • Pick your 2 Free Books...

Yes! Please send me my Free Books from each series I select and Free Mystery Gifts. I understand that I am under no obligation to buy anything, as explained on the back of this card.

Which do you prefer?

❏ **Harlequin® Romantic Suspense** 240/340 HDL GRCZ
❏ **Harlequin Intrigue® Larger-Print** 199/399 HDL GRCZ
❏ **Try Both** 240/340 & 199/399 HDL GRDD

FIRST NAME   LAST NAME

ADDRESS

APT.#   CITY

STATE/PROV.   ZIP/POSTAL CODE

EMAIL ❏ Please check this box if you would like to receive newsletters and promotional emails from Harlequin Enterprises ULC and its affiliates. You can unsubscribe anytime.

HI/HRS-520-TY22

dropped onto an overstuffed couch that faced a huge television mounted on the opposite wall. The place was rather sparsely decorated, much like her bachelor brother's place, so she had few clues about the man who was helping them navigate the bowels of the dark web.

Her phone jangled, jarring her from her numb reverie. Caller ID told her the call was from her younger sister Isla. She really wasn't in the mood to talk to anyone, but she knew her family was worried, as much for her as for Fenn.

She answered the call with, "No good news."

"I was afraid of that," Isla responded. "What can I do?"

"I don't... Nothing. I can't..." Emma glanced down the hall toward the computer room when the men's voices interrupted her train of thought, such as it was.

"I'm bringing dinner to you tonight. Lexi's favorite lasagna. You need to eat, to keep your strength up, and I figured Lexi could use a treat, a distraction."

"Lexi..." Emma pinched the bridge of her nose. "Speaking of Lex, could you help Mom and Dad with her? Jake and I are working on something—I'll explain later. Cait covered for us this morning until she had to go to work, but Mom was coming over at eight to relieve her. They've had her for most of the last three days, and I know they could use a break."

"Absolutely. Consider it done."

Jake appeared in the living room, and Emma sat straighter, adrenaline spiking when she saw the anxious look on his face. "Isla, I gotta go. Thanks for everything." She disconnected the call without taking her eyes from Jake. "What?"

He shook his head, shrugged.

When he dismissed her question so blithely, irritation swelled in her. "Jake? Tell me! Do we have the high bid?"

"He's working on it." Jake rubbed the back of his neck. "Maybe you should go home. This could take a while."

She shook her head so hard the messy bun she'd put her hair in came apart. "I'm not going anywhere."

"Emma…" His tone said he thought she was being unreasonable. "We're handling this, and there's no reason for you—"

"This!" she said, springing to her feet, propelled by a shot of anger. She aimed a finger at him. "This is a perfect example of you shutting me out. Fenn is as much my child as yours, and you will not sideline me in bringing her home!"

"Sideline you?"

"You've been pushing me away and shutting me out for months! Even before Fenn ran away." She knew this was not the time to air her grievances…again. But her emotions were all roiling at the surface, and every new crack in her composure allowed the seething brew to bubble out. "Do not try to shut me out of this, Jake. I won't allow it."

Jake's jaw tightened, and he shifted his weight, jerking his chin up and flattening his mouth as his nose flared defiantly. "I was offering you the chance to get some rest. Clearly you're stressed out," he said, his tone harsh, "and I don't need you here if you're going to just pick fights." Then under his breath, "Like you've been doing for months."

Emma bristled. "Oh, hello, Black Pot," she said with sarcasm dripping, "meet Kettle."

Jake screwed up his face. "That…doesn't even make sense!"

"You know exactly what I mean!"

Brody charged into the room, frowning. "Hey! Both of you chill! This isn't helping."

Jake spun away with a grunt of frustration. "No, it's not."

Emma dropped back onto the couch and buried her

face in her hands, shame and regret washing over her. She knew arguing would accomplish nothing, would even hinder their goal of finding Fenn. Why had she lashed out? She had to find a way to bite her tongue and put her personal hurt and squabbles aside...for Fenn's sake if nothing else.

"Guys?"

Emma looked up at the sound of Ben's hesitant voice. Jake turned toward Ben. "What's happened?"

"Well, you weren't outbid this last time." Ben divided a wary look between Emma and Jake. "But the auction's not over. It could go higher."

A prickle of embarrassment inched down her spine. He'd obviously heard the yelling. He couldn't have *not* heard it.

"How much?" Jake asked.

Ben winced as if reluctant to deliver bad news. "Forty-one thousand."

Jake groaned, and his face blanched. "Where the hell am I going to come up with forty-one thousand dollars?"

"I'm, uh...you said to keep upping the bid until..."

"I know. I—" Jake blew out a long breath. "That's our life savings. I don't even know..."

"It's fine." Emma stood and gave Ben a confident nod. "Thank you. We appreciate your help, more than words can ever say."

"Of course." Jake gestured his agreement with one hand. "We'll figure the money out."

After an awkward moment of silence, Brody said, "So...now what? What's the next step?"

Ben cleared his throat. "I thought I'd start working from a different computer, trying to track the IP address for the auction, hack the account for the user that posted the auction..."

"What do we do?" Emma asked.

Ben twisted his mouth. "I'd say start rounding up those funds. If the auction ends and you can't pay, this is all for nothing."

Jake's shoulders drooped, and he braced a hand on the wall.

Ben and Brody left them alone in the living room, returning to the computer room. Emma stared at Jake's back, his dejected posture boring into her heart.

Emma dragged herself from the couch, never before feeling so boneless and dejected. She moved up behind her husband and put one hand on his back. The warmth of his skin seeped through the soft cotton of his shirt, a comforting reminder of what it was like to be wrapped in his arms, his skin against hers, while his body heat enveloped her like a protective blanket. She missed that sense of security, that feeling that all was right with the world, that belief that together they could do anything. That was what their lovemaking had been about. Not as much about sex, although it was certainly gratifying and full of pleasure, but more about reconnecting, bonding, refilling her soul with the man who was her heart and breath.

A pang twisted inside her, squeezing her lungs. When was the last time they'd made love? The last time they'd had that physical, spiritual, essential reminder of their vows and commitment to each other?

As day after day passed with Jake coming home late, her being angry, both being tired and disconnected from each other, they'd drifted apart in more ways than one. They'd let the weight of their problems, the pull of life's chaos drive a wedge into the core of what should have held them together.

Jake stepped away from her touch, and her hand dropped to her side. He stalked down the hall toward the computer room. The silent rebuff stung. But why wouldn't he pull away from her when she'd just lambasted him?

"Jake, wait."

He stopped, but didn't turn.

"If ever there was a time we needed to be a team, to work together, to present a united front," she paused, then added, "the way we used to...it's now."

He faced her now, a scowl on his face. "Ya think?"

Shoving down the tartness his sharp tone evoked, she tried again. "I'm trying to apologize for yelling. I don't want our personal problems to stand in the way of us working together to bring Fenn home."

The heat in his expression cooled a few degrees, but his tone was still tight as he grumbled, "Should go without saying."

She tipped her head in agreement. "So...truce? Can we resolve to work harder to set our differences aside for the sake of our daughter? We'll work together better if we can put a pin in our disagreements...for now."

Again he gripped his nape and rolled the tension from his shoulders. Once upon a time, those actions would prompt her to volunteer a neck and shoulder massage. Another kindness and connection that had been missing from their marriage of late.

He bobbed a nod and exhaled harshly. "Of course. Truce."

After they'd taken their seats in the computer room again, Ben said, "Your bid is holding for now. Roughly two and a half hours left."

Brody tugged his bottom lip with his teeth. "I know this is a smarmy auction and our Fenn is being sold like chattel, which makes it all the more disagreeable to discuss the mechanics of what we're doing, but..."

Emma swallowed the bile that rose in her throat, remembering the horrid, heartbreaking images of her baby girl displayed like—

"Jake, you need to have the funds ready. Can you start

moving it now?" Brody's businesslike question allowed Emma, with effort, to refocus her thoughts for a moment. "If you win the auction and can't pay... God knows what happens to her then."

Chapter 11

Jake held his brother-in-law's gaze while ice filled his veins. As sickening as the idea was of losing all the money he'd busted his ass to stash away for his family's protection and provision, the notion of losing Fenn because he didn't have enough was even harder to stomach.

"The inability to pay might tip her captors to the fact that you're not their usual sort of buyer." Ben leaned back in his desk chair and drummed his fingers on the padded arm. "We need to be sure your buy goes through or they could get spooked."

Jake pressed his mouth in a hard line, tensing his jaw as he scrambled mentally for a work-around. "I can move money around, scrape up most of it, but I'll probably have to move some from the company accounts or—"

"No, Jake…" Brody sighed. "You just got cleared of the false charges of embezzling from your company. Don't do anything wonky with your company funds."

"To get my daughter back? I'll do *wonky* times ten if I have to. I don't care!"

Raising a hand, Brody said, "I have some savings. It's yours. I can send it to your account in a matter of minutes. And I know Mom and Dad would do the same. As would Isla or Cait. I'm sure of it."

"Brody…" Love for her brother's kindness shone from Emma's damp eyes. Her family had proven over and over how much they loved and supported her, starting with the way they'd rallied around Emma and him when she'd gotten pregnant in high school. As a young couple with nothing but starry-eyed dreams and a baby on the way, her family had given love, home and unrelenting support. If she divorced him, he'd be losing more than just his family. He'd lose her family. That acknowledgment stung.

"Protect your company. We'll figure this out," Brody said.

Jake held Brody's gaze, his eyes growing damp. "Thank you. That's…"

Brody clapped Jake on the shoulder. "We all love Fenn and want her back from these creeps. Money is just a thing."

"Just a thing…" Jake mumbled under his breath. He scrubbed both hands over his face then pulled out his phone to open his banking app.

Money is just a thing.

Knowing Jake's history, the hard times his family had lived through, Emma realized Jake couldn't easily embrace such a dismissive philosophy. She'd seen how hyperfocused on saving his business, providing for his family and building a nest egg for security he'd been over the years. That responsibility had been even heavier in recent months, when their livelihood had been threatened by an embezzler within his trusted staff and false charges had been levied against Jake. Being unable to take care of his family had always been Jake's greatest fear. That he'd confront that fear to get Fenn back spoke of the depth of his love for their daughter. And because of her own fathomless love for Fenn, she appreciated Jake's sacrifice with a wrenching ferocity.

For the next two hours, Jake transferred funds from all of their personal accounts and many loans from Emma's family until they'd accrued a staggering sum in the account positioned as the payment portal for the auction. When, at five minutes before the auction was set to end, the bid Ben had entered on their behalf hours earlier still held, a flare of hope lit in Emma's core. Maybe, God willing, just maybe they would actually get Fenn back through this cockamamie scheme.

"Four minutes," Ben announced as they watched the digital countdown on the screen.

"Ben, will you do one more huge favor for us?" Jake asked.

Brody's friend glanced at him. "What's that?"

"It's just that after all this that we've done to find her and pull the money together to get her back, I'd hate to blow it all because anywhere along the way the monsters holding her got a sniff that something was off."

Emma shifted her gaze to Jake. "What are you saying?"

He popped his knuckles and bit the inside of his cheek. "They can't know her parents were behind the buy until she is safely in our possession again."

Ben narrowed a wary look on him. "Yeah, so…?"

"Three minutes," Brody said.

"Wherever they want us to go to retrieve her, however they tell us to claim her, it has to be you that goes."

Emma caught her breath. Jake was right. But, damn, she wanted to be the one to bring Fenn home. She glanced at Ben to read his receptiveness.

"You do understand this auction and anyone participating is breaking the law? If the feds show up at the transfer, they'll be much more lenient toward the girl's parents than some shmuck who says he was helping a friend."

Emma's face crinkled with desperation. "I know it is asking a lot, but how do we risk blowing this whole thing because Fenn realizes it's us and tips our hand or they recognize us somehow before the trade is made, or—"

"We will have your back in every way possible. Our testimony to what happened should it be needed, bail money, travel expenses and…" Jake hesitated only a moment to send Emma a quick glance "…reward money. Compensation for all you're doing."

Ben winced. "It's not about payment."

"But you'll have it. I swear," Emma said, leaning forward to grip Ben's hands. Her expression pleading with him.

Ben's cheek bulged as he ran his tongue around his mouth and furrowed his brow in contemplation. "I supposed I could. I just…"

Emma hadn't realized how anxiously she'd been waiting for Ben's answer until her breath whooshed from her like the plug being pulled on an overinflated tire.

"Two minutes," Brody said, and *bam* the tension was back.

For the next ninety seconds, Emma paced, prayed, worried.

She glanced to the computer-side chair where Jake had his head bowed, his hands fidgeting.

When the counter reached thirty seconds with their bid still in place, Emma joined the others in hovering around the monitor. Every second seemed to drag. Her heart was beating twice as fast as the clock was counting down.

Twenty. Nineteen. Eighteen.

"Geez, this is nerve-racking," Brody muttered, then cast an apologetic look to his sister, as if realizing his stating the obvious helped no one.

Twelve. Eleven. Ten...

Then Ben cursed.

"What?" Jake rasped.

Emma saw it. A new higher bid had been entered in the final seconds.

"Bid again! Hurry!" Jake crowded even closer to the computer desk, as if he could reach through the monitor and stop the calamity unfolding before his eyes.

Five. Four. Three...

Ben hurriedly typed in a new bid and hit Enter.

Error. Bid must exceed $1000.

Two...

One...

"Damn it!" Ben shouted as he typed again and hit Enter.

Horror froze Emma's pulse. "What happened?"

Auction ended.

NØtar@11Ø5 held the winning bid at $100,000.

Emma gave a choked sob. "No!"

Ben groaned, and his shoulders dropped. "I mistyped. In my hurry to enter the new bid, I mistyped. God, I'm sorry. So sorry!"

"So...that's it?" Jake asked numbly. "This Notar at 1105 person won?"

Brody flopped back in his chair and whispered a curse word.

Emma's breathing grew ragged and uneven. "Fennie. Button. No..."

* * *

Jake braced an arm on the back of Ben's chair when his legs wobbled. "But…we had the money… We had the high bid for…"

Turning, he staggered to the desk chair across the room and sat on it as his head spun with shock and dismay. "We lost her. Our baby girl…"

"So…" Brody rasped, "Now what?"

Emma buried her face in her hands, sobbing. "Nooo! No, no, no! Fennie…"

Her wails reverberated inside Jake. Guilt and grief twisted and choked him. If he hadn't been so loud and hadn't woken Fenn the other night…if he'd answered his phone sooner the day she went missing…if he'd been more certain to assure Fenn she was loved and safe and…

Ben slammed his fist down, the sound jarring in the small room.

"No," he gritted and scooted his chair closer to the desk. "We don't quit. That's for sure. I can start by finding out all I can about this Notar 1105 person." The techie's fingers flew over the keyboard, and he scrolled his mouse clicking through screens, his expression fierce and determined as he worked.

Jake held his breath and sent Brody a querying look.

His brother-in-law shrugged. "What are you doing?" No answer. "Ben?"

"No promises, but I can try to get in the buyer's account. Maybe track the location of the computer that posted the auction listing. Or the location of the computer that made the winning bid."

"You can?" Jake asked.

Ben glanced up briefly. "I said no promises. I'll find out as much as I can…" He kept working, casting only occasional glances toward Jake when he'd paused for a second or two, waiting for a web page to load. "This could take a while…" *Tap, tap, tap, click.* "If you have something else you need to do…" *Click…tap, tap.*

Something else to do? The only thing he had to do, the only thing that mattered was finding Fenn.

And that effort, Jake thought with a despairing groan as he buried his face in his hands, had reached a dead end.

Chapter 12

After an hour, when Ben had still not come up with anything tracing the auction or the parties involved, Brody
finally convinced Jake and Emma to go home to wait for
news. Their hovering over Ben's shoulder, asking, "Any
progress?" every ten minutes wasn't helping.

But sitting on the front steps of their porch, watching
Magic, the black feral cat they fed, sleeping in the sun-
shine wasn't any easier on Emma's nerves. She felt numb.
Paralyzed with grief and horror. They'd lost the auction.
Fenn had been sold. Sold!

Where was she? Where would they send her? Who was
this sick NØtar@11Ø5 person that had bought her?

A shadow fell over her as Jake approached from the
yard. He'd started chopping wood again to burn off frustration and anxiety when Brody dropped them off. Isla
still had Lexi, and Emma knew they needed to retrieve
their youngest soon. But at the moment, she just needed
to…mourn.

Jake sat on the steps next to her and exhaled his fatigue. After several silent moments, he grated, "This is a nightmare."

"I wish," she answered, her voice monotone. "You can wake up from a nightmare, but this…"

Jake's cell phone rang, and he snatched it out. "Yeah?"

Emma went perfectly still, not daring to breathe, to blink. Please, God, let this be Fenn…or some hope…

"You did?" Jake's face brightened, and he lunged to his feet. "What did you find?"

Adrenaline surging, Emma followed him inside the house where he hurried to her desk for a notepad and pen.

"Where's that?" he asked as he scribbled an address and circled *Tennessee* on the notepad.

Without waiting for Jake to get off the phone call, Emma raced to the bedroom to get her purse and phone. If Jake had an address related to Fenn's abduction, they would be headed out to that location. Now. No packing. No questions. No hesitation.

Jake was already in his truck, starting the engine, when she opened the passenger door and climbed in. He sent her a what-are-you-doing look.

"Don't even try to stop me from coming with you," she warned as she buckled her seat belt.

"But Lexi—"

"Will be fine with my family. I'll call them from the road to tell them where we're going." She clung to the arm-rest as Jake sped out of the driveway and onto the narrow lane. "So…where *are* we going?"

"Ben traced the seller to a house in East Tennessee. It's a long shot, but…"

Emma nodded. "Hurry."

"Are you sure this is right?" Jake asked four hours later as they navigated down a rural, pothole-filled road in Tennessee. He scanned the rolling farmland and saw no sight of life other than a few black-and-white cows swishing their tails from the shade of scattered trees in green pastures. "I don't see any buildings. Not houses or barns or stores…"

"According to the GPS app, we're getting close." Emma glanced again at the phone in her hand, and the blue dot marking their progress along a thin black line on the map.

Then they crested a hill, and on the downward slope of the hill, beneath a small copse of oak trees sat a clapboard house with a sagging porch. The exterior had been white at one time, but now bore only badly peeling paint, mildew, and the patina of time and sun. Missing shingles checkered the roof and one window shutter hung at an angle beside a dusty window. The driveway, such as it was, was choked with weeds and pocked with rocks and ruts.

Emma sent him a puzzled look. "According to the app, that's it."

A light breeze stirred the tall grass surrounding the ramshackle house, but nothing else moved or gave signs of life. Jake drove his truck past the house slowly, studying the shadows, not taking the lack of activity for granted. Was this place a dummy location? A spot somehow spoofed by technology to mask the kidnappers' real location? But then, wasn't an abandoned house the perfect spot to hide for a few days if you were up to no good?

After the initial drive-by, reconnoitering, he turned the truck around a short distance down the country road and stopped on the edge. He drummed his fingers on the steering wheel and frowned. "I didn't see signs of life. Did you?"

"No." Emma wiped her palms on her jeans and sent him a nervous glance. "But we need to check it out. We gotta go inside. What if Fenn's in there alone? Tied up…or…"

"I know." Jake drew a deep breath, battling down the

twinges of doubt and anxiety as he changed gears and checked for oncoming traffic. "We should be prepared for her not to be alone. Open the glove box. My gun is in there."

After a nervous glance, she gave a quick nod. "Right. So…how will this work? Do we just walk up to the door and ask to be let in?" Emma asked, her tone incredulous. "Is that really our plan? If the owner is connected to the human trafficking ring, they're hardly going to welcome our intrusion and questions."

"We can pretend we're lost and asking directions," Jake offered.

"Directions won't get us inside," Emma countered. "What if we ask to use the restroom? Or tell them we need a phone because our cells are dead or without a signal?"

Jake nodded. "Sure. That could work."

On their second approach to the house, Jake turned in the bumpy dirt path that led onto the property. He parked in the side yard, out of the view of the front door and windows.

After he cut the engine on the truck, he said softly, "Hand me the gun. I'm not going in this place totally exposed and vulnerable."

Emma extended the handgun toward him. When he reached for the pistol, she didn't let go. Instead, she leveled a determined gaze on him. "*We* will not go in exposed. I didn't come this far to be told to wait in the car."

He sighed. "Emma…"

She waved a hand to silence him. "I'm going in with you. Period."

From her purse, she removed her keys, where a vial of pepper spray was attached in a small leather case. Unsnapping the top of the case, she readied the spray nozzle and shouldered open the passenger door.

He banged the steering wheel in irritation. Why did

she have to be so stubborn? Didn't she understand how dangerous this could be? That he was trying to protect her? He couldn't stand the idea of anything happening to her—especially on his watch.

He hurried to catch up to her as she crossed the yard. "At least get behind me, huh? I don't want you in the line of fire if I have to shoot."

With a nod, she conceded the point and let him take the crooked, creaking steps to the porch first. Jake approached the front door, eyeing the windows further down the porch, while a feeling like spiders on his neck crawled over him. Emma huddled close as he opened the screened door and knocked on the solid door behind it.

They waited.

No response.

He knocked again, shouting, "Hello? Anyone there? We need to use your phone."

When they still received no answer, Jake tested the doorknob. "Locked. But..." He rattled the knob harder, applied his shoulder to the door...and it gave way.

"Um, Jake..."

He pushed the door wider and craned his head to scan the interior from the threshold. Then took a step inside.

Emma grabbed his arm. "Wait. Jake, this is breaking and entering. Do we really want to cross that line?"

He set his jaw, his gaze fierce. "To get Fenn back? I do." He twisted his mouth as if considering something, "But now's your chance to stay outside, in case things do go sideways. We still have Lexi to think of. She needs a mother."

Emma exhaled sharply and muttered, "Damn it, Jake. Don't lay that on me now! I'm here, and I'm all in, whatever it takes to get Fenn back. Lexi is safe. Lexi is with her family. Fenn is not. Fenn is my priority until she is back where she belongs."

Jake frowned and, sidling in with his back to the wall, took another step inside the ramshackle house.

Swallowing hard, Emma stepped into the dusty foyer of the house on his heels. Moving from the sunlight into the unlit home felt like walking into the bowels of a cave, of a dungeon. She shivered involuntarily and inched closer to Jake as he crept forward. In the living room, a sparse few items of ratty furniture lined the walls. "Hello? Anyone home? We need to borrow a—"

The clacking sound of a shotgun being racked greeted them. Emma froze but for her fingers curling into the shirt on her husband's back.

Jake spun toward the sound, raising his pistol in a two-handed grip. "Don't."

Floorboards creaked as a middle-aged woman with a long-barrel that was almost bigger than she was appeared from the adjoining room. "I know how to use this."

Emma gawked at the frail woman with frizzy blond hair and sweatpants that were at least one size too large for her. Skinny arms with sun-weathered skin shook as she pointed the weapon at them.

"We don't want trouble," Jake said. "Put the gun down, ma'am."

"Not so long as you got that thing aimed at me," she replied, her voice thin and scratchy, a smoker's rasp.

Emma held her breath. She wasn't ready for Jake to disarm, not knowing who else might be in the house or what other weapons.

As if echoing her concerns, the squeak of a door and quick thump of footsteps preceded the appearance of a teenage boy behind the woman.

"Who are you?" he asked angrily. Though he was tall enough to pass as an adult, the boy's face, still soft with rounded features and marked with acne, skewed Emma's age estimate down. His hair was the same sun-lightened blond as the woman's and needed to be combed.

"W-we don't want trouble," Emma said, raising her hands, but staying half-behind Jake. "See...we got lost and needed to use your phone."

"Ain't got a phone," the woman said, "Now, go on and git."

In a soothing voice, Jake said, "Nobody needs to get hurt. Just set the weapon on the floor and move back from it." He eased forward a step or two. Slowly. Smoothly.

The double barrel of the shotgun had begun to droop, but when Jake moved toward the thin woman, she jerked it up again. "Stop there. I'll shoot ya."

"I'll take it, Mama," the man-child said, stepping forward to take the shotgun from the woman's hands. She passed it to him silently. The muzzle's aim never left Jake and Emma. "Y'all need to leave here 'fore I fill you with buckshot."

"We're not leaving until we get answers," Jake said. "Put the gun away, and we'll talk."

"I don't have nothing to say to you." The boy's eyes narrowed. "And I will shoot you if you don't leave. Right now!"

Jake shook his head slowly, stayed calm. "We're looking for someone and have reason to believe—"

"I said leave!" The boy straightened his back and tensed his arms as he stared down the sights of the shotgun.

Emma saw the impasse and scrambled mentally for a way to shift the standoff in their favor. She knew Jake was fast, but was he faster than the teenager's trigger finger? Even a delayed reaction could result in a fatal discharge of the shotgun.

Behind Jake's back, Emma shifted her keys with the pepper spray to her palm.

"Be ready," she whispered, barely above a sigh. Jake

inclined his head a microscopic amount, letting her know he'd heard.

Keeping her arm still and her eyes focused on the boy, she gave her wrist a hard, underhand flick, lobbing the keys to a far corner of the room. They landed with all the jangle and clatter she'd hoped.

Eyes wide, the teenager jerked the muzzle toward that corner.

And Jake pounced. He closed the distance to the shotgun in two large steps, seized the barrel, and shoved it toward the ceiling.

The boy cussed. The woman gave a cry of dismay. An earsplitting blast reverberated in the empty room. Plaster and dust rained down. With his pistol in one hand and his other keeping the shotgun pointed up, Jake could only twist his body and dodge the teenager's flailing elbows and butting head as they grappled.

After a heartbeat of stunned immobility, Emma surged forward to aid Jake in the battle for control of the shotgun. But so did the teen's mother. She slapped at Jake and pulled his hair. Rage for the woman's assault on Jake bloomed hot and red in Emma's gut, and adrenaline fueled her. She rushed into the fray, tackling the woman from behind and wrestling her to the ground.

The woman's head thumped hard on the floor, and she reached groggily to cradle her temple.

Emma shoved away from the other woman, regaining her balance. When her opponent rolled to her back, her eyes dark with venom, Emma shouted, "Stay down!"

The grunts behind her drew her attention back to Jake's one-handed struggle.

"Jake, give me the gun!" she called as she sprang to her feet and grabbed for the pistol.

Jake held the handgun barely out of the tall teenager's

reach and grappled to hold the kid back as he angled the weapon toward Emma.

Quivering from the inside out, Emma trained the weapon on the woman who was clambering back to her feet. "I said stay down!"

But the woman rose to her knees, glaring defiantly. When she spotted the weapon Emma held, she balked. Briefly. Then started to rise again.

Emma knew she needed to quickly regain the upper hand in this situation. She knew she couldn't really kill anyone, but the woman had to think she'd be willing to. So she angled the weapon toward the floor near the woman and fired.

The woman yelped. The boy stilled, yanking his gaze toward his mother. "Mama!"

Jake seized the opportunity to wrest the shotgun from the kid and shove the boy back against the wall. "Lie on the floor!" he commanded.

When the boy didn't move, Jake repeated the command, pointing the shotgun at the kid's chest. "Do it! Now! Both of you!"

The brook-no-resistance tone of Jake's voice sent a ripple of something unfamiliar through Emma. She'd never seen this iron and blood, war commander side of him. The man who'd gently rocked their daughters to sleep and read fairy tales with cartoonlike voices was now the embodiment of authority and steely will. A warrior on a mission to rescue his daughter. To protect his wife. The ripple swelled to a wave and coalesced in her core, warm and proud.

"Go on," Emma said, the pistol trained on the woman. "Down. I'd do what he said, if I were you." When the two finally complied, she added, "It didn't have to come to this. We don't want trouble. We just need answers."

Jake eased closer to Emma, the shotgun still at the

ready. When he was beside her, he said quietly, "I'm going to search the place. You okay with watching these two, keeping them on the floor until I get back?"

Emma swallowed. She didn't want Jake leaving her alone with the mother and son, but short of tying them up—which seemed radical and hostile—she saw no other choice. She bobbed a stiff nod.

"Who else is here?" Jake asked the pair.

Silence.

"Answer me!"

The boy angled a glare at Jake and swore at him.

"The sooner you tell us what we need to know, the sooner we get out of your hair. Please." Emma split her gaze between the two and decided she'd get farther with the woman, talking mother to mother. "My daughter was kidnapped by some very bad men. Men who want to exploit her innocence. Sell her. Prostitute her. Degrade her." She fought against the knot forming in her chest. Now was not the time to get overwrought with emotions. She had to focus, be strong, for Fenn. "Please help us find her before it's too late."

"Can't help you," the woman mumbled.

"Can't or won't?" Jake asked, his tone still angry.

Emma shot him a look that begged him to let her handle the conversation. Jake scowled and a muscle at the corner of his eye twitched. After another beat of tense silence, Emma asked, "Is anyone else here? Please! We don't want sneak attacks that end up with someone getting shot by mistake."

The woman pursed her lips, then snarled, "No. No one else."

Emma met the woman's eyes, trying to assess her honesty. "Truth?"

"If someone else were round, don't ya think they'd have

shown by now? That we'd've called on 'em for backup?" the woman said, her tone bitter.

Jake, apparently satisfied by the woman's answer, headed into the next room, leading with the shotgun like a soldier clearing an insurgent's lair.

As Jake disappeared from view, Emma kept the gun trained on the teen. She assumed the boy was the bigger threat, more likely to try to overtake her. And that the mother would be less likely to try anything if doing so put her child at risk.

But holding the two at the business end of Jake's pistol left her cold and unsettled at her core. She doubted she could bring herself to shoot either of them if the need arose. In order to keep her hostages in line, though, she had to maintain a facade of grim determination and intent.

She had to remember why she was there, why they were in this untenable position. Fenn. For Fenn she would eat broken glass or walk through fire. Or drive hundreds of miles to a remote farmhouse and hold strangers at gunpoint. The things a mother would do for her child...

Emma took a slow, deep breath and as she tried to refocus, her last thought hummed through her brain again. Things a mother would do...

She met the woman's eyes squarely, remembering the boy calling her "mama." "This is your son."

A statement, not a question.

The woman narrowed her eyes warily and said nothing.

Emma relaxed her stance, though the gun remained steady. She flashed a grin. "He's pretty tall for his age. And handsome. I bet you have to fight off all the girls."

The mother cast a glance toward her child, and a hint of a grin flickered at the corner of her mouth.

Bingo. Compliments about her children were kryptonite for mothers. Maternal pride was one of the strongest elements on earth...next to maternal love.

"He did well just now. The way he stepped up to defend you. I know you're proud of him."

The woman's expression grew wary again, but she couldn't hide the shimmer in her eyes that answered, *Yes. Very proud*, even if she didn't speak the words.

"What's your name?" Emma asked the boy.

"Doug," the boy said at the same time his mother said, "Don't say nothin'."

"Doug. That's a good name. A strong name." Emma smiled at the pair, then took a deep breath before venturing further with her plan. "Do you have other children?"

The woman lifted her chin a notch, her brow furrowed as if weighing whether it was wise to answer. "Yeah. I got a girl."

Emma's pulse spiked. She nodded. "Yeah. Me, too. I have two daughters. One's at home. My baby, Lexi. She's four."

The look in the woman's eyes softened as if remembering when her own babies had been that young.

"And then there's Fenn. She's fifteen. She's got my mother's eyes, and my husband's stubbornness, and the gentle soul of an angel. She's good with her little sister. Real protective of her and patient." Emma had to pause and swallow hard against the knot of emotion that threatened to choke her voice. "Fenn is witty, and fierce. She loves reading and is a terrific swimmer and an animal lover. She and her sister have been begging us to get a cat. I don't know why we haven't. Just…distracted by other things lately, I guess." Emma resolved then and there to remedy that lack if they got Fenn back. No…*when* they got Fenn back.

"She's beautiful, inside and out," Emma continued. "She's everything to me. Both of my girls are. My heart. My breath. My reason for facing each new day, even when life is hard and disappointing."

She saw a glint of moisture in the woman's eyes, and her hope lifted. She'd made the connection she'd hoped she would.

"Fenn is who we're looking for. We got information that she might have been here. Or that someone who knew something about where she was had been here."

And just like that, the door she'd cracked open with the mother slammed shut. The woman's jaw tightened, and she blanked her eyes as she turned her face away.

"Please!" Emma heard the crack in her voice as she continued, not bothering to hide the emotion behind her plea. "If you know where Fenn is, if you know how we can get her back, if you know…anything, please tell me! Please help me get my baby girl home!"

She studied the woman in the taut silence. A tear escaped the woman's right eye and rolled down her cheek. She didn't bother wiping it away as she rasped, "I can't tell you anything."

"But you know something. Don't you?" she pushed.

"Leave it alone."

"Leave what alone? What do you know? Please. You're a mother. You understand how my heart is breaking, don't you? How desperate we are to get—"

"Of course I know!" she growled. "That's why I can't say nothing!"

Emma wrinkled her brow. "Meaning?"

The blonde woman shook her head, her mouth pressed in a tight line as if she regretted saying what she had.

Emma moved closer, clapping her free hand to her chest. "Help me get my girl back. Please help me. Please—"

The woman snapped her head around, her gaze pained and sharp as she narrowed her eyes at Emma. "If I help you— If they find out I helped you—"

"They? They who?"

The woman drew a shaky breath. "The men who have my daughter."

Emma gasped. "What?"

"If they find out we said anything, they'll kill my Ruby."

Chapter 13

Jake moved through the old house, the anxious drumbeat of his heart pounding in his ears. He moved slowly. Quietly. He checked each new room with a cautious glance around the doorframe before moving inside. The woman and her son could deny all they wanted there wasn't anyone else around. He would take nothing for granted. He kept the shotgun poised and ready.

One room after the next revealed much the same. Casual clutter, threadbare fabrics and mismatched particleboard furniture...and no Fenn. Nor did he find any signs of any kidnappers or sex trade operation. He was growing despondent over the lack of clues when he found a room on the second floor that had a folding table set up in the corner by a window with a desktop computer, a printer and a full ashtray. His pulse jumped, and he rushed over to wake the monitor with a tap of the keyboard.

The screen that came up was blank except for two white bars asking for the user ID and password. Jake sighed. Not much chance he could guess the log-in information, but surely the woman or her son could provide the information.

He returned downstairs to the spot where he'd left Emma and the homeowners. The scene he found surprised him. Emma and the woman were both crying softly. The teenager remained grim-faced and glaring at the pistol Emma kept trained on him.

"Em? What's happening?"

"They have her daughter. Ruby Haynes. The girl we met with the dyed hair," Emma said without looking at him. "She refuses to tell me anything out of fear for Ruby's life."

A fresh blast of adrenaline kicked through Jake. "So they do know something? The kidnappers were here?"

"She won't say."

Jake raised the shotgun and stormed closer to the woman. Getting in her face, he rattled off questions, his body shaking with the spike of energy. "Was Fenn with them? Where did they take her? Who are they?"

The woman refused to meet his eyes. She set her jaw, and her nostrils flared with defiance.

"For God's sake, answer me!"

"Go to hell!" the boy groused.

Jake shifted his attention to the teenager. "What's the password for the computer upstairs?"

"None of your damn business." The kid lifted his chin and squared his shoulders in challenge. He'd clearly figured out that neither Emma nor he had the ill scruples to actually shoot him or his mother. That didn't bode well for cooperation, and Jake needed to get on that computer. He needed to know what it might have been used to arrange. A search history. Programs recently open.

A dark web auction.

"Please. If we work together, maybe we can rescue both our Fenn and your girl," Emma said, appealing to the woman. "I know you're scared. I'm scared, too. And I'm

sick with worry. But think about how much more frightened my Fenn is. She's just fifteen! They auctioned her
off like a piece of property to a man whose only interest in her was to take her virginity. To rape her and steal
her innocence!" Emma's voice cracked as her volume and
passion rose.

Jake had to steel his nerves not to let the horror of the
reality Emma described sideline him again. He'd spent
enough time grieving, fretting, stewing. In this moment,
he had to focus on action. Concentrate on maintaining
command of the volatile situation.

"If we promise to do everything in our power to protect you, to help find your daughter after we rescue Fenn,
will you help us?" Emma asked.

"After you rescue Fenn?" the woman repeated, frowning. "You're not going to find her. They're long gone. Left
here this mornin'."

Jake tensed but said nothing at the further confirmation
they were on the right track. "We won't let anyone know
how we found her. We won't expose you or your son to
any danger, if you—"

"Your being here puts us in danger! What if they're
watchin' the place? What if they come back and—" The
woman cut herself off with a shake of her head. "And
that ain't our computer. We don't know no password or
anything. They brought it. Left it. They mean to be back.
They've been using this house for months, saying that
'cause it's outta the way, nobody'll mess with them. They
have more privacy to conduct their business."

"Why haven't you called the police on them? Stopped
them from using your house?" Emma asked.

The woman whipped her head toward Emma with an in-
dignant scowl. "You deaf or something? They have Ruby!
They swore they'd kill her if we called the cops or did anything to screw them over."

"We tried to find my sister, when they first took her," the boy volunteered. "But Tommy found out and...beat Mama and me near to death. That was last summer. Tommy said they moved Ruby to another state after that."

"Hush, Doug! You've said too much!" the woman grated.

Tommy. Jake made a mental note of the name. It wasn't much, but they were building a sketchy profile of the people who'd taken Fenn.

Daniel Monroe. DJ. Tommy...something.

Jake flexed and balled his fist in frustration. These crumbs were too little, coming too slowly. They had to locate Fenn before the monster who bought her could— He cut the thought off, unwilling to carry the ugliness any further.

He stepped close to Emma and whispered into her ear. "Look, I know you can't kill either of them if they give you trouble, but you can shoot them in the foot or leg or something. Hmm?"

Emma looked askance, her eyes dubious. "They won't give me any problems," she said, full voice, clearly addressing the woman and son more than Jake, "because they know if they don't cooperate, we'll go straight to the police when we leave and turn them in. We're on the same side. We all want our daughters home safely." She drilled the woman with a stare that said, *Right? Right.* Then to Jake she asked, "How much longer do you need? If they're not here, shouldn't we go?"

"You should," the boy snarled.

Jake stroked Emma's cheek. "I want a few minutes with the computer. Maybe I can get in, find something. I gotta try. And I want a closer look in the other rooms. There's got to be something here that will help us." With a hitch of his head to the other two, he asked Emma, "You good here?"

She nodded, and he returned upstairs. He checked all the rooms again and still found nothing he could discern as useful or telling. Once back in the room with the desktop and printer, he sat down with the shotgun across his lap and woke the screen again. He tried the most obvious and overused passwords first.

ABCD1234.

Password1234.

Qwerty1234.

And all the variations of these: 1234password, 9876password, xyz123, etc.

No luck. Finally, seeing the futility of spending valuable time on endless attempts breaking into the computer of criminals with enough computer savvy to run an auction on the dark web, he shoved the chair back and stood.

Before returning downstairs, he needed to neutralize the teen's shotgun. He unloaded the buckshot shells and looked for a place to discard them. He found a wastebasket under the table where the printer sat and tossed in the shells. Instead of the loud thump he expected the shells to make when they hit the wastebasket, he heard a muffled crunch of paper.

Curious, Jake pulled the can out and discovered a pile of crumpled paper in the receptacle. He reached in and pulled out a few wads of the balled paper. The first few were nothing of interest—an invoice from a shipping order for blue jeans and men's undershirts, restaurant coupons, the title page for a term paper on George Washington, an article from an online blog about the best ways to clean your kitchen appliances. Tossing these aside, he dug out more sheets, not really sure what he was looking for…until he found it. A sheet that had obviously gotten jammed in the printer making the paper crumple and the text slant and overwrite. But despite the misprint, what he held in his hand was clear. An attempt to print an airline boarding pass. To Orlando, Florida. For a flight leaving Nashville today.

Quaking inside with revived hope, Jake folded the discarded printout and hurried downstairs.

He handed the boy the emptied shotgun, then took Emma by the arm. "C'mon. Time to go."

"Did you get on the computer? Learn something?" Emma asked, falling in step with him.

Rather than answer her, he turned to the woman and teenager. "I think for both our sakes we should agree that we were never here. The kidnappers won't hear about it from us, and the cops won't hear about it from you. Understood?"

The boy frowned and looked at his mother, who hesitated only a moment before she nodded. "You were never here."

"Good." He pivoted on his heel, but when they reached the door, Emma stopped and turned back toward the woman.

"Ruby was in North Carolina this past weekend. Near Valley Haven with a man named Daniel Monroe. That's all I know, but... I hope it helps. Once we find Fenn, we won't rest until these people are stopped. I promise you that. Mother to mother."

The woman raised a hand to her heart and nodded. As tears spilled from her eyes, she mouthed, *Thank you.*

Jake's breath stuck in his throat. Emma's compassion and grace were among the many reasons he'd fallen in love with her. Rather than harbor resentment toward the woman for her part in Fenn's abduction, she'd seen Ms. Haynes's humanity.

Taking Emma's hand, he led her outside and hurried to his truck. When they were ensconced in the cab and backing out of the rutted driveway, Emma asked, "Where are we going now?"

Jake backed onto the rural road, shifted into Drive and gunned the engine. "Airport. We have a plane to catch. We're going to Florida."

Chapter 14

When they reached a location with better cellular service, Emma searched for the closest airport with soonest flights to Orlando. In their case, this proved to be Knoxville with a brief layover in Atlanta. Next she arranged for a rental car to be waiting on them when they arrived at the Orlando airport, and booked a hotel room for three nights. A start. They could extend their stay as needed beyond that. Having left town on this goose chase without so much as a toothbrush, she next ordered a few essentials—a change of clothes including undergarments for both of them, toiletry items and healthy snack foods for energy on the go—from a superstore with pickup near their hotel. These tasks done, she chuckled mildly as she set her phone aside. "Access to the world in your palm. Pretty amazing, huh?"

"Hmm?" Jake cast a confused look at her.

"Just musing over the power of the internet and a cell

phone. Where were you just now? You clearly weren't here with me."

"We need to tell Smith what we've learned. He can alert the FBI field office in Orlando and get all the law enforcement parties involved on the same page."

"He's going to tell us to stand down again."

"Probably. But we're not going to. He can arrest us later if he wants to for interfering or...whatever." Jake leveled a determined stare at her from the driver's seat. "I'm not going to quit looking for our daughter for any reason. Are you?"

She shook her head. "Not a chance."

While Emma called Officer Smith and left a detailed message on his voicemail, Jake returned his gaze to the interstate and drummed his fingers on the steering wheel. "Em, we're making progress. They may be crumbs, but they're a trail. I intend to keep following that trail until we stop finding crumbs."

Emma's heart swelled. She was well familiar with Jake's persistence, the boundless love he had for his children and his dogged pursuit of any goal he felt worthy of his attention. That's how he'd built a successful construction company from the ground up. How he'd survived false charges of embezzlement last year. Those traits were on full display now and would serve them well.

She recalled, too, the glimpse she'd had of Jake earlier in full soldier-on-a-mission mode. The authority, strength and decisiveness of his actions hadn't really surprised her, but her response to him had. The sheer power and command he'd wielded made her ovaries quiver. She reached over and stroked a hand on his shoulder, giving the muscles in his neck a squeeze. "I have to say, Mr. Turner, you were quite impressive back there. I don't believe I've ever seen you quite so...tough. Warrior-like."

He snorted. "Oh yeah. So tough…against a woman and teenage boy." He shook his head.

"They had a shotgun. And you took command of the situation without anyone getting hurt. It was…kinda sexy."

Jake blinked and shot her a startled look. A grin. "Really?"

She moved her hand to his leg and squeezed his thigh. "Really."

He inhaled deeply and cleared his throat. "You were pretty badass yourself, Mrs. Turner."

Emma barked a startled laugh. "For a housewife slash design consultant, you mean?"

"For anyone. You were impressive. I have to say…you surprised me, babe." He lifted her hand from his leg and kissed her palm. The light abrasion of his unshaven chin brushing her tender skin sent ripples of pleasure through her, shorted the wires in her brain.

"We make a good team," he said, with a side-glance and a half smile. He squeezed her hand before he released it to return his hand to the steering wheel. She studied his profile in the rapidly dimming sun, and her heart thumped a slow, wistful rhythm.

"We used to," she said under her breath…but clearly loud enough that he heard.

Jake shot her a dark look. "What does that mean?"

Emma leaned her head back on the seat and sighed. "Forget it. Now's not the time."

He twisted his mouth in frustration, and banged a fist on the dashboard. "So when is the right time, Emma? After you've drifted completely away from me? After the divorce goes through the courts?"

"Jake…" She closed her eyes. "Please, not now. I'm tired. And worried about Fenn, and…"

"I think now is the perfect time to discuss this. We're

alone. We have forty minutes before we reach the airport. And you brought it up, so…let's have at it."

She angled her head to meet his irritated frown. "Can we discuss things without devolving into shouts?"

He rocked his head side to side, stretching his neck muscles. "If we can't, then maybe we don't have any business staying together." He squeezed the steering wheel and gave a curt nod. "I promise to be civil."

"Civil," she muttered sadly. "I think the fact we have to agree to be civil is an example of how far we've fallen. We used to be on the same page. We used to be a team. We talked. We shared. We cooperated. We *communicated*. Without yelling."

"And you're saying we're not a team anymore? You don't think we're on the same page?"

"Not like we used to be."

"People change, Emma. We weren't always going to be the eighteen-year-olds with stars in their eyes that got married back then. Life, maturity, parenting…we grew up."

"But growing up doesn't mean we have to grow apart," she countered.

"No. It doesn't. And I didn't think we had. Sure, we've had a rough patch lately. Things have been difficult at work, and I've had a lot to juggle." He cut a quick glance to her then back to the road. "You know that. I don't think it's fair that I be punished for the extra hours and sweat I've put into keeping my business afloat and food on our table."

"I'm not trying to punish you, Jake. Where do you get that?"

"Oh, I don't know…maybe because you kicked me out of our home because I've been working late most nights for the last few months?"

She scowled at him for the deeply sarcastic tone he used. "That's not why I asked you to move out."

"Really? That's the vibe I got."

"I asked you to move out because our fighting was scaring the girls." She waved her hands. "Case in point. Fenn ran away."

"So we're back to this being my fault?"

Emma curled her fingers into her hair. "Geez, Jake. I did not say that. We're both to blame. We both yelled. We argued instead of solving anything. We let our anger build up instead of fixing what was wrong. I accept my part in that. Can you?"

A muscle in his jaw flexed as he clenched his back teeth. He blew out a long breath, and his countenance relaxed. "Sure. Of course." He rubbed a palm on his cheek, and his eyebrows dipped in concentration. "What do I have to do to fix things?"

She rolled her eyes and gave her head a small shake. "Do you hear yourself?"

He cut a baffled glance at her. "What do you mean? I'm trying to work things out. I want to fix this. I thought that's what you wanted."

"I do. But you keep saying I. My. Me. If we're truly a team, it should be we. Us. Our."

"So your issue is with my pronouns?" he asked, his tone aghast, sarcastic.

Emma took a moment to set aside the prick of irritation. Losing her temper wouldn't advance this conversation. And it was critical that Jake understand her if they were to have any hope of salvaging their marriage. "Please, Jake. Don't pretend you think I'm being that literal. My issue is your pronouns appear to be an indication of your mindset, your reference point. Your attitude."

Jake pulled a face that spoke for his frustration. "Emma, I don't—"

She put a hand on his arm to stop him. "Let me walk you through my view of things. Okay? Just…listen. Really listen."

He flipped up his hand. "Okay. Listening."

"In recent months especially, but increasingly over the years, I've felt more and more left out of your life. Left out of your decisions, your struggles, your work."

He angled a quick glance at her. "The construction company? But that's—"

"Something we started together," she supplied. "We dreamed about it together, saved up to invest in it together, worked side by side to get it off the ground. I was the company's first bookkeeper and receptionist, remember?"

"Of course, I remember."

"So can't you understand how I feel part ownership in the business and its operation? It's something we did together. You run it now, but it's important to me, too. For lots of reasons."

This time when he flipped up his palm, she took it as conceding her point. But...

"Tell me what you just heard, what you're taking from what I just said."

His dark eyebrows snapped together. "What?"

"I want to know that you really understood my point."

He pulled a face and grunted. "Emma."

"It's called communication, Jake. I just want to know if you really understood what I was asking of you."

He twisted his mouth then nodded. "Fine. You want me to...use inclusive pronouns and keep you more informed about what's happening with *our* company."

She swallowed her groan of frustration. Based on the earnestness of his expression, he really was trying to grasp her meaning. She took a beat to gather her composure, choose her words. "That's part of it, yes. But I want to be included in all parts of your life and decisions regarding our family. I want us to communicate better, share more, work as a team again. I feel like you've slowly pushed me out of your life. As if you consider me just the person who takes care of your house and children."

He wrinkled his nose and frowned at her. "That's ridiculous! I don't do that. I haven't—"

"Jake!"

"What?"

She growled under her breath. "I'm trying to tell you how I feel. What the last few months…years even…have been like for me. It is my truth. My feelings. They are not for you to judge or criticize or call me wrong. They just… are. What I need is for you to hear me. Acknowledge my feelings. Try to understand how I see things."

"So it's up to me to fix everything between us? Everything is my fault because of how you perceive I've wronged you?"

"God, no! Don't be defensive!"

"You just said your feelings are the truth. That somehow they're all that matter, no matter how warped and one-sided they are."

"That's not what I meant!"

"I'm supposed to just accept that, because they're how you feel, that automatically makes you right and me wrong?"

"No! Stop twisting my words!" Emma felt tears of anger, futility and frustration building inside her. Her hands shook with the unspent adrenaline stirred by her turbulent emotions. "Jake, don't be deliberately defensive and obtuse."

"Obtuse? What, now I'm too stupid to understand anything?" The hard lines in his face and flash of fury in his dark eyes told her the discussion had gone off the rails.

"I didn't say stupid. I said obtuse. There's a difference." Too late, she heard the condescending tone of her voice. She wished she could haul it back in, but that toothpaste was out of the tube. In a calmer voice, she said, "*Obtuse* means...slow to understand."

"So I'm not stupid, I'm *slow*," Jake grumbled bitterly. "I'm sorry if I don't have your vocabulary. I don't have time to read all the books you do while I keep the construction company afloat."

Emma pinched the bridge of her nose, fighting back her tears. After a moment of silence to gather her thoughts, calm herself, she said, "You've never been especially good with verbal things or writing. I'm the artistic, creative, literary one."

He snorted harshly and sent her a dark glare. "Wow. Em, that's..."

"True."

"Low."

"You didn't let me finish."

He laughed sourly. "Please, pile on more."

"I was going to say, that while I'm—call it right-brained— you're good with finances, business, mechanics, structure and logic...left-brained stuff." She watched his face, waiting for him to register what she was telling him, praying it soothed his hurt feelings. "There's nothing wrong with being better at one skill set over another. Few people are good at everything."

She reached for him and squeezed his forearm. The sinewy strength beneath her hand tensed momentarily before relaxing. When he finally glanced at her, she twitched a strained smile. "That's why we made such a good team for so long. Between us we had all the bases covered."

Jake heaved a deep sigh and shook his head. "Well, maybe it takes more than having all the bases covered to make a marriage work."

Pain sliced to her marrow. Was he not even willing to try to understand? To work with her and look for common ground? It seemed not. And his rejection flayed her heart. "Jake…"

He pointed to a sign at the edge of the interstate. "We're almost to the airport."

In other words, discussion closed. Emma wrapped her arms around herself as a chill seeped through her, more convinced than ever she was fighting a losing cause.

Chapter 15

They made their flight with only a few moments to spare. Since they were traveling without luggage, they were able to bypass the front counter and headed straight for security check-in with their e-tickets. Their flight was already boarding. Due to having purchased their tickets last minute, their seats were not together.

When Emma asked the man in the row with her to trade seats, Jake stopped her. "No need. I'll sit back here and meet you at the gate after we land."

The look Emma gave him was somewhat hurt, but she schooled her face, clearly uninterested in causing a scene. Turning down the aisle, Jake found his seat at the back of the plane and buckled in. He didn't mind the separation. In truth, he wanted the time alone with his thoughts, time to process the information they had so far about Fenn's kidnapping and to digest his most recent conversation with Emma about their marriage.

Leaning his head back on the seat, he closed his eyes…

and let regret wash through him. Why had he gotten so defensive with Emma? Defensive and resentful seemed to be his trigger emotions, his go-to reactions with her of late, even with minimal provocation. Emma's surly mood the past several months, her drumbeat of demands and the growing, palpable discord at their house had primed him to instantly snap back. He tended to assume the worst and shut out his wife's complaints like a turtle protectively ducking into his shell to avoid the barbs that flew at him whenever he was home.

Because, today, he was already edgy and angry about the bastards who'd taken Fenn, his mood hadn't helped the conversation they'd had in the truck either. Neither of them had had more than a couple hours of sleep in days. His nerves were still as tight as a tension wire after the armed standoff at the rural house, and he was all too mindful of the running clock to find his daughter before the perv that bought her could assault her.

So when Emma had raised touchy subjects with him, things he needed time and composure to sort through and reason out with her, he'd felt attacked. And he'd snarled and lashed out like a cornered bear. Not his finest moment in an ongoing series of crappy behavior.

He wanted to work things out with Emma. Of course he did. But he was in strange territory and a bit lost how to navigate. She'd always been his sounding board to vent his ire, the one safe person he could allow to see his anxieties and doubts. Having her shoot poison back at him made him reluctant to be open. Having been shut down more than once in the last few years because she was preoccupied with the kids, her family, her work had discouraged him from sharing.

She wanted communication, unity and teamwork? Jake mentally rolled his eyes. Well, that takes two. Recently, when he'd tried to reach out, he'd received rejection, impatience and grumpiness. Who needed that? He had enough on his plate keeping the company afloat through an economic downturn, dealing with an employee's betrayal and lost contracts. He didn't need the added stress of Emma—

He groaned and pinched the bridge of his nose. *Stop. Just stop.*

At some point the cycle of blame and negativity had to just…stop. He had to quit sounding like Fenn in one of her teenager grumps and be the father, the husband, the responsible and caring family man he was supposed to—

"Are you all right?" his seatmate asked.

"Pardon?" Confused, Jake turned with a creased brow to the older woman who'd been knitting to pass the time.

She eyed him warily—and with a touch of maternal concern. Folding her hands over the yarn and needles in her lap, she asked, "Are you airsick? Should I call the flight attendant?"

Jake shook his head and forced a smile. "No. I'm… fine."

"You moaned and were pressing your fingers in your eyes," the woman explained. "I thought you might be feeling sick."

He shook his head. "Not sick…exactly." Then, without knowing why, he added, "Just frustrated. Stressed. I fought with my wife before we boarded, and I acted like a jerk."

The woman gave him a lopsided grin. "Well, at least you recognize it. That's half the battle. Now you only have to apologize and admit to her she was right, and everything will be fine." Her smile brightened, and she gave him a playful wink.

Jake arched one eyebrow. "What if she's not right?"

"Maybe she's not, but if you want to have sex tonight, you'll tell her she was right and let her have her way."

His eyes widened, startled to have this stranger speaking so frankly and audaciously about his sex life or lack thereof. Just the suggestion of having sex with Emma sent a whirl of heat through his blood. He couldn't remember the last time he and Emma had been intimate—indication enough that it had been far too long. Now he gaped at the woman beside him like a guppy, his mouth opening silently as he searched for an appropriate reply.

The woman picked up her knitting again. "Oh my. I've rendered you speechless." She chuckled as she cast Jake another quick, teasing glance. "Honey, the fact that the fight has you this upset tells me you're not a lost cause. You're only in trouble when you don't care enough to be upset after a fight."

"I… I guess."

"Oh, I *know*. I've been married to my college sweetheart for thirty-nine years. We've seen a fight or two, I promise. And he's spent the night on the couch many nights. But here's the thing you've got to remember." She leaned a little closer as if sharing a secret just for his ears. "They say marriage is a 50-50 partnership. But they're wrong. Sometimes it's 60-40 or 75-25, and one of you has to step up when the other needs help."

"True."

She gave his hand a maternal pat, adding, "Change is guaranteed. That's when you depend on the constants— your love and commitment—to get you through. But no matter where the odds fall—whether 50-50 or 75-25—you both have to be giving one hundred percent. Marriage is hard enough without one partner phoning it in."

Jake gave her a polite nod and smile, and, thankfully, the woman returned to her knitting and allowed Jake to return to his brooding. But he did mull her advice. His own mother had died years earlier, and he wondered what she would have said to him if he'd asked her for guidance through this tricky quagmire his marriage was in.

He stared out the window at the blue sky, and the blanket of clouds below them. He remembered the first time he'd flown and the plane broke through the clouds to the infinite sunshine. He'd been struck by the reality that the blue sky and sunlight were always there, permanent. The clouds were only temporary, changing, an inevitable part of the environment and nature. But fleeting.

That truth tugged at him now, as if some higher power were trying to tell him something.

He wanted to believe that beyond the gray clouds that surrounded his marriage, the shadows lurking in his life right now, there were brighter, more promising times ahead.

Deep in his core, a spark of hope warmed him. As determined as he was to bring his daughter home, to surround Fenn with all the love and nurturing she needed to recover from her experience, he was equally intent on sorting through the tattered pieces of his life with Emma and restoring his marriage. He still loved Emma, and that was enough reason to keep fighting.

Chapter 16

Jake was one of the last people off the airplane when they arrived in Atlanta. Not surprising. He'd been sitting near the back, and she'd always known him to be the gracious guy who let others go first. His gaze scanned the waiting area at the gate, looking for her, and Emma lifted her hand to catch his attention. Immediately, she heard Fenn in her head, groaning, *Mo-om, stop. I see you. Geez. You're so embarrassing.*

She hiccuped a sad laugh, promising herself that if they got Fenn home—*when* they got Fenn home—she'd be careful not to embarrass her daughter ever again. She twitched a private grin, adding, "Or maybe not."

When Jake reached her, he pulled her close and gave her a kiss. "I'm sorry."

Emma shrugged. "I haven't been waiting long. I knew you were in the back."

"No, I mean… I'm sorry. For being a jerk in the truck. For losing my temper again. For… Aw, hell. Who knows what all I've done? I'm just...sorry. Next time we talk about things, I promise to listen. Really listen."

Emma blinked, startled by his apology. When she tried to respond, her throat tightened, and she could only squeak. "Me, too."

"Come on. Let's find a board that says where our connecting flight is." Jake put a hand at the small of her back, gently guiding her from the rows of seats in the waiting area and into the flow of passengers rushing to restrooms or connecting flights.

As they merged with the bustling mass of humanity, an older woman dragging a rolling carry-on smiled at them and mouthed, *Good luck.*

"Thanks," Jake replied quietly and gave the woman a nod.

"Who was that?"

"My seatmate."

"You told her we were looking for Fenn?"

"No."

"Then what was the 'good luck' for?"

He gave her shoulder a squeeze. "Oh...she just gave me some...hmm, call it motherly advice."

Ordinarily, Emma might have pressed for more explanation, but conversation wasn't easy as they wove through the stream of people in the long concourse. After some distance, Emma spotted a newsstand and sundries shop. "I'm going in here for a sec. I need something to calm my stomach. Want anything? A snack or some water?"

Jake twisted his mouth as if considering her question then shook his head. "No thanks. I'm gonna check that flight board—" he pointed down the concourse "—and I'll meet you back here."

Emma nodded and made her way into the brightly lit shop that smelled of magazines and newspaper print. She scanned the shelves of touristy baubles featuring Georgia peaches, the Atlanta Braves and magnolia blossoms while the twang of country music played from the overhead speakers. When she located the small display of single-dose packages of pain medication and stomach remedies, she selected packets of antacid and acetaminophen, just in case her headache returned, and took them to the checkout.

She'd paid for her items and was on her way out of the shop when the twangy tune ended and a new song began. The dulcet notes of a keyboard struck her heart as if the piano wires were inside her, vibrating as each one was struck. The tender love song had been played at her and Jake's wedding. They'd danced to it at their senior prom. They'd sung it to each other in the car when life had been simpler and looked rosier. If any song could be called "their song," the ballad playing from the store speakers was it.

Emma's breath lodged in her throat. She stood stock-still, frozen in place just outside the shop as the heart-rending notes and lyrics flowed over her with bittersweet familiarity. On some level, she was aware that she was blocking traffic, people jostling her as the flow of the crowd shifted around her. But all she could see were the snapshots of her past that flickered in her mind's eye.

Jake in his rented tuxedo, looking like her personal Prince Charming at prom. Jake in scrubs, encouraging her as she struggled through labor and delivery. Jake flashing his winning grin as the minister told him he could kiss his bride. And Jake, hands dirty, skin damp with perspiration, as he built Fenn a tree house worthy of the daughter of a construction company owner—like the life and home he'd built for them, brick by brick, one nail at a time, by the sweat of his brow. As the music continued, the highlights of her years with Jake spun out like a movie in her head. Good days and bad. Sickness and health. Financial struggles and spending splurges on vacations to the Grand

Canyon or Dollywood when Fenn was five. So much history. So much love. All over—if the divorce papers she'd filed earlier in the week were signed and finalized.

Over...

Emma's breath stuck in her lungs.

Jake found the electronic flight board simply by looking for the spot in the concourse where traffic backed up as people stopped to stare at the giant screen on the wall. He located their flight, memorized the gate number and the on-time notification, then pivoted to head back to meet Em. He was almost back to the newsstand where he'd left Emma when something out of the corner of his eye caught his attention. As if the face in the billboard had shouted at him. As if a voice deep inside him told him to look. As if, on some level, he'd been watching for, waiting for the display to appear. A strange tingle raced up his back as he faced the large sign with the vulnerable face and wide eyes staring out from the photograph. An advertisement for an advocacy group, but also a public service announcement, a plea.

"Human trafficking is real. If you see something, say something," the billboard read. Jake could only stare at the dark, sad eyes of the woman featured, her hands bound, the shadow of a man looming over her. Tearing his eyes from the woman's hypnotic gaze, he shifted his attention to the smaller photos below the main image. Girls of all ages, races and nationalities were posted with brief descriptions of their physical appearance, date they'd gone missing and last known location. Some of the young women on the display had been missing for years. One girl was only eleven years old.

A few days ago, when he'd first learned what had happened to Fenn, who had taken her, he'd thought of these billboards. Now, seeing them again in living color as he made what was likely a fool's errand to Florida, he could only stare at the faces with a sick feeling in his soul. Here he was, pursuing the tiniest of leads to track his daughter down, and he had to wonder if some day Fenn's picture would be posted here with dates decreeing she'd been gone from her family for months. Years. *Dear God...*

A sour taste filled Jake's mouth, and he pinched the bridge of his nose to hold back the sting of tears. What an unimaginable nightmare...

Pain wrenched in Emma's chest. Rooted to her spot by the parade of memories, by recollections of all the things Jake had meant to her through the years. He'd been her champion, confidant, co-parent and best friend. How would she do life without him at her side?

As if some internal radar sensed him near, she turned her head and found him a few dozen steps down the concourse. He stared at something on the wall that she couldn't read from her angle. His expression was bereft, and an answering pain arrowed to her core. His pain had always been hers, too. When he'd sliced his hand with the jigsaw three summers ago and had to get stitches, she'd swear she felt every prick of the needle in the ER. When his mother had died, she's cried the tears he'd told himself he didn't need to shed. They'd spent too many years reading each other's thoughts to not realize something had him deeply disturbed. But what?

As if he, too, sensed her, he angled his head and met her gaze. With a deep inhale, he started toward her, his eyes never leaving her as he dodged other travelers and moved inexorably toward her, pulled by an invisible cord. From inside the newsstand their song continued playing, each note digging deeper into her soul, a melodic entreaty to heart. *Fix this.*

Yes, he'd hurt her, pulled away from her, lost sight of

the course they'd set for themselves when they'd married. But she'd made mistakes, too. No matter what else happened in the coming days, weeks, years…she had to find a way back to the man she'd loved for almost twenty years.

As he neared Emma, Jake realized tears were streaming down her cheeks. She hadn't moved since he spotted her standing just outside the news shop. His pulse spiked. Something had to have happened to evoke this flood of tears. She'd been fine, if a tad airsick, when he'd left her. So what…?

He hastened his pace, dread pooling in his chest. Had she gotten bad news about Fenn? When he reached her, he cupped a hand under her chin and swiped at tears with his thumb. "What? Emma, tell me what's happened?"

"H-happened?" She blinked, gazing up at him with a puzzled knit in her brow.

"You're crying." He dried more of the dampness from her face, concerned now because she seemed dazed. "Em, what's going on?"

"Nothing. I— Listen…" She lifted a hand weakly to point toward the ceiling.

Stilling, he focused his attention on the noises around him. Gate agents down the concourse calling for boarding. Low conversations of passing travelers. The whirring motor and whiny honk of an electric airport transport vehicle.

Gripping Emma's arms, he guided her out of the path of the handicapped transport vehicle that needed to get past her. As they stepped closer to the store, out of the flow of pedestrian traffic, he heard the closing chords of a familiar song. Emma had called it "their song" once, and he didn't protest. He liked the song well enough, and he was glad to let Emma have any romantic notions about their marriage she wanted. No harm, no foul. He found his wife's sentimentality regarding such things endearing.

Now, looking into her damp, red-rimmed eyes, his heart lurched. "Our song?"

She nodded, then glanced down as she seemed to shake herself out of whatever spell the music had cast over her.

"That's all?" he asked, relieved that she hadn't received tragic news or been victim to a crime. "That's why you're crying?"

"All?" Hurt crossed her face, and he realized belatedly his comment probably sounded condescending.

"Hell, Em. When I saw you crying, I thought you'd gotten bad news about Fenn. Or you'd been mugged or…"

Using the back of her wrist, Emma dried the rest of her face. "No. The song, it caught me off guard. My defenses were down, and I… I just…" She tipped up her chin, a sorrow in her eyes that cut him to the marrow. "What happened to us, Jake? We used to be a team. We were in sync. We had dreams and faith in each other and…"

Jake took a step back as if she'd shoved him, the ache inside him swelling. "Had. Is all that past tense for you, then?"

She lifted one shoulder, her expression bewildered. Lost. Hurting. "I don't know. I miss us. The *us* we used to be."

A man sped past, bumping Jake with the oversize duffel bag swung over his shoulder and reminding Jake where they were. Moving back close to Em, he gripped her shoulders, drilled her with a hard look. "I want to finish this conversation. We *need* to have this conversation." He paused and took a breath, swallowed the acid in his throat. Wrapping her in a secure embrace, he whispered, "But not here. Not now."

He needed time to gather his thoughts before he presented his case to Emma about where he saw fissures in the relationship. That was not a discussion he looked forward to. He put it down as one more difficult task he needed to tackle in order to rebuild his family. He knew, probably better than most people, how a house would slowly crumble without a solid foundation. How cracks in the ceiling and walls let all manner of unwanted elements in the house. Vermin, cold, contamination. While he'd been preoccupied with keeping the roof over their heads, he'd allowed cracks to form and grow. Repairs were overdue.

He pressed a kiss to Emma's forehead, took a step back and hitched his head toward the far end of the concourse. "We have a flight to catch."

Fenn trudged beside Tommy through the Orlando airport, her head down, her heart cold. The cheerful images of cartoon characters awaiting so many visitors to that airport were like salt in her wound. Memories of visiting Disney World with her parents a couple years earlier taunted her. Those had been golden days, just as the billboards in the airport now promised. Tears stung her eyes, and terror scraped through her.

Tommy had warned her, graphically, what would happen to her, to her family, if she tried to signal a flight attendant or police officer. If she tried to escape or speak to another passenger.

Were they idle threats meant to keep her in line or real danger? Fenn had been weighing that question since they left the house in the boonies, waited through hours of maintenance delays to board their plane, then endured the flight to Florida.

Among the ways Fenn had imagined losing her virginity had been a crazy spring break trip to Florida with her friends when she was in college. She'd find some hot guy on the beach who'd sweep her off her feet, and she'd sleep with him under the stars with the music of the ocean waves breaking to serenade them. Or her first time would be on her honeymoon before she boarded a cruise ship to the Bahamas. Or with her high school boyfriend, with whom she'd fallen deeply in love and ended up sharing the rest of her life. Never, in all her romantic imaginings had she ever considered that she'd be kidnapped, dragged to Florida to be handed off to some sick old creep who'd bought her online.

She shuddered and swallowed the bile that rose in her throat. Throwing up would draw attention to her, and Tommy had made clear she should do absolutely nothing, *nothing* to draw attention. When she'd sneezed at the Nashville airport and the old man beside her said, *Bless you,* Tommy had sent her a glare that chilled her to the bone.

Her hands might not be bound, but she was tethered to Tommy as surely as if he had her in chains. Still, despite all the warnings, Fenn waged an internal battle, weighing the possibility of bolting away from him or shouting for help. Of somehow passing a secret note to another passenger or making her desperate situation clear through facial expression and eye contact with the flight attendant. But the pain Tommy had inflicted before they'd reached the airport as he'd issued his warnings lingered. Her scalp ached from where he'd pulled her head back by her hair. Her shoulders throbbed from having her arms twisted behind her. And her stomach bore the lasting effects of his fist in her gut.

But more terrifying were threats of harm to her family. Tommy's words haunted her. Thanks to them finding her wallet in her backpack, DJ and his thugs knew where she lived. They'd seen her pictures of Lexi and her parents. Knew her family owned Turner Construction and Cameron Glen.

One step out of line and they would kill her parents. Take Lexi for their sick prostitution ring. Burn every cabin at Cameron Glen to the ground with her family inside. With one tap of his finger on his phone, Tommy could send a text that would condemn her family. As scared as she was, as horrible as the fate that awaited her in Florida, she couldn't give Tommy any reason to hurt her family. She had to be brave in order to protect them.

And so, with her heart in her throat and her stomach knotted, she marched silently beside Tommy down the concourse toward the exit. For the most part, she kept her head down, her eyes on the floor, afraid that Tommy might misinterpret her scanning gaze as something it wasn't. But so that she didn't trip, so that she didn't walk into a trash can or miss a turn Tommy took, she had to raise her eyes now and then. And that was how, as they stepped off an escalator and made their way across the baggage pickup area toward the exit, she spotted a familiar hairstyle, clothes and body build at a car rental kiosk. At first, she thought her eyes were playing tricks on her, that her wishful thinking and silent prayers had manifest in delusions. But when the woman with her back to her turned, Fenn's body flashed hot and cold at the same time. She froze where she was and struggled to find her voice. "Mom…" she rasped, too low to be heard over the din of the crowd. Then louder. "Mom!"

Chapter 17

Emma fumbled in her purse for her wallet so she could show the rental car agent her driver's license, credit card and proof of insurance. As she dug, a female voice rang over the cacophony of crowd noise, of tired, crying children and the rumbling luggage conveyors. "Mom!"

Her heart jolted, and she raised her head, glanced over her shoulder. The voice had sounded like Fenn's. She scanned the busy lobby, her heart in her throat, but the cry didn't come again. She couldn't be sure which direction the voice had come from.

As a family decked out in matching T-shirts filed past Emma, a girl about eight years old called, "Mom, when are we going to eat? I'm hungry!"

Emma sighed, shoulders slumping as she realized she was by no means the only woman in the airport that went by Mom.

Jake strolled up, having used an ATM to get extra cash, and asked, "Everything all right?"

"I thought..." Emma shrugged and pulled out her wallet. "Never mind." She passed the rental agent the information he needed. "Let's just go. This noise is giving me a headache."

The instant Fenn called out, Tommy seized her arm, his fingers biting into her muscle so hard she thought he might break the bone. "Shut up!"

He shoved her outside to the bustle of taxis and buses and luggage carts.

Fenn fought his grip, straining to look past the heads in the crowd to find the woman she'd been sure was her mom. She blinked hard trying to clear the tears that had instantly bloomed in her eyes and now obscured her vision. Had she imagined her mom? Was it wishful thinking? Wasn't this her last chance to find help before being hidden away again in a stuffy motel room until the creep who bought her showed up?

Mom, if it's you, please see me! Please help me! Someone help! Please, God, I promise to be good from now on!

Once Tommy had dragged her a few yards past the main driveway, into a parking garage, he angled his phone toward her, showing her the text waiting to be sent. His thumb hovered over the send button. "Didn't I tell you what would happen if you stepped outta line?" Tommy growled. "You want me to send DJ to your house to kill your family? 'Cause he'll do it."

Fenn shook her head and wiped her face with her free hand. "N-no."

He glared at her. "This is your last chance, girlie. Don't blow it."

With that, he hauled her deeper into the parking garage until they reached the section where a fleet of rental cars waited. Tommy showed the attendant in a kiosk a computer printout. It was scanned and returned with a key and rental agreement. Five minutes later, Tommy was behind the wheel of a small sedan with Fenn slumped in the passenger seat, and they drove out into the Florida moonlight.

The glow of the rising moon shone brightly over the unlit and sparsely developed stillness of Florida's central plains. Jake cast a wistful glance at the night sky as he drove from the airport toward the business district in Orlando. Another day had passed without finding Fenn.

Their rental car had that "new car" smell, and his long legs felt as if they'd been folded into the cramped driver's seat. His knees bumped the underside of the dashboard when he moved his foot from one pedal to another. But he didn't care.

He was in Florida. Finally. The flights and layover had seemed interminable.

Now he and Emma had to figure out their next step. At some point, as their plane passed over Georgia, Jake had accepted the sick and grievous reality that they probably wouldn't find Fenn before she was passed off to Nøtar@11Ø5. The chances of locating his daughter before she was violated by the pervert were slim. That truth rotted in his gut and gnawed his heart.

But...

Jake swallowed hard as bitterness filled his throat.

But...

He gripped the steering wheel tighter as he swore to himself he was not leaving Florida without Fenn—one way or another. They'd help Fenn heal, get her the best doctors and counselors to guide her through this trauma. He would show his daughter all the love and tenderness and patience he possessed.

Fenn would be all right. She just had to be. He refused to believe anything else or he feared he'd crack. Losing his daughter...

No! It simply couldn't happen.

She was strong and resilient and had the entire Cameron clan to surround her with support and love.

"She's going to be all right. Isn't she?" Emma asked from the other side of the dark car, echoing his thoughts. "Tell me we'll find her, Jake. Tell me our girl's going to be okay."

The fear and uncertainty in Emma's voice ripped at his soul. "I'll do everything in my power to bring our baby home, Em. I swear it."

His job was to protect his family, above all else. How had he let this danger and terror slip past him while he dwelled on his wounded pride, his pursuit of a bigger, better, more expensive lifestyle? Providing for his family didn't only mean earning money for food and electricity. He had a duty to provide other things of more importance than finances.

A sense of security. An assurance of his love. A freedom from fear and doubt. Perhaps greater than any failing of fiscal shortfall was the prospect of leaving his family feeling vulnerable or hurting.

And clearly the women he cared most about in the world hadn't felt provided for in those key ways or his daughter wouldn't have run away. His wife wouldn't have filed for divorce.

He cut a glance to the beautiful woman beside him. The woman who'd stolen his heart in high school and only made him love her more every day as he'd seen her bear his children, start her own interior design business, and prove again and again how capable and loving she was.

"I'm sorry," he whispered. "I meant it when I said it earlier."

Emma met his glance, the headlights of passing cars reflecting in her eyes and dashboard lights casting her face in harsh shadows. "For what exactly?"

"I let you down. I let all of you down. You, the girls, your family."

Emma frowned and gave her head a small shake. "What do you mean? How—"

"Well, we certainly wouldn't be where we are—searching for Fenn in Florida or facing divorce—if I'd been the husband and father I should have been."

Emma sat taller in the seat and lifted her chin. "True."

He turned his eyes back to the road, his chest aching.

"But…" she added, covering his hand with hers on the steering wheel, "I will not let you take full blame for the condition of our marriage or anything else that has happened in the past several months. Or the last few days."

He sighed. "Emma, you were right about—"

"Jake, listen to me. I won't… I *can't* blame you for avoiding me, staying at work late. I know I was…hard to live with. Bitchy."

"No, Em. I—"

"Hey. I heard myself. I know I was harsh and critical, and I complained. I hated the words and tone that I heard coming out of me. I tried to stop them, but when I opened my mouth, it was like a backlog of poison just…" She gave a grunt of disgust. After a beat of silence, she added, "For someone wanting more open lines of communication and to be more a part of your life, I hardly approached it with the kind of salvo that welcomed discourse and cooperation." She turned toward him, her tone softer. "I'm sorry, too. I'm afraid I took my fatigue and frustrations out on you." Her breathy sigh reached him, curling in his core like a wisp of hope. "I guess I can't blame you for wanting to avoid me, avoid coming home."

"I didn't avoid coming home," he shot back, his response a knee-jerk defensiveness he'd honed in recent months. But…in truth, he was reacting to the slash of pain deep in his soul. Because her assessment was the truth. He had avoided her.

She cut a look toward him that called him out, said she knew better. "Really?"

Be honest with yourself at least, his conscience nagged as he stared at the dark road they traveled.

Okay, yeah. He'd dodged the uncomfortable atmosphere at home and Emma's recriminations by staying at work, later and later. He'd added fuel to the fire that was destroying his marriage by doing the very thing she'd said over and over had her worried and angry.

"In hindsight, I realize that I lashed out…because I was hurt and mad and frustrated," Emma said, rousing him from his own thoughts. "I admit I didn't handle things well. Not at all. I see that now. Maybe I even saw it when it was happening and was too stubborn or emotionally wounded to take a step back." When she raised her gaze to his, Jake's chest warmed and something like relief balled in his throat. "I'm truly sorry, Jake."

He reached for her cheek and stroked her skin with his thumb briefly, before again fixing his attention on his driving. "Your brother thinks we should see a marriage counselor. Maybe…maybe he's right."

"Would you go? I've suggested that before and you refused."

Jake scrubbed a hand through his hair. "It still feels weird. Awkward. I have a hard enough time telling you about my feelings and my fears. How am I going to spill it all for a stranger?"

"Only you can answer that, Jake."

He bit the inside of his cheek, mulling the dilemma, reviewing his choices and past actions for several minutes as they drove through the night-darkened outskirts of the city.

"Don't you trust me anymore, Jake?"

"Trust you?" Her question caught him off guard. "I—

of course I trust you. What does that have to do with any of this?"

"If you trust me, truly trust me to guard your secrets and protect your heart, why can't you share your thoughts and fears with me? We used to talk about everything together. We dreamed and planned and shared our doubts and concerns. We exchanged ideas and worked out solutions to our problems together. Don't you remember? Like that night we sat out on the dock by the fishing pond *all night* discussing how much you hated your job at the real estate office and deciding how to finance your own construction company. We covered more than just your career that night. We talked about our hopes for Fenn, the right timing to have another baby, and the fact that you felt beholden to my parents for providing our house without charge. You said you wanted to pay them rent so you wouldn't feel like a freeloader."

He nodded. "I definitely remember that conversation. For years it gnawed at me that we were taking advantage of your parents."

"By living on the property that has been in our family for multiple generations?"

"It felt wrong somehow. My father worked so hard to provide for—"

"I know." She put her hand on his leg. "I remember your reasons. But that's my point. You had an issue, a concern, and we talked it out. We haven't done that in… months. Years."

He acknowledged her assertion with a nod. A shrug. "Life is different these days."

"The kids and the company certainly keep us busier."

He gave a gruff chuckle of agreement.

"So we have to work all the harder to make time for us. For our marriage."

Jake heard a pleading in her tone that clawed at him.

Wasn't Emma, their marriage, their family the most important thing in his life? Why, then, had he not given it priority? Before he could respond, Emma pointed to an exit sign.

"This is us, isn't it? Turn here."

"We're there," Tommy said. "Don't give me or the client any trouble."

Fenn sat up taller in the passenger seat and looked around. They seemed to be at some sort of playground, but since it was after dark, the place was deserted. Except for the guy with wire-framed glasses getting out of the car next to them. *The client.* The man who'd bought her. The man who intended to take her virginity.

She shivered despite the heat.

"No trouble," Tommy repeated, his finger in her face. "No more stunts like you pulled at the airport, or your little sister will be the next on our auction block."

The airport. Fenn thought about the woman she'd seen at the car rental kiosk and her heart clutched. Was she missing Mom so much she was imagining other women were her mom? Was it possible her mom was here, had somehow found out she was being brought here? That seemed impossible. Much too unlikely. And it hurt so much to think about her mom and dad. She was alone and had to take care of herself.

"I hear little kids bring in even more cash than you did," Tommy said with a leering grin.

Fenn glared at Tommy with every bit of anger and hatred she'd nurtured over the past several days. "Stay the hell away from my sister."

Tommy arched one eyebrow. "Clean up your language. Cursing hardly fits the image of innocence the client is looking for."

"Screw the client," she shot back.

Tommy cracked a smarmy grin. "Yeah. You will."

Fenn felt the blood drain from her face, realizing what she'd said, what Tommy meant. She had to swallow hard not to whimper. She wanted so badly to present a brave face. Remain defiant. She'd done meek and afraid when she was first taken. Maybe that was a natural reaction to the situation when she'd been confused and numb with shock. But now...

Now everything in her told her to fight. To be smart. To pay attention and keep her guard up. She had to be ready if ever an opportunity presented itself. But how did she do that and still protect Lexi and her parents?

Tommy opened his door. "Stay put until I say. I'm going to check things out."

He climbed out, clicking the door lock on the key fob as he left.

Fenn was glowering at Tommy's retreating back when a knock on her window startled her. She jerked her gaze to the window where the client stood, bent at the waist, grinning a dorky smile and giving her a finger wave.

Tommy grabbed the guy by the back of his button-down shirt and hauled him away from the rental-car window. Through the glass, she could hear bits and pieces of the conversation between the two men.

"...late. What hap—" the client said.

"Flight delays. Arms up."

"What?"

"Search you...or wire."

"I'm not—"

Tommy moved aggressively toward the man, sticking his nose in his face. "Do it."

The client raised both arms, and Tommy patted him down, head to foot, then lifted the guy's shirt to reveal a paunchy white belly.

"Satisfied?" the client intoned dryly.

"You have…"

"…until I knew…"

"Well, she's…" Tommy hitched his head toward Fenn, and when the client glanced her way again, Tommy sidled between Fenn and the other man, blocking his view. "…need proof…"

When her own panicked breathing made it difficult to hear, harder to glean bits of information that might help her if she escaped—*when* she escaped—Fenn held her breath. Didn't even move so that the squeak of the leather seats wouldn't interfere with her listening.

The men both pulled out phones. The client flashed his screen toward Tommy, and Tommy placed a call, saying, "Got it? Yeah? 'Kay." He then leaned close to the client again, poking him with one finger. "Remember. She's… loan. If you—"

The client swatted Tommy's hand away. "I know the drill. This isn't…rodeo. She'll be…"

After rolling his shoulders and giving the other guy another long hard look, Tommy clicked the key fob and yanked open the door beside Fenn. "Get up. Time to go."

Fenn didn't move. Better the devil you know…

As long as she stayed with Tommy, she wouldn't be molested. Her kidnappers valued her virginity too much.

But within seconds, when she didn't budge, Tommy grabbed her arm and jerked her out of the car. She stumbled as he dragged her toward the client's car and opened the passenger-side door of the low-slung sports car. "Get in."

The threats of harm to Lexi, to her parents, echoed in her head, and she dropped onto the seat. Tommy crouched beside her, and in a quiet snarl, he said, "I'll be back for you in two weeks. If I get a report you did anything to upset the client, there will be a price to pay."

"Two weeks?"

Tommy smirked. "You didn't think this was a one and done or some kind of permanent vacation, did you?"

"I—"

"When Mr. Johnson's time is up and you're all broken in, you go to work with the rest of the girls."

Fenn's stomach clenched. She hadn't considered what came after...after...

The client climbed in the driver's side, and a cloud of cologne followed him in.

Tommy stood and closed the car door, leaving Fenn sealed in the tiny front seat with *Mr. Johnson*. The fumes of his cologne were so overpowering she wanted to gag.

Then the man, who looked to be older than her parents but not as old as her Grandpa Cameron, reached for her, tucking a wisp of her hair behind her ear and smiling. "Hi, Layla. You can call me Bill."

Fenn shuddered at his touch and shrank back as far as she could in the confines of the little sports coupe. She was as sure his real name wasn't Bill as she was hers wasn't Layla.

"Don't be scared, sugar. I'm not going to hurt you." The guy smiled again and cranked the engine. "You'll see. We're going to get to know each other and have some fun. It'll be great."

In the darkness, she had trouble fully assessing his facial features, but the glow of the blue lights from the dash revealed a balding pate framed by dark hair and thick eyebrows just above the squarish lenses of his glasses. Other than a pooched belly, he wasn't overweight, but he was still bigger than her. No doubt stronger.

"My name's not sugar. Or Layla," Fenn said, lifting her chin.

The man shifted the sports car into Reverse and gave her a bland smile. "For the next two weeks, your name is whatever I say it is."

* * *

After collecting the groceries and clothes Emma had ordered from her phone earlier in the day and checking into their hotel, Jake and Emma dropped wearily on the king-size bed in their room. Emma stared at the obscure hotel art on the wall across from her and rewound her thoughts, trying to reorganize and find the strength to take the next step. Except…what was the next step?

"So we're here," she said, angling her head toward Jake. "Now what?"

"Good question." Jake pulled his phone out of his pocket and grunted. "Damn. I forgot to take my phone off airplane mode. Seven missed calls."

The reminder sent Emma digging in her purse for her phone.

Jake played his messages on speakerphone. The first was a spam call about his car's warranty, but the next was from Officer Smith. "Mr. Turner, please call me in regard to the investigation of your daughter's kidnapping. We need to talk."

Emma's stomach swooped. "Oh God. That sounds serious. Bad." Dread squeezed her chest, and she clutched at Jake arm, needing something to steady herself. "What if…"

Jake shook his head firmly and gripped her shoulders. "No. Do not assume the worst!"

But the anxious look in his own eyes said he was fighting to stay calm, battling down doubt demons himself.

Emma raised her phone with trembling hands and was scrolling to bring up Officer Smith's number when Jake's next message played. Emma's mother. "Hi, Jake. It's Grace. Just wanting an update." She paused, the sound of her mother's voice a balm she hadn't realized she needed so desperately. "Emma's phone went to voice mail, too, so… Oh. I have a little sprout here that wants to say hi."

Then a small voice that tugged at Emma's heart. "Hi, Daddy! Nanna and I made Scottish cookies today! She said they're called shortbread. I ate five! When are you coming home?" Then Grace's voice again. "Oops. I didn't know Nanna had let her eat so many. Well, call and check in when you can. I know you're busy doing everything you can for Fenn, but...we're worried and...well, that's all. Bye."

Emma closed her eyes, wishing so hard that they had good news to report to her mother. Wishing she were home at Cameron Glen eating shortbread with her daughter. Wishing she could turn the clock back even one week...

Before she'd filed for divorce.

Before Fenn had run away.

Before everything she loved felt as if it were slipping away from her, shattering at her feet.

"Jake, Officer Smith again. Call me." The message from Jake's phone yanked her back to the present, and spurred back into action, she found the policeman's number and called.

"Smith here." The Valley Haven officer said by way of greeting.

Emma swallowed hard as she set the phone to speaker. "It's, uh... Emma Turner, Officer. You asked us to—"

"Where the hell are you?" the man barked.

Emma blinked, startled by the question...and yet not. She met Jake's eyes, and he took the phone from her, saying, "We're in Orlando. We followed the clue we had about where the kidnappers had taken—"

"Hell and damnation, Turner!" the officer shouted, cutting Jake off. "Stand down! You are not helping your daughter by interfering with the official investigation! Do you understand that the FBI is involved? That your meddling—"

"Hey!" Jake barked back, "Without our meddling, as

you call it, the FBI wouldn't know that she'd been held in Tennessee, or the username of the man who bought her, or that she's likely in Florida being passed off to the creep who bought her, even as we speak! We're the ones doing all the work to find—"

"Really? Do you really think you're smarter than the FBI and their resources?" Smith shot back, his tone testy.

"Maybe not smarter, but certainly working a step ahead," Jake snapped back. "And the faster Fenn is found, the better our chances of saving her from being raped!"

"Just because you are not in the loop on every detail of what's happening in the investigation does not mean we are a step behind. You can blow everything if you tip off the wrong person or—hell, I don't know. What I do know is you need to back off. Come home and leave the investigation to the professionals."

"I can't do that. I'm not leaving here without my daughter."

"Then you will be arrested for hampering an FBI investigation."

Emma's eyes widened, and she balled the bedspread in her hand.

"Look, I convinced Special Agent Harmon not to arrest you at the Knoxville airport, to give me a chance to talk you down. But if you don't give up your wild goose chase and let law enforcement do their work, you stand to be jailed, fined—" He sighed harshly. "Just stand down, Turner. I won't—"

Jake disconnected the call and tossed her phone on the bed. Scrubbing his face, he marched across the room and back again.

"What are we going to do, Jake? You heard him. We could be arrested!"

He nodded, his expression grim. "Then we need to find Fenn before that happens."

Chapter 18

Fenn peered through the windshield of the sports car as "Bill" pulled through a tall iron gate and up the circular drive of a monstrous house. In the dark of the night, she couldn't tell much about the place except that it was big. Like, really big. Huge. "You live *here*?"

She hated the awe in her tone and quickly schooled her face to hide the curiosity and fascination she knew had to be in her expression. Hostile indifference was what she needed to go for, she'd decided. Don't let him see fear. Don't be docile or cooperative or show weakness.

Be strong. Resist. And commit as much detail to memory as she could. Anything that could be useful from car tag numbers, to names, overheard conversations, her surroundings, her captor's habits. Like her literary heroes, she had to *smart* her way out of this.

Bill sent her a smug grin. "You like it?"

She gave him a silent glare. A shrug.

He parked in front of the grand double doors of the main

entrance, and as soon as he cut the engine and headlights, a man in a dark suit came through the front doors and down the landing steps to the passenger-side door.

Bill got out and circled the sports car while the man in the suit opened Fenn's door. She didn't move, only stared suspiciously at the second man. He was younger than Bill, and like the house, the guy was big. Really big. Not fat, just...*big*. Mostly in his shoulders and chest, as if he lifted weights. And he was tall. Dark hair, cut short like a soldier's. His grim expression stood in stark contrast to Bill's goofy grin.

"Well, come on." Bill waved a hand encouraging her to get out of the car.

Instead, she crossed her arms and leveled a flat look at him.

Bill sighed and sent the big guy a quick look and jerked his head toward Fenn. The big guy stepped forward, grabbed Fenn's arm firmly and dragged her to her feet.

She swallowed hard, a sense of foreboding crawling up her spine.

"This is my assistant, Vince," Bill said, looking stupidly proud of himself for having a gorilla-sized assistant. "Vince, this is my niece, Layla."

Fenn's head snapped toward Bill. *Niece? What the—?*

"Please show her to the upstairs guest room and make sure she's comfortable." Bill turned to her now with that dorky, chilling grin. "I know you're tired after your trip. Sleep well, and I'll see you at breakfast."

With that, Bill turned and walked up the steps and inside the huge home.

Vince waved a hand toward the same door. "After you."

Fenn balked. She cast a glance around the shadowed lawn that was surrounded as far as she could see by a high stone wall. If she tried to escape, if she bolted, right now, back down the curved driveway toward the iron gate—

Vince made a grumbling sort of noise in his throat and took her by the arm again. She struggled against his grip, trying to dig her heels in. Without success. The burly guy led her inside a marble-floored foyer with a massive crystal chandelier. Geez, Bill sure liked big stuff.

As Vince hauled her toward a wide staircase, she said, "Wait! I'm… I'm not his niece."

Nothing. Just another rough tug as they started up the polished hardwood steps.

"Did you hear me? I'm not really his niece!"

"Humph," he grunted.

"He kidnapped me! I don't—"

"Look," Vince said, his voice a deep grumble. "I don't care if you're his niece or the Queen of Sheba. It's not my job to ask questions."

"But I need to get out of here. I don't want to be here! If I could just call my parents or—"

"No phone."

She frowned as she stumbled up the stairs beside him, his forward progress unrelenting no matter how many times she pulled back or tripped. "No phone? In this whole huge place? What about a cell phone? Do you have—"

"You don't get a phone," Vince said in a bored monotone. "No phone. No computer."

"But I have to get hold of my parents. Or the police. Please, I—"

They'd reached the top step, and with a harder yank, Vince jerked her close, bending to put his flat nose near hers. His dark eyes narrowed to a menacing glare. "Listen to me, girl. Nobody's callin' the cops. Just do what you're told, don't make trouble, and you'll be outta here in a few weeks. As long as you do your part, the boss man won't hurt you. But if you give him any flak, I will make you sorry. I am not your friend. I work for him." He gave her a quick, hard shake. "Got it?"

His long fingers bit into her flesh, and despite her best efforts to appear brave and aloof, tears puddled in her eyes. She didn't have a chance to answer his probably rhetorical question before he was again dragging her forward. They moved down a hall with plush carpeting, passing a number of closed doors until they reach one no different than any of the others. Fenn had to wonder if there were other girls shut in the other rooms. Or members of Bill's real family. Or more goons hired to keep Bill's prisoners in line.

Vince pushed her inside the plush bedroom, decorated with cherry furniture, pale gray carpeting and what she'd heard her mom refer to as chintz upholstery on the maroon print chairs. A queen-size bed with a pink duvet and frilly matching pillows hogged the center of one wall. Louvered accordion doors opposite the bed seemed to indicate she had a closet, while artwork featuring flowers and Grecian women in flowing robes decorated the remaining walls. The folding doors of a seven-foot-tall armoire were open to reveal a flat-screened television and selection of DVDs.

Fenn goggled at the bedroom. It was a far cry from the seedy motel room where she'd spent two days with DJ or the bare closet where she'd been kept yesterday. She sent Vince a look of confusion.

She was being treated like she was, in fact, Bill's niece, come to stay for a pleasant holiday…if overseen by a giant, glowering guard. "I don't get it. What…?"

"Boss man wants you to make yourself comfortable. Make yourself at home." Vince delivered the lines in a gruff manner that contradicted the words. "You want anything—food, movies, blankets…whatever—you push this button here," he said and pointed to a device on the wall that looked like the security system pad they had at home, "and I'll answer. I'll get it for you."

Fenn frowned. Something didn't add up. Bill had

bought her for her virginity, hadn't he? Didn't that mean he intended to—

She cut the thought off, not wanting to give it even an inch in her brain. "But..."

"I'll be back at seven in the morning to take you down to breakfast. Be ready. Boss man doesn't like to be kept waiting." With that, Vince marched out of the room and closed the door behind him.

Fenn heard the *snick* of the door being locked, but just to be certain she tested the knob. If the fancy bedroom and promises of anything she wanted to be more comfortable had cast any doubt, the unyielding doorknob left no question. She was Bill's prisoner.

In their hotel room, Jake paced, burning off restless energy as he worked to focus his sleep-deprived brain on their next move.

"They can track credit cards, so we have to assume they know we've checked in here," Emma said, pulling off her short-sleeved blouse without fully unbuttoning it.

Jake, trying not to be distracted by the sight of his wife's lush body as she changed into her silky new bra and panties, nodded. *If you want to have sex tonight...*

Since his seatmate to Atlanta had spoken those words, the idea of making love to Emma hadn't been far from Jake's mind. Early in their marriage, every fight had ended with great makeup sex. Considering how much fighting he and Emma had done in the past several weeks without making up, they were due for a hot, earth-shaking night of passion.

Jake sighed, glancing at the king-size bed in the beautiful hotel room—that they were abandoning, unused.

"And our phones," Emma said, nudging him from sensual daydreams of stripping her out of that pink demi-cup and covering her head to toe in nibbling kisses. "Even with 'location' and 'data' turned off, I've read they can track your phone. As much as it sucks, we'll have to leave—" She stopped abruptly when she glanced up at him from tearing the tags off her new pair of jeans. "What?"

"Hmm?"

"You're staring at me funny. What's—" Then her attention slipped to his groin, where he had a full erection. Color crept to her cheeks, and she released a tremulous breath as she glanced away. "For God's sake, Jake, this is hardly the time."

He gave a quiet, wry scoff. "Well, my body isn't aware of that. It's only reacting to what I'm seeing." He stepped closer, brushing her hair behind her ear. "And I'm seeing a woman who's still so beautiful to me in every way. A woman I miss. A woman I still burn for."

Leaning in, he placed a soft kiss on her lips.

She caught her breath, and her body stilled, except for the fluttering pulse at the base of her throat. Then she whispered, "Jake, we don't have time for this."

Like a splash of icy water, her words doused him, dropped him back in the cold reality of their situation. "Of course."

Stepping back, he finished undressing, discarding his airplane-stale shirt and jeans, and shifting his focus to how to dodge the police, locate his daughter and keep his sanity until his mission of rescuing Fenn was finished.

Ten minutes of fervent planning and strategizing later, Jake and Emma had finished changing into their new outfits, T-shirts and jeans, chosen for comfort rather than any hint of fashion. They left the dirty items scattered about in the hotel room, establishing it as their apparent home base, just in case—when—the FBI or local police showed up to arrest them. Knowing their cell phones could be tracked, they left those hidden in the room as well, hoping to recover them later, once Fenn was safe.

As they left the hotel lobby, they stopped at an ATM to withdraw even more money to use in lieu of a credit card. Cash in hand, they found a discount department store where they purchased a burner phone, then drove to a random non-chain motel in the sprawling suburbs. They paid cash for a room, registering under the name Jones. Their only stipulations for the new room were clean sheets and working Wi-Fi in the room.

Jake would have settled for just the Wi-Fi and sleeping in the rental car at that point. A sense of urgency pressed down on him, and the menacing sensation of a ticking clock marked each passing minute in his mind's clock. "We need a plan, Em. A plan! What are we doing *here*, when Fenn is *out there*!" He pointed a tense finger toward the door.

"I'm well aware of that." Emma raked her hair back from her face and squeezed her eyes shut. Then grabbing the burner phone, she tapped the screen. "I'll call Brody and see if Ben has found anything new. I'll give him this new number, and we can work from there."

Jake paced the motel room while Emma spoke to her brother, half listening to her side of the conversation and half dwelling on the problem that, although they were in Orlando, they had no clue where Fenn was or how to look for her.

Wild goose chase, Office Smith had called their efforts to track Fenn down. He muttered a curse under his breath. Smith was right. They were working completely blind at this point. They had nothing. Despondency sank over him so hard and fast his knees gave out, and he dropped on the edge of the soft, sagging mattress.

"Thanks. I understand. No. Of course." Emma's shoulders drooped. "Love you, too, Brod."

Silence reverberated in the room, telling Jake that Em either had no news...or bad news she was reluctant to share. When her warm hand rested on his slumped back, Jake angled a glance at her. "Anything?"

"Ben has reached the limits of what he feels he can do without getting himself in serious trouble with the Feds."

Jake grunted acknowledgment.

"He confirmed that the person with the Rat At...*whatever* username was working from a computer in the Orlando area. So...there's that. But..."

"So we've narrowed down the search for this monster to a population of a couple million," Jake said dryly. "Great."

Emma wrapped her arm around his shoulders and rested her head against him. "We'll figure something out. We have to."

"Yeah."

They sat like that for several minutes, minutes that felt like an eternity, knowing every second that passed brought Fenn closer to disaster. Assuming they weren't already too late.

Then Emma tensed. Her grip on him tightened, and she gasped as she straightened. "I have an idea!"

Jake stared at his wife, incredulous. "You're kidding, right?"

"Do you really think I would joke when our daughter's life is at stake? Besides, it worked before!" She turned both hands up, as if she were stating the most reasonable argument instead of proposing a ridiculously reckless plan that would put her life and virtue at risk.

Jake shook his head. "Last time we were just asking questions. You weren't posing as a prostitute!"

"If I thought simply asking questions would work again, I'd try it. But we've moved to a whole different level of criminality with kidnapping and human trafficking and dark web auctions. The people involved will be far more protective of their operation and—"

"No."

Emma blinked. "No...what?"

"My wife is not going into some seedy area of town posing as a prostitute. It's too dangerous. The answer is no."

She straightened her spine and pulled her shoulders back. "Excuse me, but I don't need your permission. If I want to do this to save my daughter, I *will* do it."

"Emma, for God's sake! Be reasonable." Jake stomped across the floor of the small room and curled the fingers of both hands into his hair. He felt control of the situation slipping away from him, and he hated the idea of Emma being put at risk. Of men slobbering over her, even if she wasn't really going to sleep with any of them. Why was she being so damn obstinate and foolhardy?

"Do you have a better plan? How are we going to find Fenn if we don't go to the source? Or as near to the source as we can under the circumstances."

Jake set his jaw and clenched his teeth so hard he thought he might crack a filling. "No, Em. I forbid it."

She scoffed. "Forb—" She aimed a finger at him and scowled. "You can't forbid me!"

"Look, I can go to a strip club or shady bar somewhere and ask questions. Maybe I pose as a john who likes virgins and wants to know where I can get that kind of action."

She wrinkled her nose and sneered, "Ew! You did not just say that to me!"

"Em, just...forget the vernacular. It's so much safer if I go alone. You wait here, and I'll see what I can—"

"No, Jake. That's not how this is going to work. Not this time. I won't let you shut me out or make this decision for me." She clapped a hand to her chest. "I will take whatever risk I have to if it brings Fenn back." She grabbed her purse from the bed and headed to the motel room door. "We don't have time to argue about it either."

"Em!"

She stopped but didn't turn around. "What?"

"Your clothes scream 'soccer mom,' not 'hundred-dollar blow job,'"

He saw her shudder at his crudity. Good. Maybe she'd think twice about charging off to the seedy side of town without fully thinking things through.

After a moment of silence, she angled a glance at him, her eyes bright with inspiration. "We passed a mall a few blocks before we got to the motel." She glanced at her watch. "Most malls close about 9 p.m. If we hurry, we still can get in."

"And what? Shop at Sleazy 'R' Us?" he groused.

She gave a short humorless laugh. "You clearly haven't taken Fenn shopping for school clothes lately. Skimpy, tight and far-too-sexy for our teenager is all too easy to find at any number of stores in the mall." She hiked her purse strap higher. "Now, are you coming with me or not?"

Chapter 19

Jake was extremely uneasy with how hot his wife looked. With the clothes she'd found at the mall, Emma had definitely shed the soccer mom persona. She wore the leopard print miniskirt, spike heels and sheer black camisole well. As they got out of the car at the downtown Orlando strip club, the last thing he wanted to do was let Emma go inside looking that sexy. Instead, he wanted to take her back to their hotel room, either of them, and have the kind of wild sex the clothes implied. But about the time that thought crossed his mind, he'd felt guilty and a little disgusted with himself for being turned on by the kind of blatant sexualization that fueled the industry into which his daughter had been kidnapped.

Then he reminded himself he was drooling over his wife, and he wavered between "of course I'm hot for my wife" and "damn it, the mother of my children should not be objectified like this."

"We shouldn't walk in together," she said, dabbing at

the come-hither red lipstick she'd applied in the car. "I don't want your looming presence and brooding glare to scare off possible informants."

"Emma…" he said in a discouraging tone, even though he saw her point. "I don't like anything about this."

When she turned to him and flashed a commiserating smile, his attention zeroed in on her eyes. The mascara she'd applied reminded him how impossibly long her eyelashes were and the smoky gray eyeshadow along the edge of her eyelid made her irises appear an even clearer, more heart-stoppingly blue than usual. Dear God his wife was gorgeous! Whether dressed and painted to heighten her sex appeal or makeup-free and cuddled up in flannel jammies, Emma shone. And the truth was, as lovely as her physical appearance was, what the losers in this strip joint would never know that Jake did, was how purely beautiful she was inside, too. She was kind and compassionate. Smart and creative. Endearingly clumsy at times. Firm but fair when disciplining the girls. Funny, generous—

"Jake!" She snapped her fingers in front of his face. "Focus, please. We might be going in separately, but I need to know you've got my back."

He drew a long, deep breath, and capturing her face between his hands, he planted a deeply possessive kiss on her lips. When he pulled back to meet her eyes, his voice was gruffer than he'd intended. "I will always have your back, Em. *Always*."

She blinked, looking a little stunned. Before she backed out of his grasp, she used her thumb to wipe her lipstick off his mouth. "Thanks, babe."

Emma headed inside then, and Jake watched with a crazy mix of desire, pride and horror. Her curvy hips swung in the sultry way that came naturally to women in crazy-high heeled shoes. She glanced back at him from the doorway of the strip club. Loud music and cigarette smoke rolled out to greet him as she entered, and in the pockets of the dress pants he'd acquired at the mall, his hands fisted. He paced the parking lot, mentally counted out two minutes, then steeling his nerves, he headed inside. His part in this charade was to pretend he was a wealthy businessman in town for a convention and looking for the means to satisfy a fetish.

His stomach curled at the thought of the predatory appetite he had to fake—the same predilection that some perv in town intended to slake on his daughter. As he moved toward a table by the stage where a naked woman twirled on a pole, he exhaled, shook the tension from his hands and searched the dimly lit room for Emma. He spotted her at the bar, where she'd taken a stool and leaned toward the bartender in conversation.

He found an empty table, and a cocktail waitress with a pierced eyebrow and wearing a dress cut low in front and high on her legs appeared soon after. "What can I get ya?"

"I, um—"

"Two-drink minimum," she rushed to add when he fumbled. "Only paying customers get to stay and watch the show."

"Bourbon and coke, then."

The waitress hadn't been gone ten seconds before another woman, a blonde showing even more skin than the waitress sidled up to him. She sat on the table, right in front of his chair, and gave him a sultry glance. "Hey, sailor. You by yourself tonight?"

"Uh, yeah." He looked the blonde over, as if interested, and couldn't help mentally comparing her to Emma. Emma won in every way.

"Want some company?" the blonde asked, even as she slid into his lap.

Jake sent a guilty glance toward the bar. Emma looked over at that moment, as if she felt his stare, and he didn't miss the little frown that puckered her brow before she turned away.

The blonde wiggled a little in his lap and ran her fingers through Jake's hair. "Enjoying the show, sugar? 'Cause I'll get my chance to dance in another hour."

Jake clenched his back teeth and forced a grin. *Play your part...*

"Well, it's a good warm-up, but..." He rested a hand just above her waist and could feel her ribs. Geez, she was skinny. Not like the curves Emma had. He thought about stroking Emma's womanly shape and heat prickled in his veins. "I'm actually kinda hoping to get a particular itch scratched tonight."

He didn't miss the wariness that flitted in the blonde's eyes before she pasted on a fake smile. His chest ached for the girl—because she was more a girl than a woman. She might be old enough to work in a place like this but, damn... He wanted to throw his shirt over her and send her home to her parents.

"Oh yeah?" the woman-child said. "What kinda itch?"

Jake opened his mouth, and when a sour taste filled his throat, he closed it. Taking a breath, he tried again. "I like virgins."

"Oh my gawd!" huffed a blonde woman as she joined a small group of waitresses and "hostesses" conferring at the bar next to Emma. "Is it a full moon tonight? The crazies sure are out!"

Emma sipped her Diet Coke, shamelessly eavesdropping on the women. She needed an excuse to mingle with the women and see what she could learn about...well, anything useful.

"Come here, honey. Tell Brenda all about it." Another woman with long black hair twisted into a single skinny ponytail draped an arm around the blonde's shoulders.

"How crazy are we talking? Regular crazy or call-the-bouncer crazy?"

"Mostly regular crazy," the blonde replied, then cast a quick glance over her shoulder toward the table where Jake sat. "But that guy at table nine? Don't let his clean-cut, handsome face fool ya. Totally skeevy."

Internally, Emma bristled, wanting to defend Jake. *He is the salt of the earth! The best, kindest, most loving, hardworking man—*

"Get this," the blonde said, leaning toward the other women and lowering her voice such that Emma had to strain to hear what she whispered. "He asked where he could get a virgin. He's got a *thang* for little girls."

Emma's Diet Coke went down the wrong pipe. She sputtered and coughed, drawing the attention of the clutch of women.

"You okay, hon?" Brenda asked.

Emma wiped her mouth with her cocktail napkin. "Yeah," she rasped, then seizing her opportunity, added, "I just…well, I wasn't trying to listen, but…geez! Did you say that guy asked for a virgin?"

The blonde gave her a wary look then shrugged. "Yeah. We get creeps in here pretty often, but…" With another dismissive shrug, she angled her body away from Emma.

"I mean, come on," Emma said, as if the blonde woman's body language hadn't just shut her out, "He came in *here*, looking for a virgin?" She laughed wryly. "That's kinda like looking for icebergs in the Bahamas, isn't it?"

That comment earned her more wary looks and a scowl or two.

Emma backpedaled, still speaking loud enough for the women to know she was addressing them. "How much was he offering for the virgin? For the right price, I could pretend to be whatever he wanted, huh?"

Brenda tilted her head. "And who are *you*?"

Emma took the wary question as an invitation to join the women and moved from her barstool to stand closer. "Oh, I'm... Em—mily. Emily. But I go by..." Emma paused only a half second as she scrambled for a name, but in that brief hesitation, Brenda stepped in front of her.

"You vice?" she asked even as she snatched up the front of Emma's top, ran a hand along the underside of her bra.

"What are you doing?" Emma said sharply as she jerked back.

"Checkin' for a wire. You pop up here asking questions and listening where you aren't invited, I'm thinking cop."

Emma's skin flashed hot, and she worked at keeping her composure. She leaned into her offense at being intimately searched, snapping, "I'm not a cop!" Straightening her camisole, she added in a calmer tone. "I'm a dancer. I go by Cinnamon when I dance."

The blonde gave her a sneer and a haughty look. "*You're* a dancer?" She tipped her head toward the stage and poles. "That kind of dancer?"

Emma lifted her chin, feigning confidence. "Used to be. Paid for night school dancing a few years back. Now I need the cash again, so... I'm here to talk to the manager about a job." She smiled, hoping her lies didn't show in her expression. Jake had always told her she was the world's worst liar, that because she hated duplicity, it showed in her eyes.

"Greg know you're here?" Brenda asked, lifting one eyebrow as if challenging her. "I can get him for you, if you want. But I don't think he's hiring. He doesn't have enough work for the girls he's got."

"Oh." Emma flapped a hand. "Well, that guy looking for a virgin might be my best chance after all, huh?" One of the women, peeled away from the small group and headed back out into the tables. Before she lost the other women's attention, Emma added, "So what do you do when you get guys like Mr. Skeevy out there?" She jerked her chin toward Jake, then lowered her voice. "I mean, does your boss run a side business in fetishes like that?"

Brenda frowned. "Hell no! You can't have shit like that happening around here. You'd get the whole place shut down. Greg runs a legit operation."

"Mmm." Emma nodded. "Right. I get it. I guess I'm still just kinda freaked that that kinda stuff is for sale. I mean, you know it is. But then a guy like that comes in, and it makes you wonder. Where do creeps like him go to get fetish stuff like that anyway? Especially around here. This is hardly the fetish capital of the world."

"Are you kidding?" Brenda scoffed. "Everywhere is the fetish capital of the world. Men everywhere are scum. Some women, too. People are the same everywhere."

The blonde and another waitress drifted away, leaving Emma alone with Brenda.

Ooo-kay, she thought as she watched them walk away. She'd pushed too hard. Or was too transparent. Or—

"Now, if you've got money," Brenda was saying, "you can get anything you want for a price."

Emma faced Brenda. "Money, huh? Must be nice."

"Huh, yeah. I heard about this one guy, like some prince or oil tycoon in the Middle East or something, had a thing for American women. He'd fly them to his place in Iran or Saudi Arabia or wherever by the dozens for orgies. *Pff.* Those girls got paid thousands of dollars, wined and dined and treated like royalty for one weekend before he'd fly them home, so he could get a new batch."

"Whoa. Crazy."

"Right?" Brenda sipped from a highball glass then slid it toward the barkeep. "And I hear there's a guy here in town, like a muckety-muck higher-up at one of the banks that pays for young girls and keeps them at his house for like weeks, months at a time—"

Emma's heart lurched, and it was all she could do not to gasp.

"—pampering them and telling himself he's making them fall in love with him before he sleeps with them. As if he can justify what he's doing if he can tell himself it was mutual. Consensual."

She struggled to keep her face schooled, even. But…a banker who bought young girls?

Emma pulled a face she hoped looked scandalized instead of eager. Titillated instead of disgusted. Curious instead of desperate. "Really? A local banker? Which bank?"

Brenda glanced out at the floor where the women who'd been at the bar earlier were now giving lap dances and flirting with customers. "I don't know. Coulda been any of 'em. We get those bigwigs in here every now and then. They're good tippers."

"Hmm. I bet." Emma's mind was racing. A banker who bought young girls…

Warming to her topic, and clearly seeing she had piqued Emma's interest, Brenda added, "This other guy I heard about—I forget where he was from—New Orleans? Las Vegas? Anyway…he had a mama fetish. Liked older women and…"

Brenda continued, but Emma's mind was elsewhere. Her gaze sought out Jake's from across the room, and as if he sensed her attention, Jake looked up at that moment. His eyebrows drew together in a deep V of concern, and he rose from his table. Started toward her.

Emma's ears were buzzing with adrenaline and the thumping bass of the music from the speakers as she moved away from the bar. Her eyes were fixed on Jake's when a man about fifteen years her senior stepped in her path and stopped her with a hand on her hip.

"Hey, sweet cheeks. You work here?"

Emma recoiled a step. "Uh, no."

"Well, can I buy you a drink?" he asked, undeterred.

"No, you can't," Jake said, yanking the guy's shoulder to haul him away from Emma.

"Hey, pal, I saw her first." The guy tried to shrug out of Jake's grip. "Go find someone else."

"No, *pal*," Jake replied tightly. "I saw her first. As in twenty years ago. In high school. Before I married her." He snarled each phrase through clenched teeth. "Get away from my wife."

The older guy glanced at Emma as if for confirmation, and she nodded.

With a derisive snort, he threw his hands up and walked away. "Whatever, man."

"Well," Jake said grimly, watching the other man walk away. "I guess our cover, such as it was, is blown now."

"Doesn't matter." Emma squeezed his arm. "I think I found something."

Chapter 20

"A banker? Geez, Em, do you know how many banks there are in this city?" Jake swiped a hand down his face and groaned.

"Well, it's something! It's more than we had two hours ago!" she shot back. Pressing her lips in a thin line of frustration, she turned away to fasten her seat belt.

Jake gripped the steering wheel and squeezed his eyes shut, struggling to tamp down his own frustration and lingering disgust with the man who'd come on to Emma inside. "I know. I know. I wasn't criticizing." He faced her and furrowed his brow. Her pale blue eyes gleamed in the low light from the parking lot security lamps. "We've essentially narrowed the field of suspects from millions to thousands. Assuming your tip about this banker was right. And that he's still in town operating as usual. And assuming that's even him who has Fenn. And assuming that—"

"I get it, Jake. It's not much. It may be nothing. But…" She sighed and wrapped her arms around her middle. "It gives us something to follow up on tomorrow. Right now, are we going to try another strip club or one of those bars?" She pointed down the street where neon signs blinked in the windows of other establishments where questionable transactions could be happening.

Jake stared at her silently for long moments, increasingly uneasy with their mission tonight. Finally he whispered, "I wanted to rip that guy apart just for touching you. For the slimy way he looked at you."

Emma shivered. "Yeah, well… I had dressed the part."

Jake moved his gaze to the door of the strip bar and grunted.

She reached for his cheek and stroked a hand along his jaw. In a tone as soft and warm as a Carolina summer, she whispered, "My knight in shining armor."

Ducking out of the shoulder strap of her seat belt, she leaned over to brush a kiss on his cheek. Before she could move back to her side of the car, he caught her, cradling the back of her head with one large splayed hand and tracing the line of her chin, her jaw, with his other. Tugging her close, he pressed a deep kiss to her lips, full of longing and unspoken apology.

His body stirred, surging with desire and need. Far more than the overt sexuality inside the strip club, Emma spoke to everything male about him. He wanted to protect her, fill her, love her in a way that was more than carnal, more than something innate. She'd attracted and inspired him, excited and challenged him in ways he couldn't explain logically from the day they'd been assigned to the same history project in Mrs. LeBlanc's sophomore class.

She didn't resist him. In fact, she leaned in, moved nearer, raising both her hands to frame his face. She returned his kiss hungrily. When he tested the seam of her mouth, she parted her lips, and her tongue tangled with his. He lost himself in her, reacquainting himself with the woman he'd made love to thousands of times over the years, yet who, in this moment, tasted like something new and promising.

He reached under the filmy camisole to stroke her heated skin, more silky and smooth than the finest lingerie. Familiar, and yet it had been so long, too long since they'd made love.

Where had he gone so wrong? How could he have taken anything about her for granted? He missed her, missed so many things about her.

"Me, too," she whispered without moving her mouth from his.

He stilled, opening his eyes to gaze at her flushed face, wondering if he'd spoken his thoughts or if she'd just read his mind. Neither would surprise him.

She curled her fingers in the hair at his nape and drew him close again, drawing deeply on his lips.

Someone knocked on the passenger-side window and gave a crude sounding whoop. "Yeah, man! Get it!"

Jake jerked his head up and watched a guy—young and obviously sloppy drunk—stumble up to the door of the strip club, pausing long enough to give Jake a thumbs-up and a goofy grin. He pulled his mouth, his brow into an irritated scowl, until Emma rubbed the wrinkle at the bridge of his nose with her index finger.

"Forget him." With her hand on his cheek, she tugged his face back toward hers. She gave him one more kiss, then slid back to the passenger's bucket seat. "Let's go to a couple more places before we pack it in tonight, huh? See what we can find out about this banker?"

Jake drew a long slow breath, hating the slap of reality as it returned. As much as he wanted to take Emma to bed, reconnect with her on every level, sate the hunger clawing him, he still had a job to do.

Fenn was still gone, still in danger. They were still in

a rush to find their daughter before anything grievous happened to her, before the police or FBI found him and Emma and made them stand down. Jake cranked the engine of the rental car and nodded. "Right. Let's go."

Emma touched his arm, and sent him a look that said she was in analytic mode. "But not one of these dives. If we're looking for a banker, someone with money, maybe we should be at high-end places. The bars at the best hotels downtown. Swanky roof-top restaurants or nightclubs where designer drugs are sold and escorts flaunted, and the management looks the other way because their clientele have more money than God."

Jake let his gaze travel over her sultry attire. "But you're..."

Emma looked down at herself and twisted her mouth. "Hmm. Right." She reached for the sack of their regular clothes on the back seat. "You just drive. I'll come up with something appropriate by the time we reach downtown."

He shifted into Reverse to back out of the parking spot but paused long enough to kiss Emma once more. "By the way, babe, good work in there. You got us our first good lead in a long time. Well done."

She seemed stunned by his praise, a fact that shamed him. He resolved to tell her more often how much he valued and admired her work, her creativity, her contributions to the family. He completed the Y-turn, backing onto the street and gave her hand a squeeze. "Let's go find that banker."

Chapter 21

Fenn woke to the sound of the bedroom door being unlocked. Even as she blinked away the cobwebs of the restless night, Vince entered the room and approached the bed. Adrenaline jolted through her, obliterating the remnants of sleep and kicking her heartbeat into a frantic, scampering rhythm. She sat up and clutched the covers to her chest. Her breaths sawed from her, fast and shallow.

"Told you last night that the boss wanted you down for breakfast. Why aren't you ready?"

"I... I didn't h-have a way to s-set an alarm."

Vince gave her a deprecating look and pointed at the boxy clock on the nightstand. "What do you call that?"

She gave the clock a quick look. "Oh. I... I didn't know those things had alarms. I've always used my phone."

"Ignorant kids," Vince scoffed, then yanked hard on the covers and frowned again. "You haven't changed?"

Despite the provided dresser and closet full of clothes, Fenn had opted to sleep in the clothes she was wearing, stale as they were, and she was glad of it now as the huge intimidating man hovered over her. Her clothes might be dirty, but they were *her* clothes. Under the stale smell of airplanes and sour stink of nervous sweat, she could still detect a hint of the laundry detergent Mom used. Of home. Of the cedar that lined the drawers of *her* dresser in *her* room.

Vince consulted the clock by the bed. "You've got four minutes to get cleaned up and in some other clothes before I take you downstairs for your breakfast with the boss. So get crackin'. Either you wash and change clothes, or I'll do it for you."

His expression said he wasn't bluffing. Heart in her throat, Fenn darted for the closet and grabbed the first sundress she saw. Pulling clean panties and a sports bra from the dresser, she hurried into the bathroom to wash up, not having time to wait for the shower water to get warm. She was just pulling the dress on when Vince busted through the bathroom door and grabbed her wrist.

"Time's up. Let's go."

He led her down the hallway to a different set of stairs from those they'd used the night before. Not having been allowed to get shoes on, Fenn's feet sank into the plush pile of the carpeting on these stairs. They emerged in a room with tall glass windows that looked out on a manicured back garden, sprawling patio and sparkling swimming pool. Bill was already seated at a round glass table loaded with fresh fruits, pancakes, scrambled eggs, toast and jelly, bacon and sausage, and a pot that held a pale mush she assumed was oatmeal.

Bill stood, giving Vince a disgruntled look and sending Fenn a smile that left her decidedly uneasy. "Good morning, Layla. You're late."

Vince pressed his mouth in a taut line. "Apologies. She

was still in bed. I gave her time to wash and dress in some-thing clean."

Bill grunted and pulled out a chair for Fenn. She sat and avoided eye contact with Bill.

Vince left, leaving her alone with Bill. Fenn sat on her hands, shivering in the blast of air-conditioning on her wet hair and bare shoulders.

"Help yourself to whatever you'd like," Bill said with a wave of his hand over the bounty. "If you don't see what you want, let me know, and I'll do what I can to have it for you tomorrow."

Fenn should have been starving, but her gut was tied in knots. Fear precluded any form of appetite. "No, thanks. I'm not hungry."

"You sure?"

She bobbed a quick nod.

"Suit yourself," Bill said, tucking into a stack of pan-cakes. "How did you sleep?"

"I didn't. Not much anyway."

Bill glanced up, a tilt to his head. "The bed okay?"

Fenn shrugged.

"I can have a pillow topper put on the mattress if—"

"The bed's fine!" Fenn snapped, not knowing where the spurt of irritation strong enough to fuel her challenge to him came from. "What is your deal? Why are you being so nice to me? You bought me in some smarmy auction, and now you want to play house? Pretend I'm your niece or something? That's sick!"

Bill set down his fork. "It would be sick if I were to treat you like some trashy skank from the street." He paused, folding his hands over his belly. "Which is why I choose to take this time to get to know you. To court you." He flapped one hand. "Oh, I know. That's a stuffy old-fash-ioned term, but I like the idea of winning your affection through kind gestures, gracious hospitality…a little spoiling maybe, before we take our relationship to the next natural step."

He flashed her a lopsided grin she knew he intended to be coy, but it came off as creepy. Everything about Bill and his captive girlfriend fantasy was creepy. Even if she'd been his age and not young enough to be his daughter, his tactics were perverted.

Fenn shook her head and tried not to cry. Or vomit. Or lunge from her chair and scratch his eyes out. "Never. No amount of spoiling will make me want to do anything with you. You're vile."

Bill's eyes grew flinty, and his hands gripped the arms of his chair so tightly his knuckles turned white. He inhaled deeply. Exhaled. "Nevertheless, I paid good money for you, and you will do my bidding over the next several weeks."

"And if I don't?" she heard herself snap back.

Stop it! Shut up! What are you doing? a voice in her head screamed.

Bill rocked his head side to side as if releasing the tension in his neck. "Oh, you will. Vince will see to that." He picked up his fork again and stabbed another bite of pancake. "I will be gone until dinnertime. Work, you know? But Vince and my cook, Estelle, have been instructed to do everything possible to make you feel at home. Have whatever you want for lunch. Take a swim in the pool. Watch movies in my home theater. I have gym equipment in the basement you may use. A library. Hot tub. Tennis court."

"God," Fenn whispered. "You *are* rich. Where'd you get all your money?"

He sent her a flat look. "That is a rude question. But if you must know, I never married. I never had the expense of a gold-digging wife to drain my accounts, so I could spend it on a lifestyle I wanted."

Including bought women and kidnapped girls, Fenn

thought and clamped down on the words before she spoke them. She'd already rankled her host, and her time here would go better if she stayed on Bill's good side. For now. "How am I supposed to do any of that stuff—use the pool or movie theater—if your goon has me locked in the bedroom?"

Bill nodded. "Good point. I'll tell Vince you are free to explore the grounds at will. But know this, I have security cameras. The property is well secured, and Vince will be monitoring you in case you were harboring ideas of trying to leave the premises."

"Yeah, I get it. I'm your prisoner."

Bill's phone rang, and he lifted the mobile device from the table by his plate. "Excuse me. I need to take this."

She watched him stride into the next room then stared at the bowl of strawberries and cut melon. *His prisoner.* A renewed pang of homesickness and dread rung her stomach like a rag.

She missed her family, even missed school. Would she ever get back to Cameron Glen? To her house and parents and friends?

Her thoughts drifted back to the airport, to the woman in the car rental line. If it had been her mom, maybe rescue was on the way. Maybe she only had to hold on, stay safe, for a little while longer before the police, her parents, someone rescued her.

And maybe she'd imagined it all. Maybe fatigue and fear and wishfulness had conspired to conjure the thing she wanted to see most in the whole world. What were the chances her mom and dad could track her down, find her in this random rich guy's house?

Small as that chance was, Fenn clung to it. Prayed for it. She had to keep that hope alive and stay strong. No matter what, she would not, could not give up.

* * *

"This is hopeless," Emma said with a sigh. "We don't even know that she's still in the city, if she was ever here to begin with. Orlando could just have been the closest airport, cheapest ticket…or whatever. She could be anywhere, Jake!"

She turned and stared despondently out the window at the passing scenery—nameless buildings, crowded parking lots and low-hanging clouds heralding a late morning rainstorm.

After a late night of downtown hotel bar hopping, they'd gotten a precious few hours of sleep before heading back toward the bank crowded downtown to see what the upscale coffee shop breakfast crowd might reveal. Clearly the trip was a long shot, but they hoped by lunchtime bartenders or waitresses would share secrets about their nightlife clientele.

Emma watched one billboard after another for car dealerships, fast food and the plethora of banks pass her window like floats in an advertising parade. Pain sat on her chest, sapping her energy and crushing her hope like the dark clouds on the horizon blotted out the sun. "Where do we even start?"

"I don't know, babe. But I swear, I'm not leaving without Fenn."

A crushing reality settled over Emma, and she whispered, "Even if it costs you Turner Construction? How long can the company run without you there? It could take weeks to find her. Months!"

He sent her a bleak look, lifted one shoulder. "I guess we'll see."

"And what about Lexi? While we're down here searching for Fenn, our other daughter doesn't have either parent tucking her in at night or reassuring her she's safe and loved."

He sighed. "She has her grandparents and Nanna, her aunts and uncles."

"It's not the same, and you know it."

"Are you saying you want to go home? You could go back to Cameron Glen, and I'll stay here to—"

"No," Emma interrupted, her tone fierce. "We do this together. A team. Isn't that what we agreed last night? Didn't you mean it?"

"Yes, I meant it, but if you're worried about Lexi..." Jake turned up a palm and buzzed his lips in frustration. "I don't know how we're supposed to balance the company and Lexi while we search for Fenn, but I can't give up on our Button. I won't. I blame myself for her leaving. If I'd been a better father, a better husband..." He stopped, swallowing hard as his eyes grew moist.

"Don't, Jake. Don't take this all on yourself. We share the blame. And we'll figure it out." When he dabbed at his eyes, she glanced out the side window, giving him a semiprivate moment to regain his composure.

She watched a flock of birds settle on a power line, read the whimsical slogan on a billboard for Taraton Bank, glanced idly at the Fiat that passed them. And frowned. Something unsettling niggled in her brain. At first she dismissed it as a general pessimism born from her conversation with Jake. Something about Lexi? No. The construction company? Closer. The feeling had come after—

She gasped. "Jake!"

"What?" His tone reflected the same alarm that hers had.

"Pull over. Or...or turn around. I think I'm onto something!"

Jake didn't question Emma. When she instructed him to get off the highway and go back the way they came, retrace their steps, he did. Even she couldn't say for sure what she was looking for, but he trusted her instincts. Any clue or hunch was better than the nothing they'd been working with.

"How far up am I going before I turn around?" He glanced at her and found her leaning forward in her seat, her head swiveling from one side of the road to the other, searching for…something. "Em?"

"I saw something that…stirred a memory or felt off. I can't explain exactly, but I've heard it said that when we quiet our mind, our subconscious speaks to us. Something we missed rises to the top and…" She gasped again and pointed out the windshield. "There! Taraton Bank!"

Jake wrinkled his brow and guided the car to the shoulder of the road where he stopped with the billboard in front of them. "What about it?"

She grabbed a pen and the rental car receipt from the glove box and wrote on it. N.O.T.A.R.A.T.

Something hot flowed through Jake, and his pulse accelerated. "What is that?"

"If zero is substituted for an *o* and the *at* symbol is A. T.—Taraton backward is Notarat!" she exclaimed. "As in NØtar@11Ø5! That woman I met last night said she'd heard of a bank bigwig who liked young girls. Virgins. What if NØtar@11Ø5 is someone at Taraton Bank?"

Jake drove them back to their scruffy motel room with haste. Even before they were ensconced in their room, Emma was doing an internet search and making phone calls from the burner phone, trying to track down the hierarchy and members of the board of directors at Taraton Bank. Getting a list of names was simple enough, but weeding out who might be their pedophile was another matter altogether.

"Well, we can eliminate the women," Emma said, crossing those names off the paper-and-pen list she'd made. She ripped the list in half and gave one piece to Jake. "You track down these people, see what you can learn."

Jake pulled a face. "And how, exactly, are we supposed to figure out who our creep is? We can hardly call them up cold and ask, 'Are you the pervert who bid in an illegal auction on the dark web and purchased our daughter's virginity?'"

"True." She bit her bottom lip and groaned her frustration. "But…we can build profiles on them all. See what shakes out. I know it's a long shot, babe. But right now, it's the best lead we've got."

Jake paced from one side of the room to the other, wearing a path in the thin motel carpet. When she spun to face him, her eyes bright, she said, "Ben. Maybe Ben can get something we can't if he knows what he's looking for."

"You want him to hack into the bank's computer system?" Jake shook his head. "That'll get him flagged by the FBI real quick."

"No, but surely he knows more ways to dig up personal information or find home addresses or…hell, I don't know!" Her agitation reverberated in her voice, and Jake moved close to rest a hand on each of her shoulders.

"Deep breath, babe. We're getting closer. I can feel it. We just have to hold it together a little while longer." He kissed her forehead, and Emma gave a shuddering exhale, closed her eyes and leaned into him. "Your idea about Ben is a good one," he said, wrapping her in a hug. "I'll call your brother and have him ask Ben for his help. Meanwhile, let's start making our way down the list and see what we get."

When he made a move to back away, Emma grabbed the front of his shirt and drew him back. She closed the distance between them and circled his waist with her arms. "Hold me, Jake. For just another minute."

In an instant, the tone of the hug changed. No longer was he calming his antsy research partner. With her quiet plea, her embrace became a balm, a restoration, centering as they prepared to head once more into the fray. Emma was his home base. His harbor in a stormy life of trouble and uncertainty. His anchor.

And God, he'd missed her. Missed this...this connection.

We used to be a team...

Her words from earlier echoed in his brain. And he began to understand.

If he'd not gotten defensive, would he have realized the deeper truth of what she was explaining then, and not let the discussion devolve into an argument?

Too soon, Emma was backing from his embrace and said, "We need a cover story, something to explain why we're asking so many questions without tipping our hand."

Jake bobbed his head. "I'm listening."

"Well..." She gazed out the motel room's plate glass window to the parking lot for a moment, her mouth twisted in a thoughtful moue before continuing. "People love to talk about themselves if they think it makes them look good. Or it's for a positive thing...like an award. Could we say they've been nominated for some civic award, and we need personal information for the awards committee to review? Or tell them we're doing a profile on them for a 'top businessmen of the year' feature for a regional magazine?"

"Worth a shot."

And for the next two hours, after he'd gotten Ben started on an internet deep dive as well, they worked, calling, running search after search online, asking questions when they finally got someone on the line.

It was approaching noon when Ben hit pay dirt. "Ralston William Kingsley, the CFO at Taraton Bank, whose birthday is 11/05/1964, uses the password NØtar@11Ø5 on more than one social media account," Ben told them, an exuberance in his tone. "His home address is in a posh area in the suburbs outside Orlando. Got a pen?"

Jake grabbed the motel pen from the bedside stand. His hand was shaking from adrenaline, renewed hope. "Go."

With the help of the Google Maps app on the burner phone, Emma navigated across Orlando toward the address Ben had found for Ralston Kingsley. When they reached their last turn, they found themselves in a neighborhood for which the term *wealthy* was an understatement. The homes were spaced well-apart from each other, and every mansion was bigger and more elaborate than the next. Many had privacy walls, security gates and call boxes at the end of their driveway. Emma goggled at the homes, while her heart thumped an anxious cadence. Was Fenn being held in one of these exorbitant homes? And if she was, how did she and Jake reach her, get her out?

Jake's thoughts were clearly running along the same lines, because he sighed and flipped up his palm. "The farther we drive into this community, the bigger the houses get and the better the security surrounding the homes. Walls, gates, guards… We won't be able to just stroll up to the front door and be invited in."

"So how do we get inside? How do we find out if Fenn is being held inside Kingsley's fortress?" She bit down on her already raw and overchewed bottom lip as she mentally scrambled for something…anything that might get them inside. A lie, another pretense, obviously, because *We're Fenn's parents and we're here to take her home and have you arrested for kidnapping and rape* wasn't going to work. "Is there a way to circumvent the security systems? The cameras?"

Jake shrugged and slowed the car as they came upon a plumber's utility van driving slowly and braking at every driveway, clearly searching for the address of his service call. "I don't know. If I installed these high-end systems in the homes we build, I might have a clue, but we contract that work out. And just getting past the perimeter isn't going to be enough."

The plumber slowed almost to a stop, stuck his arm out the window and waved Jake around him. Pulling carefully into the oncoming lane, Jake passed the van and continued down the block.

"That's 3405," Emma said, pointing to the first house number she'd seen. "Kingsley's is still a few blocks."

Jake passed a mail truck, a dog walker and an older couple on bicycles before they got to the homes numbered in the 4800s. He slowed as they approached Kingsley's house, 4835. A ten-foot-high brick wall surrounded the multi-level, Spanish-inspired manse that could just be glimpsed through the iron gate across the driveway.

Tension and frustration twisted inside Emma. She wanted to leap from the car and shout for Fenn. She wanted to scale that wall and bang on the windows and doors until her hands were bleeding, if that's what it took to get her daughter back. Instead, she dug her fingernails into the leather seat of the rental car and choked back the scream that burgeoned inside her. *Hold it together. For Fenn's sake, don't lose it until she's safe again.*

Jake drove on, and Emma whipped her head toward him. "That was it. Where are you going?"

"You really want me to park in front of the place and draw attention before we have any clue how we're going to get inside to look for her? Em, we don't even know if our theory is right. We could have the wrong Taraton bank executive or the wrong Ralston Kingsley—"

He fell silent as she shot him a look expressing her doubt that there were two Ralston Kingsleys in the Orlando metro area.

"Okay, okay." He waved off his previous statement. "We have to step up our thinking. What are we going to do to get in there?"

"Jake, maybe it's time we just call the police and get them out here?"

"When we know for sure she's here, yes. But now, with no proof? Just our hunches? And think about how we got Kingsley's address. Ben hacked the man's accounts. So think about what happens in that scenario if we're wrong about Kingsley?"

"But, Jake—"

"The FBI has likely told local police to be looking for us, expecting our SOS. As soon as we pull the trigger and bring in the cops, we'll be arrested for all that hampering-an-investigation stuff Officer Smith mentioned." He shook his head. "No. It's too soon. We have to get in there and find her first." He stopped for a stop sign and pinched the bridge of his nose. "So we're back to square one, which is how to get inside. Preferably with the assent of someone on the inside to eliminate the whole trespassing factor..." A heavy sigh. "In theory."

Not leaving the intersection where they were stopped, Jake stared straight ahead, while the muscle at the corner of his eye twitched. "If I were in some kind of law enforcement instead of just a construction worker and business owner—"

Emma's heart squeezed, and she covered his hand with hers. "Don't say 'just.' You're good at what you do. The company is valuable to the community. Don't minimize that, Jake."

"But right now, it's of little help to Fenn—" His facial expression shifted suddenly from despair to intrigue and inspiration.

"Jake? What? Do you have an idea?"

He whipped the car in a sharp U-turn and headed back

the direction they'd come, much faster than he'd driven this road earlier. When he passed Kingsley's house, he didn't so much as give the estate a glance.

"Jake? What are you—"

"Hang on, Emma. I don't know if this will work, but…" His gaze swung from one driveway to another as they backtracked, until he muttered "bingo" under his breath and pulled the car in behind the plumbing company's utility van they'd passed earlier. Without a word to her, Jake slammed the car into Park and hurried out. The plumber, who was at the open cargo end of his van, glanced up as Jake rushed toward him. Not wanting to be left out of whatever Jake was scheming, Emma joined her husband as he conversed with the plumber.

"…but I need a way to get inside and have a look around—"

The man's hands shot up, palms toward Jake. "No. Sorry, bud. I don't want any part of anything shady—"

"It's not shady. We're not here to hurt anyone or do anything illegal, we just have to know if our daughter is there!"

The plumber continued to shake his head. "Look, I feel for you, man. But I can't get involved with something that—"

"Do you have children, sir?" Emma cut in. "A daughter?"

The man frowned and shifted his gaze to her. He stared silently for a moment before answering, "No. I have three boys. Five, seven and ten."

Emma nodded, her eyes filling with tears. "And I know you love them, would do anything for them."

"Of course I would. That's not the poi—"

"If it were your child, one of your boys, or if you had a fifteen-year-old daughter that had been kidnapped and sex trafficked, wouldn't you want a citizen in a position to make a difference, someone who could *help save them* to get involved?" She wasn't sure what Jake's plan was, but if Jake needed this man's assistance for his plan to work, she'd beg the plumber on her knees for help.

"I'm not asking you personally to do anything except loan me your truck and your coveralls, for a couple hours at most. I just need a way inside."

The man seemed to falter, the stubborn lines of refusal in his face softening.

Jake reached in his back pocket and opened his wallet to the cash they'd gotten from the ATM earlier. Extracting a few bills, he showed them to the plumber. "I'll give you five hundred dollars right now for use of your van, your cap and coveralls for the next two hours."

The plumber's eyebrows shot up, his interest clearly piqued.

"You can take out whatever tools you need for this job first." He waved a hand toward the house whose driveway they stood in. "Meantime, you can hold on to my credit card, my driver's license—whatever you want—as collateral. I will bring your van and uniform back in two hours. I swear it."

The plumber, whose coveralls' name patch declared him to be "Chris," rubbed his chin. His mouth compressed in a thin line of exasperation, and he narrowed a dark look on Jake. "Two hours."

"Two hours. Maybe less."

With a harsh exhale, the man bobbed a nod. "Deal."

Chapter 22

"Jake, damn it, no! I thought we had an understanding!" Emma grated two minutes later as she watched her husband, now wearing the plumber's cap and coveralls, march toward the driver's side of the utility van. "I'm coming with you! Do *not* shut me out of this!"

"No way, Em. You're staying here." He firmly pushed her back from the door and shut it behind him after climbing in.

Tears of fury and frustration burned in her eyes, and she tried to open the van door, only to have him snatch it back and lock it from the inside. "You're staying here, where it's safe."

She growled and fisted her hands. "Do not pat me on the head and push me away as if I'm some child needing to be shielded. Fenn is my daughter, too, and we agreed to do this together, to find her *together*! Both of us! I need to be there."

"Not for this. If I'm to have even a remote chance of

making Kingsley believe that I am really a plumber, there on an emergency call, I need to go alone. Plumbers don't bring their wives to calls." He cranked the engine.

"Jake!"

"How would we explain your being there? You don't figure in the plan."

"Because you didn't *share* your crazy plan with me! You just plowed ahead without any input from me *like you always do*!" The anger and tension inside her torqued tighter with every word, every move he made to desert her.

"Emma, I don't have time to fight about this. I promised Chris I'd have his truck back in—"

"Don't do this, Jake," she pleaded, her voice no more than a rasp now as old familiar feelings of betrayal, distance, abandonment swelled like a rising tide to drown her. "I swear if you shut me out now, I'll—"

"Think about it, Em. I need you out here in case something goes sideways. I don't know what I'll find. I don't know what will go down, but if something happens to me, even if I just get arrested for some reason, I need to know that our daughters still have one parent free, alive, able to finish raising them."

She gasped. "You bastard! Don't you use the girls as an excuse to justify your breaking a promise to me, for your continuing to leave me out and push me away!"

He shifted into Reverse and backed out of the driveway. He gave her one last stubborn, unrepentant look as he pulled away and headed back down the street to Kingsley's home.

Emma tipped her head back and roared to the heavens with her fury, her hurt…her fear. Jake was headed into an unknown situation *alone*…damn him! She'd thought she'd gotten through to him in recent days about his excluding her, shutting her out. During this search and rescue mission especially, like a microcosm of their marriage, they needed to be a team, support each other, work in tandem to find Fenn. But *noooo*! As usual, Jake left her out of the loop as he dreamed up his scheme and shut the door on her entirely in the implementation of said plan.

Hands balled at her sides, she paced the driveway of a stranger, steaming. She'd thought she'd made progress toward making Jake understand her feelings about being pushed away and shut out. But here she was again on the outside while Jake fought battles alone that should be a joint effort. She could have hidden in the van, snuck around the outside of the house, kept watch on the street... something! But he hadn't even given her a chance. And that stung. Deeply.

Did he not think she could contribute something valuable? Maybe, if given the chance, she could have offered insights, or alternatives that would bolster and improve his idea. Maybe she could've given the scheme a better chance of success.

Wiping tears of rage and crushing disappointment from her eyes, Emma stomped back to the end of the circular driveway where they'd parked the rental car. And discovered Jake hadn't left the keys with her. Intentionally, she'd bet. She snorted sourly. If he thought he'd keep her isolated by stranding her here without a car, he'd thought wrong.

Hiking her purse onto her shoulder, Emma set out down the posh neighborhood street—if you could call homes spaced a quarter to half a mile apart a neighborhood—and started walking the direction Jake had driven the plumber's utility van. Anger and determination fueled her. Jake might be shutting her out, but she would not sit back and do nothing. She would find her own way inside the banker's home to rescue Fenn. She would take matters into her own hands, and when she had Fenn back safely, she would move forward with the divorce. Jake had proven just now that nothing had changed. His promises of cooperation and team work were hot air. And the pain of that truth gouged her heart.

She was done. Finished. So over it.

She was so tired of this hurt and feeling of isolation. If Jake couldn't commit to a marriage where they were a team, then she was done with Jake.

Jake parked the utility van down the street a little way from Kingsley's house and, on foot, walked the perimeter of the tall brick wall, searching for the key to his plan. His entire ruse hinged on finding the main valve shutoff to the mansion from the city water supply. Well, that and counting on Kingsley to know a whole lot less about plumbing than he did about banking.

After a few minutes of poking around in bushes and pampas grass, he located the box that housed the utility knob. He muscled it off and rose to dust his hands on the coveralls.

That done, he approached the iron gate at the end of Kingsley's driveway. Pushed the call button. Once. Twice. Then as he was reaching to jab it a third time, a gruff voice asked, "What?"

"Hi, yeah… Chris Jones with Greenway Plumbing. The city hired us to track down the source of a leak that's causing pressure drops in the city pipes. I need to come in and check your plumbing. Are you Mr. Kingsley?"

"No. Go away," the voice said over a soft crackle of static.

"But I have to—"

The sound of a click and silencing of the static told Jake the man was gone. He pushed the button again.

"I said, Go a—"

"Just check your sink, any faucet, and tell me if you have water," he blurted before the gruff man could cut him off.

Silence. Then, "Hang on."

Jake tapped his thumbs against the steering wheel of the van and waited impatiently for an answer.

Then with a click and a buzz, the iron gate opened with the creak of rusty metal.

A mixture of elation and anxiety stirred in Jake's gut. He'd earned entrance to the home, but how did he get free from observation to search for Fenn?

Emma was damp with sweat by the time she reached Kingsley's driveway. She peeked through the iron gate and spotted the plumber's van parked at the front door.

I'll be damned. Jake got inside. But inside could mean he was in trouble. What if the kidnappers figured out he was Fenn's father and had hurt him? Killed him? Or hurt Fenn?

She gnawed a fingernail and walked back out to the street, mulling her options. Climb the rock wall somehow? Conjure a ruse like Jake's to be admitted?

She stalked the stretch of road for several minutes until a small hatchback with a pizza store's logo magnet on the door slowed and crept into the driveway.

Emma's heart leaped, and she hustled to the small car before the driver could reach the security call box.

"Hi. Um, can you tell me who the order is for?"

The delivery driver, a young woman with short blond hair, who didn't appear much older than Fenn, hesitated, then angled the box and read, "No name on here. Just the address. Medium pineapple and bacon pizza with extra cheese. Total cost fifteen twenty-seven."

The hair on Emma's nape stood up. "Pineapple and bacon?"

The young delivery driver shrugged. "That's what it says. Doesn't sound too appetizing to me but…" Another shrug.

"But it's Fenn's favorite," she whispered on a shaky exhale.

Once again, the delivery driver reached for the intercom button.

"Wait!" Emma cried, trying to maintain her composure when everything inside her said she'd just received the proof she needed that her daughter was inside. With trembling hands, she dug out her wallet and handed the girl a twenty-dollar bill. "I'll take it inside."

The girl frowned. "I can't give you someone else's—"

"It's my daughter's. The order is for my daughter, and… I'll take it inside…to her."

"I'm not supposed to—"

"Five hundred dollars," Emma blurted, remembering the thing that had swayed Chris the Plumber. She'd offer any sum that would facilitate getting her daughter home.

The delivery driver barked a laugh. "What?"

Clearing the nerves, the impatience, the newfound hope from her throat and struggling to stay composed and appear assured, Emma said, "I'll give you five hundred dollars for your hat, name tag and the chance to take that pizza to the door."

She wanted to ask the teenager to swap shirts with her, since the golf-style shirt the teenager was wearing was imprinted with the delivery pizza store's logo and clearly completed the uniform. But women exchanging shirts in the street was much more conspicuous than Jake simply putting on Chris's coveralls.

The girl gaped at her. "Are you for real? Five hundred dollars?"

Emma nodded, improvising. "It's, uh…part of a surprise for my daughter's birthday. I'll take the pizza inside for you, and…when I'm finished with the cap and name tag, I'll bring them back to you at the store."

The girl chuckled gleefully as she unfastened the name

badge that read, Sarah. "Hells yeah. That's like two weeks' pay and tips for me."

Sighing her relief, Emma dug the cash out of her wallet, then handed it over while receiving the hat and name tag with her other hand.

As she tucked the money in her pocket, Sarah flashed a sly grin. "Deal's done now, but…truth is, I'd have done it for one hundred."

"Huh, well…" Emma secured the hat on her own head and reached for the pizza. "Life is expensive. Perhaps you should put today's windfall into savings for a rainy day?"

Sarah offered the pizza through her open car window. "You sound like my mom."

"Smart woman, your mom. Listen to her. Appreciate her."

The delivery driver gave a little wave as she backed out of the drive onto the street, and Emma turned to the intercom. Pressed the button.

"Yes?" a grumpy voice barked over the crackle of static.

"Pizza delivery."

"Pizza? No one here ordered a pizza."

Panic spread through Emma at the thought of her plan being shot down so quickly. "Wait! Are you sure? This is 4835, right? Maybe your kids ordered it?"

"I don't have…" She heard a low curse then. "Fine. I'll meet you at the door, but I'm busy so make it quick."

Emma's pulse jumped, and her hope swelled as, with a creak of iron and whir of small motors the gate opened to allow her on the property. That was a start, but now she had to scheme her way inside. At the front door, she rang the bell, and through the window panels on either side of the door, she saw a tall, burly man approaching.

When the door was yanked open, the large man with a buzz cut loomed over her, cash in his hand. Emma's stomach roiled as she laid eyes on the man. Was this Ralston

Kingsley, the ass who'd bought Fenn? He may have already physically defiled and emotionally shredded her daughter. Rage and disgust jammed her voice.

The brutish man cast puzzled glance past her, frowned. Was he looking for her delivery car? Maybe. If needed, she could bluff through an explanation why she had none. Fortunately, he seemed eager to get rid of her. He simply tossed a bill toward her and grabbed the pizza box, snarling, "There. Now get lost."

He took a step back, and Emma watched as if in slow motion as the front door swung toward her, closing. With a gasp, she swung up a stiff arm to block the door from shutting. "Wait! I just…"

The door opened again to the man glowering down at her. "What now?"

"I just…" Her mind scrambled, and like a gift, words formed on her tongue that made a modicum of sense. "Can I use your bathroom?"

The guy's eyebrows snapped together. "No." Again he tried to shut the door, and this time Emma put her shoulder into blocking it.

"Please, it's an emergency! I—"

"No!" He pushed on the door, and she pushed back, determined to get inside. Then shoved at him, trying to get past.

"Look, lady, you're not—"

Remembering the tactic too-wily-for-her-own-good Lexi had discovered and frequently used to get her way, she threw a hand to her mouth and faked a retch. "But I ate something bad and…oh God, I'm going to be sick. I—" Another fake retch. And suddenly the bulldog of a man was leaping back as if to avoid being vomited on. *Noone ever* wanted to be vomited on, and the mere suggestion it could happen swayed people to instantly give way. Emma seized her brief advantage and shoved inside, making a beeline toward the back of the house, the most likely location of a bathroom.

With another scorching curse, the man shouted, "Second door on the right!"

Finding the correct room, Emma ducked inside and closed the door behind her. Shut her eyes. Tried to calm the tremors that started in her core and soon caused her whole body to shake.

Inhaling deeply, she took precious seconds to plan her next move. She was inside. Good. But gaining the opportunity to search the house undetected was an entirely different matter. As soon as it was discovered she wasn't who she claimed, wasn't really sick, she'd be kicked out. Or worse. She didn't waste the time or negative energy entertaining what "worse" might entail.

Cracking the bathroom door open quietly a few moments later, she peeked through the sliver of space toward the entry hall. The big guy stood there still dividing his glower between the hall she'd just hustled down and the rooms in the opposite direction. Then a quick glance up the wide staircase opposite the front door. She heard a crash, and with a snarl, Big Guy pivoted to hurry to the other end of the house. This was her chance.

Wasting no time, Emma slipped off her shoes to silence her footsteps and stepped from the bathroom to start her search of the house.

Jake strained to listen as Kingsley's assistant answered the door, concerned his cover could be blown and curious whether he might gain any insights or opportunities that would work in his favor. He needed to shake the burly "assistant" if he was going to look for Fenn. And then he'd heard a familiar voice.

Emma! Damn it, what was she doing? He'd told her to stay put, to stay safe, to stand by in case…

Now, not only did he have to maintain his plumber ruse, but he had to ensure that Emma was safe for whatever machination she was up to. And find Fenn.

Gritting his teeth, he slammed his hand down on the kitchen table in frustration, rattling the waiting place settings there. Which gave him an idea.

If he could distract Kingsley's man, draw him away from Emma…

He moved to the cabinets and tugged a pan out onto the floor with a loud clang. As hoped, the beefy guy with the buzz cut stormed back into the kitchen and tossed a pizza box on the table. "What the hell's going on in here?"

If he'd looked peeved before, the guy looked full-blown furious and unsettled now.

"I'm sorry. I was looking to see if there was a pan I could catch the water from the J-pipe with, and I dropped—"

"Just…hurry up and get it done," he growled. "I want you out of here."

Jake glanced at the pizza box on the table. Emma had delivered a pizza? Was there something here he needed to follow up on, something she was trying to tell him? Had she dropped off the pizza and left?

Jake nodded toward the box, from which fragrant garlic and yeast aromas wafted. "Smells good. Feel free to have your lunch. I don't want to interrupt that."

"It's not my lunch. It'll keep." With a dark glare, he folded his arms over his chest and resumed his vigilance, though now his attention seemed divided. He glanced back toward the entry hall time and again.

Jake's pulse kicked up. Did that mean Emma was inside?

"Is there a problem back there?" Jake asked as he settled on the floor in front of the open sink cabinets and flicked a hand toward the door.

He grunted. "Not for long. The pizza chick is in the bathroom barfing."

Barfing? But she'd seemed fine earlier...

The security guy's frown deepened, and he cursed. "Without water, the toilet ain't gonna flush, is it?"

When the assistant grumbled and started back toward the front of the house, Jake called, "Actually, it will. Once. The tank, you know." His comment slowed the guy for a moment, but when he turned again toward the front door, Jake added loudly, "Before you go... I—can you help me with this? The knob is stuck and...well, I can't do any of the checks until—"

A disgruntled frown dented the security guy's brow as he returned. "What's stuck?"

What, indeed? He'd blurted the first thing that had come to mind, stalling. Jake gritted his teeth, working hard not to appear rattled. *Hurry, Emma! Whatever you have in mind, do it quick.* He wasn't sure how long he could bluff and keep Kingsley's assistant distracted. But if it meant protecting Emma, giving her the time she needed to search for Fenn, he'd find a way—any way—to keep the guard occupied and buy Emma time.

Emma checked the hall at the top of the stairs in both directions before she chose to head to the right and tip-toed to the first door. "Fenn?" she whispered, then a little louder, "Fenn?"

The room, apparently a home office of some kind, was empty. She quickly moved to the next door and switched on the lights. A bathroom. "Fenn?" She checked behind the shower curtain, just in case. Nothing.

As she turned to leave the bathroom, her own reflection in the mirror over the sink spooked her. She barely caught the yelp that rose in her throat. Damn, she was tense!

Pressing a hand to her racing heart, Emma continued

down the hall, checking the next room and the next to no avail. In her brain, a clock was ticking. She knew she had precious few seconds before the behemoth watchman from the front door got wise to her ploy and came after her.

When the last door also revealed nothing but a room piled with junk and her soft calls gained no response, Emma retraced her steps and headed the opposite direction down the hall.

She noticed immediately that all the doors but one were at least slightly ajar. Maximizing her time, she headed straight for the closed door, sending silent prayers to God to help her find her daughter.

She heard noises coming from this room, voices. And music. A television maybe? Holding her breath, Emma inched the door open and peered inside.

Hyperaware of house noises that might signal Vince returning—or Bill—Fenn stiffened when a subtle creak drifted over the movie soundtrack. She'd decided after breakfast that morning that two days of captivity was two days too long. She needed to find a way to catch Vince unaware, incapacitate him and get away from this place. Her first step needed to be studying the security system. Finding a way to work around it. But how? She needed to observe Bill coming and going, see what Vince did to secure the house, try to catch him punching in the codes…

She'd spent the long night before, locked in the bedroom, staring at the ceiling and working up the nerve to venture out for her first exploration. But what if Vince caught her? She'd need a weapon against him. Searching the other rooms for a weapon was her first task. Her gut had turned and guilt had rampaged through her. She hoped it didn't come to violence, but…yes. She now thought that maybe, in the moment, she could attack Vince. Or Bill. If it was self-defense. If she had to…

Now, hearing someone in the hall outside, moving around close by, Fenn moved to the wall so she'd be behind the door if it opened. She clutched with both hands a golf club she'd found in the junk room down the hall.

The doorknob moved. The door opened. Slowly.

"Fenn?"

Shock rolled through her, immobilizing her for a moment. Was she dreaming? Was this—

Then it came again, "Fenn!"

And her mom stepped into the room.

Tears gushed to her eyes in an instant, and she choked out a relieved, "Mom!"

Chapter 23

Jake lay on his back, head under the kitchen sink where he fiddled with the J-trap. He'd bought a little time getting the security guy to crawl under the sink and twist the obviously-not-stuck shutoff valve. Now, faking other checks to the PVC pipes, Jake studied Kingsley's assistant. The man fidgeted and frowned and kept glancing back toward the foyer. When the guy touched his chest with a quick pat, Jake noticed the lump there. And his pulse tripped. *Gun.*

Hell, the risk just went up tenfold.

Finally with a huff, the security guy grumbled, "Stay here. I have to evict a pizza girl."

Jake rolled out, calling, "Before you go—"

Mouth pressed in a taut line, the guy stopped and glowered at Jake. "What now?"

"This is clearly not the problem area. Can you show me to the laundry room?"

"In a minute." He turned.

"But the sooner I finish, the sooner I'm outta your hair."

Mr. Buzz Cut seemed to consider that, but then pointed toward a door at the other side of the room. "Utility room is back there. Can't miss it. I'll be back in a minute."

"But I need you to sho—" Jake started. But his chaperone stalked away without turning.

"Damn it!" Jake muttered and jabbed a hand through his hair. He had a choice. Sneak toward the back of the house, hoping to get some searching in before Kingsley's man returned, or follow the surly guard and be ready to protect Emma if needed.

He heard an annoyed grunt from the front of the house, a door opening and slamming, a dark curse.

Squeezing the wrench in his hand, Jake hurried toward the foyer. All his instincts told him Emma was in danger, and he only had seconds to find her before Kingsley's man did.

Emma gasped and dashed to her daughter, relief and love hitting so hard, her knees nearly buckled.

"Fenn! Oh, baby, are you all right? Did they hurt you? Did they…t-touch you?" She kept her voice low as she clutched her daughter in a fierce hug.

"I'm o-okay."

"Oh, thank God. Oh, Fenn!" She pressed a dozen kisses to her daughter's head and cheeks, then held her at arm's length to do a quick visual survey for injury or evidence of abuse.

"M-Mom, I'm sorry. I'm so s-sorry."

The sight of her daughter's brown eyes, bright with tears and remorse, broke her heart. And filled her with unconstrained joy. She framed Fenn's face with both hands and whispered, "We'll talk about what you did later. For now, know that I love you. Okay?"

Fenn nodded, tears pouring down her cheeks.

An angry shout sounded from a distance beyond the

door. Fenn tensed, and a whimper escaped her throat. "That's Vince. Mom, he's coming!"

"Okay, don't panic," Emma said, as much to herself as to Fenn. "We're gonna get Dad and get out of here."

"Dad's here?" Fenn's tone warmed, as if more confident for knowing her father was close.

The reminder that Jake was nearby bolstered Emma's nerves as well. With a nod to Fenn, she guided Fenn farther from the bedroom door. In the adjoining bathroom, she pulled the burner cell phone from her back pocket and brought up the only contact she'd saved to the new mobile device. She dialed Officer Smith and prayed he would answer. One ring. Two.

He answered with a gruff, "Yeah?" and, without preamble, Emma blurted, "It's Emma Turner. We found her. I'm with my daughter."

"You found her? How?"

"Forget the *how*. *Where* is what's important right now." She rattled off Kingsley's name and address. "That's where we found her. We're still here, intending to get Fenn out and all of us away from here, but we sure would like some police backup."

"Hell, lady! Do you understand what you've—"

"Just send help!" she said, her volume rising along with her impatience. "Local police or FBI or whoever, but fast!" She hung up and jammed the phone in her back pocket again. Focusing on Fenn, she asked in a rush, "Where is Ralston Kingsley? The homeowner. The banker?"

"You mean Bill? He went to work. Or that's where he said—"

"Okay. So not here? That's good."

"But Vince…"

As if summoned when she spoke his name, Vince shouted, "Layla!"

Heavy thudding footsteps warned of his approach, and Emma shoved Fenn behind her. When the bedroom door opened with enough force to crash against the wall, Fenn gasped and crowded closer to Emma.

"Where are you?" he growled, as thumps and bangs told of his violent search of the bedroom and closet.

When his towering bulk filled the bathroom door, Emma shivered. Merciless ice gleamed in his eyes, and his expression declared war. His only acknowledgment of finding Emma with Fenn was a narrowing of his glare and a low scoff.

As he advanced on them, Emma stood as tall as she could, squaring her shoulders and setting her jaw. She had no idea how she was going to protect Fenn against this giant, but she knew he'd have to come through her to reach Fenn. She'd fight him with everything she had.

"Lady, your comin' here was a mistake."

Rage and disgust for what this man had put Fenn through overrode fear and discretion. Emma lifted her chin and grated, "No. The mistake was when you and your boss kidnapped my daughter for your sick predilections."

He grabbed a handful of her shirtfront and bent to stick his face in hers. "You know I gotta deal with you now. Gotta make sure you can't talk, can't go to the cops."

Fenn whimpered. "No! Don't hurt her! Please!"

"Shut up!" Vince barked, and with a swift thrust of his other arm, he shoved Fenn so hard she stumbled backward.

Emma saw red. "You bastard!" She launched herself at him, fingers curled like claws as she swung and scratched and screamed, "Don't you touch her! You monster!"

Viselike hands grabbed her wrists, restraining her, and he shook her so hard her teeth clattered together.

Until suddenly she heard an "oof," and he released her. Spun away with a growl of rage.

Emma blinked, trying to clear her muddled brain, her blurred vision. As she groped behind her to find Fenn, her daughter released a bloodcurdling scream. "Nooo! Daddy!"

Pain shot through Jake's skull as his head hit the wall, snapped back by the force of the behemoth's shove. His legs buckled, and he slumped to the floor. Black spots filled his vision, but he wielded the wrench blindly and swung toward the shadowy shape of his opponent. He heard Fenn scream, tried to tell her to run, but his throat didn't work.

Then another, more feral-sounding scream reached him, and as he squinted, his sight returning, he watched Emma jump on the huge man's back.

"Don't—" he shouted, but it came out a rasp. Adrenaline surged and fueled him as he clambered to his feet. *Defend Emma. Save Fenn.*

"Vince, no! Please!" Fenn sobbed.

He'd just gotten his feet under him when the giant shook Emma off his back like he was shrugging out of a jacket. She stumbled backward but stayed on her feet. Fenn rushed to her mother, crying.

His strength and clarity returning, sharpening as his fury rose, Jake squared his feet and took a defensive stance, wrench held at the ready. "You sonofabitch, stay away from my wife and daughter. You wanna fight? Fight me!"

Buzz Cut pivoted toward him, his expression enraged. "Daddy, no!"

As much as he wanted to rush to Fenn and comfort her, his first job was eliminating the threat of Kingsley's goon. But when the man Fenn had called Vince reached inside his jacket for the lump Jake had noticed earlier, his blood chilled. Vince withdrew a handgun and aimed it at Jake's head.

"I knew you weren't no plumber. Now you're gonna die."

A gun. Emma stilled. Ice burrowed to her core. *Dear God, the monster had a* gun*!*

Terror scrambled up her spine with claws unsheathed. She could not, would not let this man shoot Jake in cold blood. Despite having just been shaken loose, Emma launched herself at the man's back again. This time she dug her fingers into his eyes, locked her feet around his waist, bit his protruding ear.

A deafening blast reverberated in the small bathroom. Fenn's screams followed. Shrieks of horror and guttural fear. Emma closed her eyes tightly, dread hitting her gut like concrete.

She clung to Vince as he thrashed, trying to lose her. She refused to look. If Jake was dead, she couldn't bear to have the image of her dead husband burned in her brain. Then a familiar grunt found her ears. And a voice.

"Fenn, get out of here! Run!" Jake shouted over their daughter's crying.

A hard body part smacked Emma's side, knocking the breath from her. The butt of the gun was slammed onto her shin. As the pain from that blow raced up her leg, Vince lunged backward, ramming her against the wall. Her head hit the corner of a small shelf and her vision wavered. Her grasp weakened.

"Mom!"

"Fenn, go! Run!" she rasped with what little breath she could suck into her lungs. But Emma realized the tangle of grappling bodies, her on Vince's back, Jake trying to wrest the weapon from the goon's hands, blocked Fenn's path to freedom. With a new mission, Emma kicked free of Vince, the taste of blood in her mouth. Had she bitten her tongue or had she broken the skin on Vince's ear?

She found Fenn, grabbed her arm. "Come with me! Now!"

Her tone brooked no resistance. She hauled Fenn forward, then muscled her way past the wrestling men. Flailing arms and elbows hit her as she plowed past, clearing a path for Fenn. Once they were in the next room, she yanked the burner phone from her pocket and thrust it toward Fenn. "Take this! Get out of the house and call 911!" She reeled off the address for Fenn and gave her daughter a shove toward the hall. "Go!"

"But Dad—"

The gun fired again. Glass shattered. Both she and Fenn yelped in alarm.

"Go!" Emma demanded.

Her face wan, Fenn turned.

Emma didn't wait any longer before charging back toward the bathroom to help Jake. *Please, please, God let him be okay!*

The two men stumbled out of the tight bathroom, struggling. Vince had a beefy arm around Jake's throat and, though he seemed to be gasping for air, Jake maintained a grip on the hand holding the weapon.

Hearing the crunch of glass under the men's feet, she spotted the shards of broken mirror and scurried to find a large jagged piece. Not caring that the glass cut her own hand, she wielded the sharp triangle like a dagger. The arm around Jake's neck was her first priority. Moving behind Vince, she thrust it into his shoulder, stabbed the bulging biceps clenched around her husband's throat.

For several moments, it was as if Vince didn't notice, didn't care that she was slashing at him. Finally she jabbed the glass into his neck. Deep. Vince growled in pain. He cut a glance toward Emma, to his bleeding arm.

Releasing Jake, he swung his arm up in an arc that caught Emma under her chin. Her teeth clacked together, her head snapped back and a buzzing filled her ears.

The rubbery wobble of her legs was the last thing Emma registered before she slumped to the floor.

Oxygen rushed back into Jake's lungs as he gasped deep breaths. On his hands and knees, he battled the spots that danced in his vision, determined to stay conscious. Hearing a thump, he saw Emma crumple to the floor, and panic spun through him. He seized the new rush of adrenaline to stagger to his feet.

He raised his head, searching for his opponent, the gun. Vince still held the gun in one hand while his other hand pulled something from his neck. After tossing away the shard of glass, he clamped a hand to the seep of blood.

Taking in another lungful of oxygen, Jake lunged, shoulder first, at Vince. He caught the giant low, destabilizing his legs, making him stumble, tripping over Emma's legs. While the other man floundered, Jake went for the gun. With both hands wrapped around Vince's wrist, Jake dug his thumbs into the underside of the man's wrist.

The next moment, Jake was falling, yanked off balance by his opponent. But the gun was on the floor.

A fist smashed into Jake's ribs, then his cheek. Balling his hand and staggering back to his feet, Jake braced his legs and swung. When he connected with Vince's jaw, pain streaked up his arm as if he'd punched a brick wall. His lungs heaved, still needing air. His body ached all over. But Vince kept coming. Kept hitting. So with every last bit of his strength, Jake fought back. For his life. And for Emma's.

Fenn called 911 like her mom had told her to. But she didn't stay on the phone as the operator directed. She set the phone on the ground outside and went back in the house.

She couldn't leave her parents to fight off Vince alone. Weren't the odds better if she joined the fight? Three against one was better than two against one.

She shook from the inside out, was terrified what she'd find when she returned. But she had to help. This was all her fault. Her parents had risked so much to find her, and she wouldn't, now, abandon them.

Steeling her nerves, she climbed the stairs as fast as her trembling legs would take her. At the door to the bedroom, she peeked inside to get a measure of the situation before she barged in.

She saw blood—a lot of it—on both Dad and Vince. Somehow, Dad was still on his feet, trading blows with Vince. Mom was…

She leaned farther into the room and spotted her mom on the floor. A whimper swelled in her throat, but she swallowed it. Then Mom stirred. Sat up. Mom lifted her eyes to Dad, then glanced across the room to something else.

The golf club. Fenn had dropped it at some point in her terror. But now she had a second chance to be brave. She darted into the room, grabbed the golf club in both hands and spun toward Vince. She didn't want to hit Dad, but couldn't wait for the perfect shot that might never come.

Channeling all the fear and rage and humiliation and grief of the past several days' trauma and mistreatment, Fenn cracked the club against Vince's back.

With a howl of pain and rage, he whipped around. He paused only a split second, as if stunned to find Fenn there, before he moved toward her.

"No! Fenn! What the hell—" Dad grated, winded.

Despite the cold fear puddling inside her as Vince's

dark eyes narrowed on her, she swung the golf club again. Vince caught it with one hand and yanked it from her grip.

Fenn gasped. Squeaked in dismay.

But her mother's voice, strong and commanding, full of ice and steel, said, "Get away from my daughter or I *will* shoot you."

Both Vince and Fenn cut their gaze to her mom, who knelt with the gun clutched with both hands. Her arms shook but the gun's aim was true.

"Emma?" Dad said, easing closer to Mom, reaching for the weapon.

Mom said, panting, "I've got it. I can do it. Get Fenn."

Then Dad was rushing to her, enveloping her in his arms. After he'd hugged her and kissed her cheeks a few dozen times, Dad hustled her toward the bedroom door, down the hall. "Get out of here, Button. Get help and—"

The front door burst open, and men in black tactical gear surged up the stairs. "Hands in the air! Release the girl and turn around!"

Chapter 24

Emma sat on a garden bench in Ralston Kingsley's yard, Fenn cuddled close to her despite the warm Florida sun. Even now, thirty minutes after the police and FBI had stormed into the bedroom where she'd held Vince at gunpoint, Emma couldn't stop shaking. Neither had Fenn.

Emma glanced up to watch the police march Vince, hands cuffed behind him, to a waiting patrol car. She nudged Fenn, thinking it was important for closure that Fenn see her captor taken into custody. "Button, look. He's been arrested. You're safe."

The last she said as much to reassure herself as her daughter.

Fenn angled her head to see and gave a shudder. "Good. But...what about Bill? Or Ralston Kingsley or whatever his name is? And DJ? And the others?"

Emma met the gaze of an FBI agent who stood a few steps away. "Any news of the others involved?"

The middle-aged FBI agent with a strong jaw and somber dark eyes bobbed a nod. "Last report I had was Kingsley was taken into custody at his office. His man over there seems eager to cut a deal and is already giving up names and a history of sex trafficking that Kingsley's been party to."

A desktop computer was carried out along with a laptop and numerous paper files, and the cache of evidence loaded into a black SUV. The FBI agent looked directly at Fenn when he said, "We've got a lot of information to sift through, but I promise, we will bring in the rest of the people involved. No one is going to hurt you now."

Fenn heaved a deep sigh and muttered, "Thanks."

Emma sensed that she was being watched and turned to glance across the yard to Jake. He stood with his head bowed close to another FBI agent as he related the events that had brought them to Ralston Kingsley's home. How they'd gotten inside. Acknowledging that they'd disobeyed orders from Officer Smith to stand down.

She and Jake were in a bit of trouble there, but she trusted Jake to negotiate with law enforcement. The authorities didn't *have* to press charges. Jake was doing his best to convince the agent in charge that he and Emma shouldn't face repercussions. Considering all the facts in the bigger picture—Fenn had been found safely and significant leads to shutting down a sex trafficking chain unearthed—the FBI was leaning that way. But—

Red tape. Chain of command. Of course.

Still, they had hope.

An EMT approached, casting a worried look to Emma, her bandaged hand, and to Fenn. "Are you sure you don't want us to transport you to the hospital? You really should be evaluated by a doctor."

"We'll stop by the ER as a family soon. When we're done here." With a glance, she consulted the FBI agent, who nodded. "You said you didn't see signs of critical injuries, right?"

"Nothing critical." She extended a clipboard to Emma. "Sign here saying you declined transport."

Emma signed the papers and handed the clipboard back. Having each received a preliminary physical evaluation from the EMTs, Emma was less worried about external injuries than internal scars Fenn might have. Though she'd assured her parents she hadn't been sexually assaulted— thank God!—the whole ordeal had been trying. Terrifying. Traumatic. Fenn would need counseling. The whole family would. And Emma would see that they all got every bit of emotional help, parenting guidance and spiritual healing they all needed.

Which really left only one question in her mind. Where did she and Jake go from here? The divorce papers she'd filed were still at her lawyer's office being processed. She saw her marriage in a new light thanks to the past several days' events. But did Jake?

"Can we do the rest of this in North Carolina? I just want to get my daughter home. She needs her family around her. All of her family," Jake said.

FBI Agent Gilbert, the fed in charge of the crime scene, scratched his cheek and looked askance before his expression darkened. "What you two did was highly ill-advised and reckless."

"I understand that. But if it had been your daughter, what would you have done?"

For several moments, the fed was silent. Finally he lifted a shoulder, saying, "All right. We will have more questions for all of you as the investigation moves forward, but they'll keep." He aimed a pen at Jake's face. "Get that looked at. You could have a concussion."

Jake touched a finger gently to his swelling eye and nodded. "Hospital is our next stop."

Even from across the sprawling lawn, Jake could see bruises darkening on Emma's face. His heart squeezed remembering the terror of seeing her crumpled and still on the bedroom floor.

"Agent Gilbert?" Jake called as the FBI agent turned to walk away. "Thank you."

After a cleansing breath to help refocus his train of thought, Jake strode across the yard to his family. He stroked Fenn's hair and gave his daughter a smile. "What do you say we get out of here?"

Fenn twitched a grin. "Definitely."

One three-hour stop at the emergency room later, all three Turners had been fully vetted by the medical staff and discharged with relevant stitches, antibiotics and directions for follow-up care when they got home. Emma had a slight concussion and stitches on her hand. Jake deep contusions and a cracked rib. Fenn a three-day-old cut on her lip and cheek bruise, but no other physical harm.

Jake nearly wept when that had been confirmed by the doctor. His baby girl was safe with her family again.

Jake used the key card to enter their original hotel room, and the three of them staggered wearily inside. Jake eyed the couch that would be his bed later. It'd be cramped but he didn't care. Fenn could sleep next to her mother in the king bed tonight, and in the morning, they were catching a flight back to North Carolina. Together.

But once back at Cameron Glen, what would happen between him and Emma? That trouble was what had sent Fenn fleeing her home five days ago. As relieved as he was to be returning with Fenn safely beside him, the chilling truth remained. Emma had filed for divorce.

Fenn turned a full circle looking at the hotel room and

gave a humorless laugh. "It's sure a lot nicer than the last motel room I was in."

"Oh, Fenn," Emma said, taking their daughter in her arms again. "I can't imagine. We were so worried about you!"

That Fenn allowed her parents to keep hugging her, time and again, spoke for how relieved their teenager was to be back with them. He joined the embrace, wrapping both women in his arms and kissing Fenn's head. As they stood there, savoring their reunion, Fenn began crying.

"I… I'm sorry. S-so sorry," she sobbed.

Emma wiggled free of Jake's arms so that she could lift Fenn's chin and meet her daughter's gaze. "It was a foolish thing you did, running away. But we're going to put it behind us. The important thing is you're safe. We're going home."

Fenn split a guilty look between her parents and swiped at her runny nose. "I am s-sorry for running away, for worrying you. B-but that's not what I meant."

Jake furrowed his brow. "What else do you have to be sorry for?"

"Ruining your marriage. Driving Dad away from home."

Jake was so stunned, so gut punched by the statement, he actually staggered back a step. "What?"

"Fenn, honey, no…" Emma shook her head and stroked Fenn's hair. "Why would you think—?"

"I heard what you s-said," Fenn mumbled between sniffles. "That night you were fighting, when you stormed out of the house last week…you said it was because of Fenn and Lexi. Because of the girls…"

Emma groaned and sent him a look that stopped short of *I told you so*. But Jake drowned in guilt just the same. "Button, sweetie—" He took her shoulders and guided her to the bed where he sat beside her. "You only heard half of what we were saying. I moved out because—" He paused. He could throw Emma under the bus here, say it was because she'd kicked him out, because she'd filed for divorce, but what would that serve? In the silence of his hesitation, Emma lifted her chin and seemed to be bracing herself to take a blow. *We used to be a team.*

They'd gotten to this point in their marriage together, and it would take both of them to fix what was broken.

"Because we knew, your mom and I, that our fighting was unhealthy for you girls to hear. That we were upsetting you. I moved out so that things at home could be quieter, calmer, and so your mom and I could work on our differences in private. That is the only way you are connected to anything that was happening. I left that night so you didn't have to hear our yelling. I wanted to protect you. Not blame you. You are *not* at fault for anything…" He nudged up Fenn's chin, wiped the fat tear that rolled down her cheek. "Except bringing us more love and pride and joy than I ever could have imagined."

Emma crossed the floor to kneel in front of Fenn. She gave Jake a quick grin before adding, "Sweetie, do you know why we call you Button? How you got that nickname?"

"'Cause when Nanna saw me the first time she said, 'Well, she is just as cute as a button.'" Fenn imitated her great-grandmother's Scottish accent with a hint of a smile tugging the corner of her mouth.

"That's part of it. But for your dad and me, you were what brought us together, what linked us, bound us. The best of us, combined to make one tiny sweet thing. A teenage pregnancy could have split us up, caused problems, but we decided from the start that you were a sign we were meant to be together."

Jake met Emma's eyes then, remembering, and a bittersweet ache filled his chest. When Emma had told him she was pregnant during their senior year, he'd panicked. He'd been overwhelmed by the idea of starting a family and having so much responsibility so young. Until he'd felt Fenn kick against Emma's belly. Then he'd seen his future in sharp and brilliant relief. And he'd wanted Emma, wanted their baby, wanted the family they made, no matter the cost.

The memory of that moment, on a warm spring day sixteen years ago, rushed through him anew, the emotions as tender and powerful and focused as they'd been when he was eighteen.

His eyes, filling with moisture, locked on Emma's as she continued, "Things were rough those early years for your dad and me, but you were our button, keeping us together, keeping us working together for the family, the life we loved."

Fenn divided a look, a tremulous grin between them. Then like a candle being snuffed out, her expression darkened. With a furrow in her brow she asked, "So…what changed? Why are you splitting up now?" Pain filled Fenn's face. "Don't you two love each other and our family anymore?"

Fenn's questions cut deep, stole Emma's breath. While she opened and shut her mouth like a landed trout, Jake charged into the breach. "Of course we love each other. And we will always, without fail or conditions, *always* love you and Lexi. But parents sometimes…make mistakes… or lose their way when life gets complicated."

"So then…you're getting divorced? Just like that?" Fenn asked.

Emma's heart thumped so loud she was sure Jake and Fenn could hear it. They were all exhausted, emotionally spent and sorting out the dizzying events of the last few days.

"Honey, why don't you get a shower and get ready for bed. We can talk about all of this later once we've all rested and calmed down. Hmm?" she said, tugging lightly on Fenn's long hair. "I'll order a room service hamburger for you, okay?"

Fenn seemed hesitant to leave her parents' presence, even to go in the bathroom to shower. She bit her chapped lip and dented her brow.

Until Jake lifted Fenn's arm and pretended to sniff his daughter's armpit. With an exaggerated cough and groan, Jake pulled an expression of disgust. "Oh my gawd! It's like rotten eggs!"

Fenn chuckled and side-bumped her dad, rolling her eyes for her father's antics. "Dad! Gross…"

Looping an arm around Fenn's shoulders, he hauled her in for a kiss to her temple. "Go on, stinky face. Get cleaned up. Just save some hot water for your old man."

As Fenn slid out from Jake's arm, she wrinkled her nose. "You're the stinky one, Dad. Ew…it's like a garbage bin."

The familiarity of the lighthearted banter was a balm to Emma's soul. She snuck in another hug as Fenn disappeared into the bathroom, snagging the sack with the new clothes they'd bought her on the way to the hotel from the ER.

When the bathroom door clicked shut, Emma turned to Jake. "She's right, you know. We still have to decide what's going to happen with our divorce."

Jake's shoulders fell. "Right." In the next room the water in the shower started. Jake tipped his head that direction. "We have approximately twenty minutes when she can't overhear if you want to talk now."

Chapter 25

"Look, Em," Jake said, spreading his hands in a let's-be-reasonable manner. "I want you to know that I get it. I know it seems like I wasn't listening, when our discussions of late have gotten testy, but... I heard you and I understand your points."

Emma steeled herself for another emotional conversation. Her defenses were low, thanks to the fatigue and tumult of the day, the ache in her bones from Vince's mistreatment. But she did want to cover at least a few key points with Jake before she lost the opportunity. She sat at the head of the bed, bringing her knees up to her chest as she leaned back against the headboard. "Do you, Jake? Because when you left without me in that plumber's van..."

He bent one leg to prop on the mattress as he faced her. "What about it?"

Emma glanced to the hotel bathroom, a part of her attention listening for evidence that Fenn wasn't as okay as she presented. If she heard one peep of crying, she would break off this conversation to tend her daughter. "When you made your plan to go after Fenn, garbed as a plumber, your thinking was unilateral. I was left out."

His expression and grunt of dismay said he found her argument absurd.

She sent him a look that asked him not to be dismissive, and he took a breath, ducked his head once and said, "Okay. I'm listening."

"To me, your plan, your excluding me in something so critical to our family, to Fenn's life, was a prime example of what we've lost. I felt pushed aside. Dismissed."

"I was trying to keep you safe! For God's sake, Em. We had no way to explain your presence, and more important, we didn't know what we'd find inside, what danger we might encounter." He waved a hand as if presenting exhibit A in court. "Case in point, Vince had a gun and tried to kill us!"

Emma shuddered, remembering the earsplitting blasts when the gun fired during Jake's struggle with Kingsley's goon. "And he might have succeeded in killing you if I hadn't been there. Because he had three of us to contend with, we kept him from bringing his full bore against any of us." When Jake frowned, she added, "Right?"

He sighed and looked toward the night darkened window. "Emma, you don't—"

"And when you left, you didn't so much as say, 'Here's my plan. What do you think?' You didn't give me a chance to suggest ways I could help." She sighed. "Do you see my point?"

Jake met her eyes, his own bright with admiration and respect. Awe. His Adam's apple bobbed as he swallowed. "Yeah. I get it. We made a pretty fearsome team."

"As a *team*, Jake." She leaned forward to catch his hand in hers. "When you and I tackle something together, we have a pretty awesome track record. Surviving becoming teenage parents. Building a life from scratch. Starting a successful business. Finding our kidnapped daughter and rescuing her."

He stared down at their joined hands and inhaled deeply. "You gotta understand, though, Em. As a man, a husband, a father...my first instinct is always going to be to protect my wife and kids. If I seem to be pushing you aside, maybe it's because I'm trying to spare you from danger or worry or heartache."

Emma let that fact sink in, nodded her understanding. "Fair point. But I would rather face whatever comes our way, good or bad, with you. Beside you. Not from behind or pushed into darkness and uncertainty. That's what our wedding vows were about, babe. Sickness and health. Rich or poor. Good times or bad. You weren't meant to bear the whole weight of life's troubles for the family."

Jake's fingers tightened on her hand, and he lifted a gaze full of heartache and pain. "It's just..." He had to stop and gather his composure before he continued, "I watched my dad struggle to provide for us my whole childhood. I saw the burden it put on him, how it drove him into an early grave, and I wanted..."

He didn't finish the sentence, and she scooted closer, so she could frame his bruised face with her hands. "To follow him into the grave, working just as hard and bearing all our family's struggles alone?"

His eyebrows snapped together. "No. Of course not. I—"

She said nothing, because she could see in his expression when her words settled over him, sinking in. His mouth thinned as he obviously fought back rising emotion. "But that's what I did, isn't it? My efforts to ensure we never lived with the kind of financial insecurity I had growing up overshadowed the reality of what was happening to my family."

Again she scooted along the mattress until their thighs touched, hip to knee. She threaded her fingers through his hair, and he winced when she bumped a sore spot. "Sorry."

She started to withdraw her hand, and he caught her wrist. "No. Don't stop. I've missed your touch." He placed a hand at the small of her back and leaned closer. "So much."

They were quiet for a couple of minutes, listening to the water run in the bathroom, knowing Fenn would be back out in the room in moments.

"I was unfair to you, too," Emma confessed while they bent close, foreheads touching.

"How?"

"I let my anger stew. I let frustration and rejection become bitterness, which I unleashed on you rather than finding safer, healthier channels to express unhappiness to you. I made our home an unpleasant place for you, and I'm so sorry."

His fingers curled against her back, and he angled his head to press a soft kiss to her mouth. "Forgiven."

Another moment of silence ticked by before she said, "Jake…the divorce papers…"

He stiffened beneath her hands and regret coiled in her gut. "I will rip them up and burn them, if—"

The water in the shower cut off. They were running out of time for this private conversation.

"If?" His tone was edged with an understandable hurt and wariness.

"If I've learned anything these last few days, it's how much my family means to me. Nearly losing Fenn…nearly losing you… We need to be intentional about repairing our marriage, about setting a new course where we understand each other and listen to each other and grow past this—"

Jake sat up, his shoulders squaring. "Haven't we? Isn't that what we've just done?"

Emma clung to his arms. "It's a start. A very important and promising start. But we are too important, our family is too important to risk falling back into old patterns."

"Okay…" Jake's furrowed brow told her he was listening and trying to anticipate what was coming. She gave him bonus points for both as progress.

"Promise me that when we get home, we will see a marriage counselor, that we'll keep working on us for as long as we have to."

Jake raised his chin and cast a worried look toward the bathroom. "Fenn is going to need counseling, too. Someone professional she can trust to talk to."

Fresh pain sliced Emma's heart. "Yeah. She will."

Jake gave her a crooked smile. "Sounds like our family is going to keep the Valley Haven counseling group pretty busy in the coming months." He twisted his mouth as if something had occurred to him. "You know, Button in there—" he hitched his head toward the bathroom "—has brought us together again."

Together.

"Then that's a yes?" Hope spread through her like the first rays of sun in the dawn sky. "You'll get counseling with me?"

With a laugh that sounded suspiciously choked with tears, Jake pulled her close and kissed her. Hard. "Emma darling, I would do that and anything else you asked, for the chance to live out my life with you and our girls. I love you more than anything."

Happy tears stung Emma's eyes as she wrapped her arms around her husband's neck and returned a deep, sensual kiss. The hotel room fell away, and all that existed was the man she'd lost her heart to so many years ago in high school. A heat and passion she'd feared lost poured through her blood and stirred a longing from deep in her core. Home. This man was and would always be her home, her safe place. She would forever—

A groan cut through Emma's bliss.

"Geez, y'all. Really?" Fenn said. "Get a room!"

Jake flushed as he gave his wife a secret smile. "Later?"

Emma laughed and nodded, then leaning in for one more kiss, she whispered, "I love you, too, Jake Turner. For always."

Epilogue

Three months later

Jake was late getting home. Emma wasn't worried, though. He'd texted to say he was picking up a surprise for the girls and would be home within the hour.

Since returning from Florida and starting counseling, they'd both made an extra effort to be mindful of their actions, their words and their relationship. Little things mattered, because the little things added up to big changes, more joy, and a stronger union between her and Jake.

She was just finishing a video meeting with a client, clearing the rest of the day to focus on her husband and daughters, when someone knocked on the front door.

"I'll get it!" Lexi shouted as she tore down the hall, her sandy-brown ponytails flying.

"Wait for me, Lex," Emma called, hurrying to the door. As she passed the living room, she noticed Fenn standing near the window, frowning.

"Button? What's wrong?"

She motioned outside. "It's a cop."

Emma's heart ticked faster as Lexi yanked the door open, and Officer Smith nodded a greeting.

"Stay inside, sweetie," she said, scooting past Lexi as she stepped out on the porch. "What can I do for you, Officer?"

She held her breath. So many things concerning Fenn's kidnapping and the events that followed were still pending. As much as Emma hated the open details, she dreaded what might happen to tie off those loose ends.

Officer Smith seemed to read her anxiety and raised a hand. "Don't panic. I've brought good news, not an arrest warrant."

Emma mentally exhaled. "Do tell. Good news is always welcome here."

"I had a call today from the head of the FBI task force leading the sex trafficking investigation. With the information your family provided, along with other informants, Daniel Monroe, Tommy Yates and the rest of their crew were picked up in West Virginia yesterday."

"Good!"

Emma turned at the sound of Fenn's voice. She'd not heard her daughter follow her outside. She lifted an arm so that Fenn could tuck in for a side hug next to her. "That's great to hear. Thank you for letting us know."

"We'll still need your cooperation with the prosecution of these individuals," he added, looking directly at Fenn, "but it can be arranged that your statement is videoed, so that you don't have to face these men again."

Fenn nodded enthusiastically. "Yeah. I want to do it like that. Please."

"And…" Officer Smith faced Emma again. "As long as you and your husband continue cooperating in all aspects of the prosecution and sentencing, Agent Gilbert has assured me the FBI is willing to drop the charges related to your interference in the investigation."

"They were just trying to find me!" Fenn protested.

Emma squeezed Fenn closer. "Fenn, shh."

"Which was a key factor taken into account, I assure you." Officer Smith flashed Fenn a smile. "By the way, young lady, I have a message for you."

Fenn straightened. "From who?"

"Ruby Haynes."

Emma and Fenn both perked, standing straighter.

"Ruby asked me to tell you 'hello' and 'I'm sorry.'"

"Sorry? But she helped me." Fenn frowned. "Well, after she helped DJ grab me, that is."

"She was with Daniel Monroe when he was arrested," Office Smith continued, "and she's cut a deal for immunity from charges in exchange for becoming a key witness for the prosecution."

Emma narrowed a querying gaze on the policeman. "What about her mother and brother? They used the Haynes' house as a pit stop for their operation, holding Ruby's life over them to guarantee their cooperation."

Smith lifted a shoulder. "I can't speak to that specifically, but I'm sure, like for you and Ruby, the FBI will take circumstances and cooperation into consideration. The important thing is Ruby and the other girls with Monroe and Yates are safe. The operation has been closed down."

Emma exhaled audibly. "*That* operation. But my research says there are still so many others around the world. It's...heartbreaking and infuriating."

The policeman pulled a grim face. "That it is. But the work you and your husband are doing with the high schools is a good first step. Educating the public, teaching students awareness and prevention can only help."

Emma flashed a lopsided smile as pride swelled in her. "Thank you, but Jake gets most of the credit for starting the STOP program," she said, referring to the Sex Trafficking Opposition Program she and Jake had initiated in local schools. "He came home from Florida on fire with a mission to save other girls like Fenn. It's been our pleasure to launch the program, and we're just getting started. We intend to grow it and expand our programs in the months to come."

"Well." Officer Smith squared his shoulders. "That's all I came to say. I know it's the dinner hour, so I'll get out of your hair."

Officer Smith's squad car was just pulling out of their driveway as Jake approached in his truck. He'd barely gotten the truck parked before Lexi raced out of the house and into her father's arms, squealing, "Daddy!"

Jake scooped their youngest up in a hug. Lexi giggled as he spun with her. "Hey, princess! How's my girl?"

"A powiceman was here, Daddy!"

Jake cast Emma a concerned look. "Yeah, I saw his car."

Emma gave him a kiss, whispering, "Good news. I'll fill you in later."

Relief crossed his face, and he set Lexi on the ground to hug Fenn as well. Emma could feel the bliss that shone from his face as he held Fenn close. Since coming home, Fenn had been generous with hugs in a way she hadn't been before. They still got a little teenage attitude from her from time to time, but their daughter clearly had a better appreciation for her family. Fenn's counselor was working through a few lingering issues, but on the whole, Fenn was proving resilient, strong. Having the love and support of the Cameron clan didn't hurt. Neither did the return of peace and harmony between her parents.

When Fenn backed out of Jake's arms, he rubbed his hands together and gave his girls a sly grin. "I have a surprise for you two."

Lexi bounced excitedly. "What? What is it?"

He held up a finger to say *one moment*, returned to his truck and bent inside to gather...something. He kept his hand hidden under his shirt until he reached the girls again and revealed...

"A kitten!" Lexi and Fenn shouted at the same time, both lunging forward to be the first to hold the wiggling orange tabby.

Fenn gave her father a hopeful look. "For real? We can keep it?"

"For real. He showed up at a work site, no mama to be found, and I decided the kitty should be part of our family. What do you think?"

Lexi hugged the kitten to her chest and flashed a jubilant grin. "Yes! Thank you, Daddy. Thank you!"

Fenn smiled, too. "Thanks, Dad. You're the best."

Only then did he cut a glance to Emma. His expression was wary, as if worried about her reaction to his gift. He arched an eyebrow as he walked over to Emma and tugged her close. "Okay?"

She laughed. "Okay."

He kissed her then, long and deep, and when he raised his head, beaming with happiness, she said, "Fenn's, right. You are the best."

* * * * *

"If it's necessary," he said, undoing Banner's lead rope, "I'll take care of business."

"Maybe I should take that for you, Hayden. Since you're—"

Tossing aside his ruined hat, he gave her a look of disbelief. "Have you lost your ever-loving mind? I'm not handing you my gun. It might be your job to find these people, but I'm sworn to protect them. And you, for that matter."

"I get that, but I don't believe you're currently fit to make a life-and-death call or even to be riding."

Turning away from her, he grabbed a handful of Banner's mane along with the saddle horn and shoved his boot into the stirrup before swinging aboard the gray.

If it were anyone else, she might have missed the way he slightly overbalanced and then hesitated, recovering for a beat or two, giving her time to mount her mule to face him.

"You're clearly dizzy. I can see it," she challenged. "So please, Hayden, you need to—"

The engines' noise abruptly dropped off, but they could still barely make out the low rumble of the motors idling. With the ravine's rocky face amplifying the sound, she knew it was tricky to judge distance. Though the vehicles couldn't be far, they might be just literally around the next bend in the creek or more than half a mile downstream.

Before Kate could regain her train of thought, shouts, followed by an anguished human cry—definitely a woman's—carried from the same direction. The terror in it had Kate's breath catching, her nerve endings standing at attention.

"Call for assistance. *Now!*" Hayden ordered before kicking Banner's side and leaning forward.

Don't miss
Ambush at Heartbreak Ridge *by Colleen Thompson,*
available August 2022 wherever
Harlequin Romantic Suspense books and
ebooks are sold.

Harlequin.com

Get 4 FREE REWARDS!

We'll send you 2 FREE Books plus 2 FREE Mystery Gifts.

FREE
Value Over
$20

Both the **Harlequin Intrigue®** and **Harlequin® Romantic Suspense** series feature compelling novels filled with heart-racing action-packed romance that will keep you on the edge of your seat.

Love Harlequin romance?

DISCOVER.

Be the first to find out about promotions,
news and exclusive content!

Facebook.com/HarlequinBooks

Twitter.com/HarlequinBooks

Instagram.com/HarlequinBooks

Pinterest.com/HarlequinBooks

YouTube.com/HarlequinBooks

ReaderService.com

EXPLORE.

Sign up for the Harlequin e-newsletter and
download a free book from any series at
TryHarlequin.com

CONNECT.

Join our Harlequin community to
share your thoughts and connect
with other romance readers!
Facebook.com/groups/HarlequinConnection

HSOCIAL2021

HARLEQUIN

Heartfelt or thrilling, passionate or uplifting—Harlequin is more than just happily-ever-after.

With twelve different series to choose from and new books available every month, you are sure to find stories that will move you, uplift you, inspire and delight you.